Imagine
what ...

A boy who has grown almost to manhood on a space ship dominated by women. What will his role be when the space ship finds the promised planet and society reshapes itself?

A woman, one of a line of women who have been for six generations explorers into space. What does she feel as her daughter embarks on yet another journey into the unknown?

A man facing the entry of aliens into our world. How can he decide whether their message of love is genuine or propaganda to soften us up for an alien invasion?

These are some of the human beings in the throes of human emotion you will meet in these stories that Judith Merril calls her very best in over twenty years of science fiction writing.

THE BEST OF
JUDITH MERRIL

by
Judith Merril

**With Notes by
Virginia Kidd**

WARNER BOOKS

A Warner Communications Company

WARNER BOOKS EDITION
First Printing: January, 1976
Second Printing: April, 1976

Warner Books, Inc., 75 Rockefeller Plaza, New York, N.Y. 10019

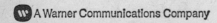 A Warner Communications Company

Printed in the United States of America

Not associated with Warner Press, Inc. of Anderson, Indiana

CONTENTS

1—Memoir

Most of the writers I know came to New York City like Moslems to Mecca; Judith Merril was born there. She was the only child of two early Zionists. Her mother had been a suffragette and was a founder of Hadassah, a liberated female frustrated at every turn by the world in which she found herself. The father was active in the group that founded the Yiddish Art Theatre, and was a writer in the Jewish educational field; at some lonely moment his problems loomed larger than his hopes, and he opted for death. His suicide left his widow with no legacy but his papers and a small child. Judith was unable for a long long time to accept the fact of his death. Her handsome, creative father was not only the person for whom she was searching, but also—inevitably—the model she was striving to emulate.

Judy wrote. She read and wrote omnivorously, compulsively, probably brilliantly. Her particular form of teen-age rebellion sprang from the realization when she was fifteen that it was her "mother's ambition for her to be a Certified Intellectual"—at which point she stopped writing, for some years. High school radicalism occupied her attention. She married a fellow activist and bore her first daughter. Comfortably sure that she was her own woman, fulfilling a woman's destiny, and free of the unending pressure at home to be what someone else wanted her to be, she discovered her own early inclinations surfacing again. She finally knew—and when Judy Merril knows something, she knows it with her whole flaming self—that what she wanted to be was, after all, a Writer.

It was 1945. Wartime. Her husband was in the navy; mine was in the army; and both were overseas. I had come to New York from the South: Mecca, where I intended first to have a child and then be a writer. Judy was a little bit ahead of me. She usually is. Within a few days of meeting, we decided to join forces and rented two cold-water railroad flats side by side in the West Village, with one adjoining wall demolished, giving us in effect an eight-room apartment with total privacy for both occupants. We shared a very active social life (our New York was full of writers—and almost every one of them wrote science fiction); our domestic life consisted of alternate responsibility for the two daughters and such details as emptying the always-full drip pan under the icebox. It overflowed a lot; so did the little girls, but we had discovered the first of the throwaway diapers, and—in memory at least—there was remarkably little drudgery involved in the experiment in communal living, "Parallax."

Judith Merril was a revelation to me. I had never before known a politically conscious female—an area where I not only did not shine, I did not exist. I had never known a woman who could outthink me as often as she could outtalk me—not always, but often enough so that I could as easily have disliked her as admired her.

None of the easy labels fitted her. I think (now) that I hardly ever thought of her as a woman. Asked then what she looked like, I would answer, "A gaunt revolutionary; extraordinary large, intense eyes and hollow cheeks with unusually high cheekbones; wavy dark hair; and an overwhelming presence." I could visualize her on the barricades more readily than I could see her in our kitchens or on baby patrol, and above all, I thought of her as central in a group of half a dozen voluble writers or seated at her typewriter like Athena in slacks pouring out incredibly good first drafts. No question but that she was a sexual person, and a very attractive one (if pressed, I would add that she had an excellent figure and good legs and was a little taller than I was, which adds up to 5′ 6″ or maybe 7″) but in assessing her I was hung up on her politicalness and intellectual elegance; I did not see her as a woman. I think (now) that this may have been because she never thought of herself as what is now denigrated as a "sex object," but only as a free and integrated person. She was not exhibiting *competitive* sexuality, the only kind I was used to; therefore I could not see the quality at all, and was continually astonished at the number and variety of men who desired her company, whereas I was moved to equal parts of hero worship and the merest beginnings of friendship. That friendship has lasted thirty years and grown to the point where, only a decade or so ago, I began to realize that I had—early on —encountered a liberated woman in my Mecca. This is the best of Judith Merril for me: she knew a lot of the answers before most people realized there might be, ought to be, questions.

"Parallax" only lasted about a year. (By then we were both seeking divorces and were shortly after remarried. Not too long after that, Judy gave birth to her second daughter, which closes that roster.)

In the meantime, and almost all the time, Judy was pursuing her ambition. Ted Sturgeon has written elsewhere a tribute to the young woman who was so determined to become what she already clearly was: a Writer.

She wrote golf stories and detective stories; she wrote secret poetry and public polemics; she worked at writing science fiction. Her first story in the genre sold to *Astounding* and made her name overnight: "That Only a Mother."

It is interesting to note that, although she has always been enormously well read and widely informed, able to discuss technicalities all night, she very seldom writes— or even touches on—nuts and bolts. It is assumed that, if there is a busbar to be welded, it will have been welded, so that the story can move on. She is much more likely to be thinking about the problems of being a particular kind of person, and the problems of communication. If there are babies in some of her stories, those babies wear diapers—and the question of how those diapers get changed under trying circumstances is not skimmed over. Back when women were being regarded as mere props to be rescued from bug-eyed monsters, Merril was addressing the question of what it might *really* be like to be a woman in the future, a woman in space; a couple of her stories were so (then) daring that she took refuge under the pseudonym of Rose Sharon. Again and again she returns to the questions raised by ESP, hoping for true mind-to-mind encounters.

There have been very few new pieces from Merril recently, and what has appeared in the U.S.A. has been experimental or explorations into the art of the translator or the old art of the book review. Her appearances within the microcosm have become rare enough so that every once in a while someone asks me—knowing that I am her agent or perhaps knowing only that I am her friend—"Whatever became of Judith Merril?" And I would like to direct them to an interview conducted by Robert Fulford (editor of the Canadian magazine *Saturday Night* and host of a talk show on CBC, an interview from which I have Fulford's gracious permission to quote.)

2—Interview

F. I guess I'd like to begin by asking you when you decided that you were going to leave the United States and come to Canada; how did you make that decision?

M. Well, it was a long, slow decision actually. I was living in England for a year in 1966 and '67. Before I went to England—like most good-guy U.S. liberals—I was against the war and I had said my little piece here and there, and I didn't take it all that seriously. But, after almost a year in London, I had reached a point . . . partly, I guess, because I was reading foreign press instead of American press, which, no matter how much you may not have believed of what you'd read at home, starts to have a different effect on you . . . but mostly it was people saying to me, "Well, how do you defend this?" and "How do you justify that?" and me saying, "Don't expect me to justify that; I disapprove of that." And after about the fiftieth time you'd said that, you started thinking, *Well, maybe I ought to be somewhere doing something about it, instead of drifting along over here.* So I went home in the spring of '67 feeling that I would either join the revolution or I would pack my goodies and go back to England to stay. And I got into a—oh, almost a kind of paralysis for about a year. Every time I decided it was time to go all out and get into something serious in the States, I . . . couldn't see how I could accomplish anything useful within any of the existing frameworks there at that time. And on the other hand, I just was not capable of the formulation I had begun to make . . . that I either have to join the revolution or I have to go back to London where I can forget that the world is coming to an end. And I wasn't able to do either one. Finally, due to a whole series of events, I wound up in Chicago for that week in '68.

F. The Democratic Convention?

M. Yeah. . . . It was in Chicago that it came to a head for me. . . . In the middle of the week I was no longer able to be a detached observer (which had been the role I'd assigned myself), nor was I ready to join the mob. What I did was to offer my station wagon and myself to the medical corps as a sort of ambulance substitute. . . . I interviewed [at the end of the week] a lot of the people who were working in the medic stations or who had been helped by them, with the idea of doing a book, which I never was able to do. . . . I was talking to a black guy who had been maced in one eye and I asked him . . . as I was asking everyone . . . where had he come from, why was he there. . . . I don't know how much of what he told me was straight, and how much of it was a put-on but he reached a point where he was talking about the possibility of a shoot-out in numbers between the Panthers and the cops the following week. And all I could think of was [*intense whisper*] "I want to be there. I want to see it happen." And I could feel this grin on my face and that was—that *was* the decision. If I was ready to

11

gloat over watching some people get killed because of the uniform they were wearing and not ready to kill them myself, then I couldn't see how I could function inside that country any longer. And at that point the idea of Canada had already hit me. . . . I couldn't quite just go where, it seemed to me, one could forget all this. Because England, London, at least, was very much in a different orbit at that time. My feeling was that in Canada I could at least offer some usefulness or assistance to some of the guys who had come—who didn't have the choices I had. . . . So we came back by way of Toronto and I guess the final little bit was [coming] back into the States from Toronto. When we crossed into Canada at Windsor, coming up, it was nothing but joy. [At] customs, the guard gave us a usual sort of Canadian smile for tourists. We felt that the air had changed completely and sort of whooped it up in the car. And when we crossed back at the—you should excuse the expression—Peace Bridge, they asked us to pull over for an examination, and we realized right then that there was no way they *weren't* going to do that. . . . The kids had plastered the car with McCarthy stickers, and we had a silk screen and stacks of posters and placards in the back and so forth. The first bag they opened was mine, in the top of which was a copy of the *Manual for Draft-Age Immigrants* which I had picked up here. . . . And I said, "It doesn't matter where I got it [when questioned]—it's absolutely legal. There's no question of duties or customs or anything like that." And he . . . took it inside, and there was a great big Thing. They searched that car—under the mats —behind the glove compartment—you know—took everyone's identification. They finally said we could go . . . but I couldn't have the book back because they had to send it to the FBI with my name and identification! As I say, if I had needed anything more, that was it. I went home and packed up. . . . [Much farther on in the interview:] I find a kind of freedom here that I can remember feeling great swells of pride and patriotism and joy about when I was a kid in high school in New York City. . . . I feel this way in Canada: the awareness, the absolute thrilling awareness of living in a free country which I had lost and which I am regaining.

3—Question and Answer

Whatever became of Judith Merril?

She went to London, and Chicago, and Canada, and Japan for a while, as well—and will go back to Japan to see Kyoto again, and live there for another while because it is another of her spiritual homes—and is a landed immigrant in Canada, seeking citizenship there, because she doesn't only talk and write and teach. She thinks; and she acts. Wholeheartedly. I think she has a little bit outgrown the provincialism of science fiction, and especially of American science fiction. But I also believe she will have more things to say within the genre.

In the meantime, it has seemed to me high time for a chronological selection to be made of the best of Judith Merril because her name has been identified with that adjective for such a long time. Hans Stefan Santesson agreed, but died untimely. It has been a joy to work to a conclusion on editing this book with Victoria Schochet . . . and I should acknowledge considerable assistance also from—Judith Merril.

Virginia Kidd

"Arrowhead" Milford, Penna., 1975

A buried newspaper item on Army denial of post-Hiroshima rumors engendered Merril's first sf story. ("Even in those days some of us automatically read certain kinds of official U.S. releases backwards.") John Campbell bought it for Astounding—October, 1948.

That Only a Mother

Margaret reached over to the other side of the bed where Hank should have been. Her hand patted the empty pillow, and then she came altogether awake, wondering that the old habit should remain after so many months. She tried to curl up, cat-style, to hoard her own warmth, found she couldn't do it any more, and climbed out of bed with a pleased awareness of her increasingly clumsy bulkiness.

Morning motions were automatic. On the way through the kitchenette, she pressed the button that would start breakfast cooking—the doctor had said to eat as much breakfast as she could—and tore the paper out of the facsimile machine. She folded the long sheet carefully to the "National News" section, and propped it on the bathroom shelf to scan while she brushed her teeth.

No accidents. No direct hits. At least none that had been officially released for publication. *Now, Maggie, don't get started on that. No accidents. No hits. Take the nice newspaper's word for it.*

The three clear chimes from the kitchen announced that breakfast was ready. She set a bright napkin and

15

cheerful colored dishes on the table in a futile attempt to appeal to a faulty morning appetite. Then, when there was nothing more to prepare, she went for the mail, allowing herself the full pleasure of prolonged anticipation, because today there would *surely* be a letter.

There was. There were. Two bills and a worried note from her mother: "Darling. Why didn't you write and tell me sooner? I'm thrilled, of course, but, well, one hates to mention these things, but are you *certain* the doctor was right? Hank's been around all that uranium or thorium or whatever it is all these years, and I know you say he's a designer, not a technician, and he doesn't get near anything that might be dangerous, but you know he used to, back at Oak Ridge. Don't you think . . . well, of course, I'm just being a foolish old woman, and I don't want you to get upset. You know much more about it than I do, and I'm sure your doctor was right. He *should* know . . ."

Margaret made a face over the excellent coffee, and caught herself refolding the paper to the medical news.

Stop it, Maggie, stop it! The radiologist said Hank's job couldn't have exposed him. And the bombed area we drove past . . . No, no. Stop it, now! Read the social notes or the recipes, Maggie girl.

A well-known geneticist, in the medical news, said that it was possible to tell with absolute certainty, at five months, whether the child would be normal, or at least whether the mutation was likely to produce anything freakish. The worst cases, at any rate, could be prevented. Minor mutations, of course, displacements in facial features, or changes in brain structure could not be detected. And there had been some cases recently, of normal embryos with atrophied limbs that did not develop beyond the seventh or eighth month. But, the doctor concluded cheerfully, the *worst* cases could now be predicted and prevented.

"Predicted and prevented." We predicted it, didn't we? Hank and the others, they predicted it. But we didn't prevent it. We could have stopped it in '46 and '47. Now . . .

Margaret decided against the breakfast. Coffee had been enough for her in the morning for ten years; it would have

16

to do for today. She buttoned herself into interminable folds of material that, the salesgirl had assured her, was the *only* comfortable thing to wear during the last few months. With a surge of pure pleasure, the letter and newspaper forgotten, she realized she was on the next to the last button. It wouldn't be long now.

The city in the early morning had always been a special kind of excitement for her. Last night it had rained, and the sidewalks were still damp-gray instead of dusty. The air smelled the fresher, to a city-bred woman, for the occasional pungency of acrid factory smoke. She walked the six blocks to work, watching the lights go out in the all-night hamburger joints, where the plate-glass walls were already catching the sun, and the lights go on in the dim interiors of cigar stores and drycleaning establishments.

The office was in a new Government building. In the rolovator, on the way up, she felt, as always, like a frankfurter roll in the ascending half of an old-style rotary toasting machine. She abandoned the air-foam cushioning gratefully at the fourteenth floor, and settled down behind her desk, at the rear of a long row of identical desks.

Each morning the pile of papers that greeted her was a little higher. These were, as everyone knew, the decisive months. The war might be won or lost on these calculations as well as any others. The manpower office had switched her here when her old expediter's job got to be too strenuous. The computer was easy to operate, and the work was absorbing, if not as exciting as the old job. But you didn't just stop working these days. Everyone who could do anything at all was needed.

And—she remembered the interview with the psychologist—*I'm probably the unstable type. Wonder what sort of neurosis I'd get sitting home reading that sensational paper . . .*

She plunged into the work without pursuing the thought.

February 18.

Hank darling,

Just a note—from the hospital, no less. I had a dizzy spell at work, and the doctor took it to heart. Blessed

17

if I know what I'll do with myself lying in bed for weeks, just waiting—but Dr. Boyer seems to think it may not be so long.

There are too many newspapers around here. More infanticides all the time, and they can't seem to get a jury to convict any of them. It's the fathers who do it. Lucky thing you're not around, in case—

Oh, darling, that wasn't a very *funny* joke, was it? Write as often as you can, will you? I have too much time to think. But there really isn't anything wrong, and nothing to worry about.

Write often, and remember I love you.

Maggie.

SPECIAL SERVICE TELEGRAM

FEBRUARY 21, 1953
22:04 LK37G

FROM: TECH. LIEUT. H. MARVELL
X47–016 GCNY
TO: MRS. H. MARVELL
WOMEN'S HOSPITAL
NEW YORK CITY

HAD DOCTOR'S GRAM STOP WILL ARRIVE FOUR OH TEN STOP SHORT LEAVE STOP YOU DID IT MAGGIE STOP LOVE HANK

February 25.

Hank dear,

So you didn't see the baby either? You'd think a place this size would at least have visiplates on the incubators, so the fathers could get a look, even if the poor benighted mommas can't. They tell me I won't see her for another week, or maybe more—but of course, mother always warned me if I didn't slow my pace, I'd probably even have my babies too fast. Why must she *always* be right?

Did you meet that battle-ax of a nurse they put on here? I imagine they save her for people who've already had theirs, and don't let her get too near the prospectives —but a woman like that simply shouldn't be allowed in a

18

maternity ward. She's obsessed with mutations, can't seem to talk about anything else. Oh, well, *ours* is all right, even if it was in an unholy hurry.

I'm tired. They warned me not to sit up so soon, but I *had* to write you. All my love, darling,

Maggie.

February 29.

Darling,

I finally got to see her! It's all true, what they say about new babies and the face that only a mother could love—but it's all there, darling, eyes, ears, and noses—no, only one!—all in the right places. We're so *lucky,* Hank.

I'm afraid I've been a rambunctious patient. I kept telling that hatchet-faced female with the mutation mania that I wanted to *see* the baby. Finally the doctor came in to "explain" everything to me, and talking a lot of nonsense, most of which I'm sure no one could have understood, any more than I did. The only thing I got out of it was that she didn't actually *have* to stay in the incubator; they just thought it was "wiser."

I think I got a little hysterical at that point. Guess I was more worried than I was willing to admit, but I threw a small fit about it. The whole business wound up with one of those hushed medical conferences outside the door, and finally the Woman in White said: "Well, we might as well. Maybe it'll work out better that way."

I'd heard about the way doctors and nurses in these places develop a God complex, and believe me it is as true figuratively as it is literally that a mother hasn't got a leg to stand on around here.

I *am* awfully weak, still. I'll write again soon. Love,

Maggie.

March 8.

Dearest Hank,

Well, the nurse was wrong if she told you that. She's an idiot anyhow. It's a girl. It's easier to tell with babies than with cats, and *I know.* How about Henrietta?

I'm home again, and busier than a betatron. They got *everything* mixed up at the hospital, and I had to teach myself how to bathe her and do just about everything else. She's getting prettier, too. When can you get a leave, a *real* leave?

Love,
Maggie.

May 26.

Hank dear,

You should see her now—and you shall. I'm sending along a reel of color movie. My mother sent her those nighties with drawstrings all over. I put one on, and right now she looks like a snow-white potato sack with that beautiful, beautiful flower-face blooming on top. Is that *me* talking? Am I a doting mother? But wait till you *see* her!

July 10.

. . . Believe it or not, as you like, but your daughter can talk, and I don't mean baby talk. Alice discovered it— she's a dental assistant in the WACs, you know—and when she heard the baby giving out what I thought was a string of gibberish, she said the kid knew words and sentences, but couldn't say them clearly because she has no teeth yet. I'm taking her to a speech specialist.

September 13.

. . . We have a prodigy for real! Now that all her front teeth are in, her speech is perfectly clear and—a new talent now—she can sing! I mean really carry a tune! At seven months! Darling, my world would be perfect if you could only get home.

November 19.

. . . at last. The little goon was so busy being clever, it took her all this time to learn to crawl. The doctor says development in these cases is always erratic . . .

DECEMBER 1, 1953
08:47 LK59F

FROM: TECH. LIEUT. H. MARVELL
X47-016 GCNY
TO: Mrs. H. MARVELL
APT. K-17
504 E. 19 ST.
N.Y. N.Y.

WEEK'S LEAVE STARTS TOMORROW STOP WILL ARRIVE AIRPORT TEN OH FIVE STOP DON'T MEET ME STOP LOVE LOVE LOVE HANK

Margaret let the water run out of the bathinette until only a few inches were left, and then loosed her hold on the wriggling baby.

"I think it was better when you were retarded, young woman," she informed her daughter happily. "You *can't* crawl in a bathinette, you know."

"Then why can't I go in the bathtub?" Margaret was used to her child's volubility by now, but every now and then it caught her unawares. She swooped the resistant mass of pink flesh into a towel, and began to rub.

"Because you're too little, and your head is very soft, and bathtubs are very hard."

"Oh. Then when can I go in the bathtub?"

"When the outside of your head is as hard as the inside, brainchild." She reached toward a pile of fresh clothing. "I cannot understand," she added, pinning a square of cloth through the nightgown, "why a child of your intelligence can't learn to keep a diaper on the way other babies do. They've been used for centuries, you know, with perfectly satisfactory results."

The child disdained to reply; she had heard it too often. She waited patiently until she had been tucked, clean and sweet-smelling, into a white-painted crib. Then she favored her mother with a smile that inevitably made Margaret think of the first golden edge of the sun bursting

21

into a rosy predawn. She remembered Hank's reaction to the color pictures of his beautiful daughter, and with the thought, realized how late it was.

"Go to sleep, puss. When you wake up, you know, your *daddy* will be here."

"Why?" asked the four-year-old mind, waging a losing battle to keep the ten-month-old body awake.

Margaret went into the kitchenette and set the timer for the roast. She examined the table, and got her clothes from the closet, new dress, new shoes, new slip, new everything, bought weeks before and saved for the day Hank's telegram came. She stopped to pull a paper from the facsimile, and, with clothes and news, went into the bathroom and lowered herself gingerly into the steaming luxury of a scented bath.

She glanced through the paper with indifferent interest. Today at least there was no need to read the national news. There was an article by a geneticist. The same geneticist. Mutations, he said, were increasing disproportionately. It was too soon for recessives; even the first mutants, born near Hiroshima and Nagasaki in 1946 and 1947 were not old enough yet to breed. *But my baby's all right.* Apparently, there was some degree of free radiation from atomic explosions causing the trouble. *My baby's fine. Precocious, but normal.* If more attention had been paid to the first Japanese mutations, he said . . .

There was that little notice in the paper in the spring of '47. That was when Hank quit at Oak Ridge. "Only 2 or 3 percent of those guilty of infanticide are being caught and punished in Japan today . . ." *But* MY BABY'S *all right.*

She was dressed, combed, and ready to the last light brush-on of lip paste, when the door chime sounded. She dashed for the door, and heard for the first time in eighteen months the almost-forgotten sound of a key turning in the lock before the chime had quite died away.

"Hank!"

"Maggie!"

And then there was nothing to say. So many days, so many months of small news piling up, so many things to tell him, and now she just stood there, staring at a khaki uniform and a stranger's pale face. She traced the features with the finger of memory. The same high-bridged nose, wide-set eyes, fine feathery brows; the same long jaw, the hair a little farther back now on the high forehead, the same tilted curve to his mouth. Pale . . . Of course, he'd been underground all this time. And strange, stranger because of lost familiarity than any newcomer's face could be.

She had time to think all that before his hand reached out to touch her, and spanned the gap of eighteen months. Now, again, there was nothing to say, because there was no need. They were together, and for the moment that was enough.

"Where's the baby?"

"Sleeping. She'll be up any minute."

No urgency. Their voices were as casual as though it were a daily exchange, as though war and separation did not exist. Margaret picked up the coat he'd thrown on the chair near the door, and hung it carefully in the hall closet. She went to check the roast, leaving him to wander through the rooms by himself, remembering and coming back. She found him, finally, standing over the baby's crib.

She couldn't see his face, but she had no need to.

"I think we can wake her just this once." Margaret pulled the covers down and lifted the white bundle from the bed. Sleepy lids pulled back heavily from smoky brown eyes.

"Hello." Hank's voice was tentative.

"Hello." The baby's assurance was more pronounced.

He had heard about it, of course, but that wasn't the same as hearing it. He turned eagerly to Margaret. "She really can—?"

"Of course she can, darling. But what's more important, she can even do nice normal things like other babies do, even stupid ones. Watch her crawl!" Margaret set the baby on the big bed.

For a moment young Henrietta lay and eyed her parents dubiously.

"Crawl?" she asked.

"That's the idea. Your daddy is new around here, you know. He wants to see you show off."

23

"Then put me on my tummy."

"Oh, of course." Margaret obligingly rolled the baby over.

"What's the matter?" Hank's voice was still casual, but an undercurrent in it began to charge the air of the room. "I thought they turned over first."

"This baby"—Margaret would not notice the tension —"*This* baby does things when she wants to."

This baby's father watched with softening eyes while the head advanced and the body hunched up propelling itself across the bed.

"Why, the little rascal." He burst into relieved laughter. "She looks like one of those potato-sack racers they used to have on picnics. Got her arms pulled out of the sleeves already." He reached over and grabbed the knot at the bottom of the long nightie.

"I'll do it, darling." Margaret tried to get there first.

"Don't be silly, Maggie. This may be *your* first baby, but *I* had five kid brothers." He laughed her away, and reached with his other hand for the string that closed one sleeve. He opened the sleeve bow, and groped for an arm.

"The way you wriggle," he addressed his child sternly, as his hand touched a moving knob of flesh at the shoulder, "anyone might think you are a worm, using your tummy to crawl on, instead of your hands and feet."

Margaret stood and watched, smiling. "Wait till you hear her sing, darling—"

His right hand traveled down from the shoulder to where he thought an arm would be, traveled down, and straight down, over firm small muscles that writhed in an attempt to move against the pressure of his hand. He let his fingers drift up again to the shoulder. With infinite care he opened the knot at the bottom of the nightgown. His wife was standing by the bed, saying, "She can do 'Jingle Bells,' and—"

His left hand felt along the soft knitted fabric of the gown, up toward the diaper that folded, flat and smooth, across the bottom end of his child. No wrinkles. No kicking. *No . . .*

"Maggie." He tried to pull his hands from the neat fold in the diaper, from the wriggling body. "Maggie."

His throat was dry; words came hard, low and grating. He spoke very slowly, thinking the sound of each word to make himself say it. His head was spinning, but he had to *know* before he let it go. "Maggie, why . . . didn't you . . . tell me?"

"Tell you what, darling?" Margaret's poise was the immemorial patience of woman confronted with man's childish impetuosity. Her sudden laugh sounded fantastically easy and natural in that room; it was all clear to her now. "Is she wet? I didn't know."

She didn't know. His hands, beyond control, ran up and down the soft-skinned baby body, the sinuous, limbless body. *Oh God, dear God*—his head shook and his muscles contracted in a bitter spasm of hysteria. His fingers tightened on his child— *Oh God, she didn't know . . .*

Ten years later, JM was into exceptional children, still. Lucky is bracketed with Henrietta for reasons of logic rather than chronology. JM's first story written around a cover: Fantastic Stories of Imagination—*April, 1962.*

The Shrine of Temptation

The name his own people called him was Lallayall. That was, of course, just his calling-name, and because it meant almost the same thing that he meant to us, we called him Lucky.

This was no transgression of courtesy, or culture-arrogance on our part. His true name, after the fashion of his people, was already long, and growing, a descriptive catalogue useful only for records and ritual occasions. A calling-name may be anything derived from the whole, so long as it suits, and the called one will answer it. Lucky was delighted to have a new nickname from us, in our language.

He was, when we came to the island, just eight years old as we reckon. His people count differently; to them, he was halfway through his Third Decade; in five more seasons, he would undergo the Apprenticeship Rites that would end his first age. Either way, he was just past the midpoint between babyhood and puberty. Like most of his race—and all others but us on the island—he was brown-skinned and dark-eyed, black-haired. Like most of his age, he was eager, questioning, rational, mystical,

27

obedient, rebellious, clumsy and courteous, graceful and quick. Like too few of them, he was generally happy and always healthy, serenely certain of parental love, highly intelligent and well-informed.

Certain of these things, and all of them to a degree, were the product of island culture. Lucky lived in a world he accepted as having been designed primarily for his own benefit and, largely, it had. Among his people, there were no fears, hungers, troubles, or questions that could not be voiced, and none—within the limits of the island's capacity—that would not be answered to the best extent of the child's understanding. All children were swift and bright; but among them, Lucky was especially blessed. Thus, his name.

He was the first in his age group to find his apprenticeship. When we came, he already knew what he wanted. A short time before that, he had spent his days, like the others, wandering from hunters to planners to makers to teachers to planters to singers, spreading his wonders and askings impartially. The others still wandered, multiply curious, questioning the weavers and fishers and carpenters, healers and painters and crafters of food. It might be three or four seasons yet until, one by one, they singled out the preferred occupations to which they'd be bound in training at First Rites.

But Lucky already knew what he wanted. Before we came, he went, day after day, to the Shrine, or the House of Shrinemen, squatting patiently in the courtyard, waiting for the chance to carry sand (for stone scrubbing) or water or polishing cloths or firewood for a Shrineman, listening in silence to such talk as was carried on in his presence, storing up questions to ask them, *hallall,* when the time should be ripe. Part of each day he sat at the feet of the Figures, self-hypnotized by gleaming amber and blue, spinning out glorious fantasies of the Rebirth.

(His own fascination with the Shrine and Shrinemen, and the weight of mystery he gave to some words and phrases—which I have tried to translate with capitals and occasional sonorous phrases in this account—led us later to a misunderstanding of some proportion. But, *hallall . . .*)

His persistence was already recognized in the village.

The other children first, then his mothers and fathers, had noticed his absence from forest, fields, and shops. Then the Shrinemen began teasing him with familiar fondness at evening gatherings and rest-day games, so that everyone started to realize what he had chosen. And if it was something of a shock to parents and teachers, the boy did not know it.

Perhaps because we settled as close to the Shrine as we dared do—perhaps out of the same fascination with the unknown that had drawn him to the Shrine—Lucky was our first and most frequent visitor, and became, either in his own person or as interpreter, our chief source of information about both the Shrine and the islanders. He did not, at first, realize that our preoccupation with the Shrine was as great as his own; we did not share his confident artlessness in question-asking. I do not know just how he explained us to himself at first, or whether he even tried. Perhaps he just waited to learn what he wanted to know—*hallall*.

It was not passive waiting. The first day, after his first attempt to speak with us, he sat in what must have been stunned bemusement for several hours, pondering the incredible fact of a second language. (We saw the squatting inward-turned boy as "a stolid impassive indigene." I blush to admit that the phrase is from my own notebook.) Then, having fully accepted that the phenomenon was not—obviously—impossible, but only previously unknown, it was he who approached us with the second overture.

We were just setting up the hand bellows for blowing foam into the camp wallforms. Lucky walked over, watched, walked away, and came back with a round stone, flattened on one side, just right to prop up the foot that kept slipping.

He held it out. We all stopped and stared. George Lazslo was quickest. He reached out and took the stone, smiling. Lucky smiled back.

"Thank you," George said.

The boy touched the stone. "Sannacue?" His small brown face seemed to turn gold with joy of his smile. "Mertz," he said, tapping the stone. "Mertz–sannacue?"

Henry started to correct him, but Jenny and I both realized at the same time that it was better to let the error ride, and not confuse the issue. (Starting as a joke, we all got to where we found *sannacue* as natural a word as *stone*.)

The principle was established, and it was astonishing to us how rapidly he learned. Jenny was our linguist, and predictably proved quicker than the rest of us in learning the island language, but when they sat exchanging names and phrases, it was she, far more often than he, who had to be told twice. Once he heard it, and was sure he understood, he simply did not know how to forget. (For her fascinating account of the process, see pp. 324-359, in "Language in the Isolated Culture," Dr. Jennifer R. Boxill, S&S, 1985).

As soon as the bare minimum of mutual language was effective, Lucky (again) initiated the next step in cultural exchange. He had been showing up at the camp just after breakfast each morning; this day he came an hour earlier, with a basket of woven reeds on his arm. It was my day for KP, and I was opening a can of bacon when he came up and touched my arm, showing me the basket. "Try my food?" he said.

The basket was filled with fresh steamed fish, still hot, each on its own new-baked half-loaf of native meal bread. At the bottom, five small pots of blue clay—the same stuff the Guardian Figure was molded in—held a savory vegetable sauce to be poured over fish and bread.

It was very good, but that seemed, at the time, irrelevant. The greatest significance of the gift was learning that our self-appointed guide and mascot was, it seemed, fully accredited in his friendship by the—so far—invisible parents and elders of the village.

I should say, "parents *or* elders," because we were uncertain. When we asked if he'd prepared the food himself, he laughed uproariously and then said, with ostentatious patience, "*Mothers* cook food." Whether he meant mothers as a class (and in this case *his* mother), or several women of the class, mother, we did not know.

Both assumptions were wrong, as it happened. He meant *his mothers*.

It took us most of six months to reach a level of communication at which mistakes of this sort could be cleared up. And from that time on, it seemed as though most of our discussions consisted of substituting closer approximations for old misconceptions. The more we learned, the more complex was what we had to learn. As for Lucky's wrong assumptions about us, they took even longer for him to recognize, and more time yet for *us* to realize he'd had them. We had been on the island the best part of a year before we gained any comprehension of the extent to which our presence had affected the boy himself. And through all that time, we so carefully leaned over backwards to avoid showing special interest in the Shrine, that we had never learned of Lucky's particular infatuation with it!

All through our second season on the island (by their time reckoning), we were pumping a steady flow of information out of the boy. We learned the basic economy and social structure of the island; how to reckon seasons, and count age and status.

He explained the system of education and apprenticeship, the courtship and marriage customs. When he did not know answers to what we asked, he would say, "*Hallall; hallall* you will know." And next day, or next week, or even next season, he would come back with the answer. Most answers, that is. Sometimes the second answer too was, *Hallall*. But then, he would add, "*Hallall, I* shall know, and then you too."

We worried, occasionally, about what was happening to Lucky, in his own village—whether his contact with us singled him out for better or worse. What we never imagined was the delight of his parents (He had nine at the time; Dr. Henry Cogswell's article in *Anthropological Review,* II, 1983, pp. 19-26, gives a brief comprehensive analysis of island family relationships) and teachers and the older people in general at the effect we had on him.

In the pursuit of the knowledge we asked, Lucky had gone back to learn himself all the things he had scorned to observe before we came; now he watched weavers and planters and netters of fish, masons and flutists and arrow-makers, with a concentrated attention that he had reserved before only for matters concerning the Shrine. The older people watched, and were pleased. They had

31

always thought well of the boy. He was marked as lucky from birth. When it had seemed clear he would be a Shrineman, they had been not disappointed so much as surprised. It did not seem quite suitable for one so lavishly endowed. Now he was learning, as they had expected, all matters of concern to the people. If it were what he wished, he would of course be a Shrineman; but they began speaking of him now as a future Firstman.

The pinky strangers ("Pinkies" was what they called us.) whose advent was otherwise inexplicable and perhaps a bit disturbing, had perhaps been sent to train a leader among the people, as the people themselves had not known how to do.

So they reasoned; at least, they decided, we *were* causing Lucky to learn what they had hoped he would, whether that was our purpose on coming or not. At the very least, it was indirectly due to us that they had made sure of his extraordinary capacities, which had been indicated as probable by various features of his birth and growth, but had never before been fully displayed. (The eidetic memory was as impressive to them as to us; and his intelligence was high, even in that high-average society. Chapter X of Dr. G. M. Lazslo's "Environment and Intelligence," S&S, 1987, deals with our findings on the island, for those who are interested.)

Two of his fathers came to thank us.

It was the first visit we had from anyone but Lucky. Out of simple courtesy, no adult would have come into our camp without some such cause. Out of simple caution, we might never have entered their village without that prior visit. It was our opening contact with the group as a whole.

The fathers were overjoyed to discover that Jennie spoke their language with some proficiency. That made it possible to dismiss Lucky and thank us without requiring him to translate praise of himself or of his friends. We told them in return how much we admired and relied on the boy—and how very pleased we were to learn that our influence had helped him adjust to his own world, and not put him out of tune with it.

This is what we meant to say, but Jennie did not

know any word in their language for "adjust" or "maladjusted." She tried "out of season," and got only smiling puzzlement. She made a long speech full of metaphor and analogy, and finally one of them said, *"Oklall?"*

Oklall, Lucky had told us, was the opposite of *hallall*. They seemed to think we were concerned about Lucky yesterday, but not tomorrow. We let well enough alone at that point, and offered food instead of conversation. Lucky rejoined us, and took obvious pride in piloting his fathers' way through the strange meal. When they left, we had our invitation to visit the village—paradoxical when we thought of it, since what had occasioned the thanks-paying was our previous inability to go in person.

If the fathers had the same thought, it would not have worried them. If we understood, as we thought we did, what *hallall* meant, we would have known they'd see no cause to worry. They had seen Lallayall's potential, displayed clearly, and were naturally content to let his nature take its own course. *Hallall,* he would learn all he needed to know. *Hallall* he would grow to his proper adult place. If he needed help or encouragement, they would provide it. The expectations they had begun to have before his preoccupation with the Shrine, expectations based on his birth and early growth, now seemed once again probable. Perhaps, as time grew closer for a Rebirth, it was necessary for a future Firstman to know more of the Shrine than was usual. His unlikely interest in Shrinemen might then mean only that he would be Firstman at the time of a Rebirth. Lallayall—Lucky—indeed! He was well-called.

As for us, we were too busy and excited with our new observing privileges, and more than that, with the news of Lucky's special concern with the Shrine, to think of the oddity of that *tomorrow-yesterday* misunderstanding. We assumed, from his fathers' manner of mentioning it, that the Shrine was not in any way taboo. It began to seem more likely that we might eventually be allowed to examine it: if a child could spend his time there freely, when his parents disapproved, it was not unreasonable to hope that visitors might be invited.

One other assumption, based on our experience of

Lucky's learning powers, proved unfounded: there was almost nothing he was able to tell us about the Shrine or Shrinemen, except just such visual descriptions as we now dared to hope might be redundant. He described the Figures, the blue Guardian on the Window of Light, and the amber Lifegiver on the scroll pedestal. He painted a vivid word picture of the reptiloid grace of the Lifegiver, the menacing power of the Guardian. About the Shrinemen and their lives he knew many minute details—but none of significance. They ate thus, slept so, conversed in the courtyard; they were celibate, wore brown robes with a design patterned on the Window of Light; they had daily rituals to say; they performed certain calculations. *Hallall*, they would officiate at the Recurrence, the Rebirth.

From the Oldest Men in the village, of whom there were three, in their Seventh Age, we learned more—if what we learned was fact. They could all recall, in young childhood, seeing the Life of the Shrine then extant. There had been no Recurrence since then, nor had it occurred in their lives, but before they were born.

In twenty-five decades, they said, the Life would Recur. It was soon, soon . . .

And saying so, they glanced significantly at Lucky. *Hallall,* a Rebirth . . .

That word again—*hallall*. In the village and fields, we heard it incessantly. It was the only no-answer a child ever got. No question was forbidden for young ones to ask—but some were not answered in First Age, and some not in Second. *Hallall,* they were told, *hallall,* ye shall know.

"When do we plant firstseed?" a child might ask.

"In the day following the third full moon of Seedfall," he would be told.

"Which seed is firstseed?"

And he would be shown.

"What comes of it?" "When do we harvest it?" "How is it stored?" "Who plants it?" "Who knows the full moon?"

All these would be answered and fully, readily. The

34

people would lay down their work, if need be, to go with a questioning child and show him the answer.

But—"Why does it grow?" "How does the Firstman know which round moon is the *full* moon?" or "Why do people seed themselves all year round, but fawns and fish only in Greengrowth Season?"

Then the answer was always, *"Hallall,"* given with a glad smile for the child who was thinking ahead of his years. First Age children were to learn only what could be seen, touched, smelled, or heard. *Why* and *Wherefore* were for Second Agers, the adolescent apprentices. So—

"Hallall, little one . . ."

It was listening to the teaching of the children that we finally came round to understand what the word meant. We had thought it was "tomorrow"—or "later," vaguely. Then for a while we thought it just an evasion, a sort of "I don't know either; perhaps some day we'll both find out." But what it meant, precisely, was, "In the fullness of time . . ."

The distinction is not nearly as much in the words as in the kind of thinking that must lie behind them. Shrine Islanders, for instance, fear death less than any society known—and this with no trace of belief in discrete immortality. In the fullness of time one is born, grows and learns, loves, weds, and begets, rears children, teaches the younger ones, acquires status, grows feeble and dies. If death comes, then one's time is full.

From the answers that were and were not given youngsters in Lucky's Age Group we also came to understand how we must have troubled him with our determined questioning about the Shrinemen. Here, too, we had progressed through a series of dead-wrong assumptions. Because Lucky told us of books and calculations, of ideographs on the Shrine (which he could reproduce flawlessly, but with no comprehension); because he had never seen books in the village, or never spoke of them; because he, the brightest of his Age Group, went daily to the House of Shrinemen, we first took for granted that the Shrinemen were priestly scholars, perhaps the guardians of an ancient culture, their role symbolized by the red-maced blue Guardian Figure protecting the "Lifegiver"—a goddess, clearly, but perhaps of wisdom rather than fertility. The reptilian appearance suggested this strongly. Henry got very enthusiastic about the correlation of snakes and divinely protected knowledge. "Rebirth" could imply a predictable renaissance—and that suggested the ugly thought that the secrecy of the Shrinemen's rites and formulae was that of an unplanned bureaucracy perpetuating itself by withholding the knowledge it had been set up to protect and disseminate . . .

When we understood what *hallall* meant, we had to revise this unhappy picture, for much of what Lucky did not know was not secret at all—just *hallall* at his age. By that time, also, we had heard from the three Oldest Men such mutually confirming details of the appearance and function of the Life of the Shrine, that the whole notion of a usurping bureaucracy became absurd. "Rebirth" was not symbol, but a literal incarnation of new wisdom, presented at intervals of roughly—by our time—eighty years. The incarnation took the form of a froglike creature at least roughly resembling the statue and relief Figures at the Shrine. (The old men recalled an identical appearance, except for color, which was gray—but they were old and remembering a strongly suggestible childhood.)

So the Shrinemen became shamans, half-ignorant half-wise witchdoctors applying without understanding some ancient formulae designed to release increments of knowledge slowly to a population reverted—for what strange intriguing reasons?—to barbarism. The near-idyllic society we saw was the planned result of this program; and the quiet patience of the *hallall* philosophy made sense now; *hallall*, all would be known. We need only wait; *hallall* . . .

But for witchdoctors, the Shrinemen were poor showmen. Neither did they do healing (any more than they governed; both of these were functions of all *other* people who lived into the Second Decade of the Sixth Age). The shaman theory began to fall apart the night George found out the man next to him at a haybringing dance was a "shaman," off duty for the party; the putative witchdoctor invited us all, very casually, to visit him at the Shrine. There had never been any taboo; no one suspected we might be interested.

We found the Shrinemen, as we had first assumed they would be, educated and cultured, in the bookish sense, far above the level of the other islanders. They were intelligent men devoted to a faith, or more, to a duty. When Rebirth occurred, it was necessary that they be on hand, trained in the formulae of sacrifice. Without their precise weights and measures and chants, the Life of the Shrine would be monstrous and harmful.

The Oldest Men, we suggested, were saying it was near *hallall* for Recurrence . . . ?

The Shrinemen nodded. They brought out a register, a long papyrus-like scroll. One fourth of its length was filled with ideographs—like those on the Shrine itself, tantalizingly like, but unlike, three different ancient languages Jenny *did* know . . .

On this scroll, they said, was the listing of dates and persons connected with Shrine Life. The first entry, in barely legible, long-faded ink, went back—they said—almost 350 decades, nearly 1200 years, as we reckon. One of them spread the scroll on a lectern, and began intoning with such singsong regularity it was evident he was reciting by rote, and not actually reading.

Yet there was an air of authenticity about their list; whether it was in the scroll or not, whether they could read the symbols or not, we somehow believed that the time intervals—ranging from nineteen to thirty decades between Recurrences—were legitimate history.

The question was—history of *what*?

The answer, of course, was—*hallall*.

If our supplies lasted until the Recurrence, we'd know what it was. Not *why*, or *wherefore*, but *how* and *what*, *when* and *who*. To the Life of the Shrine, it seemed, we were all as First Agers . . .

Thus we arrived at our last misconception regarding the Shrinemen. They were—obviously—an especially non-virulent academic breed of priest, serving their temple with civilized pleasant lives devoted to learning, discus-

37

sion, and ritual. *Hallall,* what they re-memorized every day would be of not just use, but great need . . .

Happily, by that time we understood Lucky at least better than we did the Shrine; as a result, we did not plague him with our latest errors—and plaguing they would have been, to say the least. Religion, as we know it, had no words in the Shrine Island language. *Sin, priest, faith, morals,* were not only, in complexity, subjects suitable only for adults—they were concepts unknown to the people. We did not intend to introduce them.

Since it would have been Lucky to whom we expressed these thoughts first, it is doubly fortunate we did not do so, for Lucky *was* lucky. From the time of his birth on, it was the outstanding trait of his young life.

In the calendar of the Shrine Islanders, there are three seasons to mark the year's circuit: first is Greengrowth, when the soil is renewed, when the creatures of forest and river renew life, a time of thriving for all young things. Then comes Ripening, when fawns, fish, and fruit come to full size and ripeness. Last, there is Seedfall, when pods and clouds burst to shower the land with the next season's new life, when bucks rage in combat throughout the forest, and such spawning fish as survived the nets of the Season of Ripening spawn by the thousands far up the river.

The calendar of events, of people's lives, is composed of these seasons, in sets of ten. Each Decade of Seasons has separate significance in the course of lifetime. Three Decades make up an Age of Life.

It is auspicious among the people to have Greengrowth for the ruling season of one's First Age. Lucky, born lucky in Greengrowth, would come to his First Rites, dividing childhood from apprenticeship, innocence from approaching courtship, just as the seasons changed from Greengrowth to the appropriate Ripening. Three decades later, his Full Manhood Rites would coincide with the change of the natural world from Ripening to Seedfall.

Such children were known to be fortunate in their growing, somehow in tune with the world more than others. In Lucky's case, each sign at every stage of development had confirmed the extraordinary augury of his birth on the first morning of a Greengrowth season.

38

And it was for the same reason that his early interest in the Shrine had so startled his elders: a child of his sort was seldom attracted by abstraction or mental mystery; certainly, the children of Greengrowth were too much in tune with the soil to make likely celibates.

There is a certain innocence, when you think of it, implicit in the idea of luck. A truly *lucky* person has, always, a certain natural and glorious naivete—a sort of superior unconsciousness, which can do for some people, in their acts and impulses, precisely what the well-trained, reflex reactions of a star athlete do for his body. The special ability to seize the right moment with the right hand is as vulnerable to conscious thought as the act of high-jumping would be to a man who tried to think each muscle separately into action.

So it is well that we did not force on Lucky an exercise of the metaphysical part of his mind that his keen intelligence could never have refused, once offered.

We had been almost five full seasons on the island when the second ship came. Lucky, of course, with his rare instinct, was walking in the woods when it landed, not half a mile from where it came down.

Three people emerged—three more Pinkies! Rejoicing, the boy ran to greet them, one thought predominant in his young mind: here at last was the making of a Pinkie family! (Seven is the minimum number of adults in an island household. We had never attempted to explain our marriage customs to him; frankly, living on the island, we had come to feel a little ashamed of confessing our one-to-one possessiveness. We had simply allowed them to keep their first misimpression that we did not have children because we were too few in number for a proper household.)

With these thoughts in mind, he ran forward and greeted the strangers in clear pure English, offering to guide them immediately to our camp.

They seem to have managed a rapid recovery, when one considers the shock this must have provided. Politely, they excused themselves, and announced they had come, not to join us (whom they had never heard of, of course) but to pay their respects to the famous Shrine.

Lucky led them there. On the way, they talked pleasantly with him, pleasantly but wrongly. They did not sound like Pinkies—not like the Pinkies he knew. Vaguely, he sensed something *oklall*—unripe, green, out of place and time. Gradually, his answers to the oversweet probings of the female among them became less clear, so that by the time she asked the two crucial questions, he was almost incoherent.

They did not find out how many Pinkies were on the island, nor how many others spoke English. If they had known there were only four of us, unarmed academics, and only Lucky besides ourselves who would ever know how to tell the world outside what happened, they would surely have been less precipitate. As it was, they were on edge.

He took them directly to the Shrine Window. This in itself was odd; it was bad etiquette; he should have presented them first to the Shrinemen. But he was already acting under the impulse of that strange quality of luckiness that ruled his life.

Then he found himself staring at Lifegiver, terribly torn and uncertain, not knowing why he had done such a thing, or why he had spoken to them softly, in false friendship. The amber figure glowed in double light: sunlight cascading from the unroofed courtyard, and the golden glow from inside the Window.

He—I believe it was he—said later that he did what he did just because she was beautiful: a simple act of adoration. I suppose he was confused, aware of a responsibility too large for his young shoulders, and seeking guidance of some sort. That at least is more rational than the notion that he acted then out of the pure unconsciousness of his special—lucky—nature. I know, because I watched it happen, that he moved forward in an almost trancelike manner.

(Everything from the moment of the meeting in the forest up to this point I know only from having been told. What occurred in the courtyard I saw for myself. It was almost time for the Shrinemen's evening ritual, and Henry and I were on the hilltop, with binoculars, watching.)

This is what happened:

Lallayall stepped forward and fell to his knees before the statue of the Lifegiver. He reached up, and his lanky arms were just long enough to wrap around her smooth stone legs. He gazed up at her, and then bent his head, resting it against the carvings at the top of the scroll pedestal.

At the instant of contact, the mace fell from the hands of the Blue Guardian.

The two men were fast. One jumped for the mace, one for Lucky. While the second one held the boy still, the first studied the rod and the Figure, and then reached out with the red mace and seemed to be twisting it against something on the Window. (After much discussion and examination, we came to the conclusion that it was the Guardian's eye he was twisting. The open end of the rod is exactly the shape and size of the opal eye of the Guardian.)

We did not see the Window open. It opened inwards, and our angle of vision was wrong. But we knew what was happening from the oddly expressive way the three intruders stood and stared, at the Window and at each other—questioning, triumphant, frightened, uncertain. We also saw the Shrinemen coming, a split second before the woman did. We saw her point and heard her cry faintly from down below.

The others turned to look, and all three lost their irresolution. They moved as one, taking Lucky with them. All four vanished (from our angle of view) inside the Shrine.

The Shrinemen came to a full stop in front of the Window. Had it closed again? I looked at Henry for the first time, and found him turning to look at me; it occurred to us for the first time that we ought to be doing something to help.

"You stay," he said. "I'll get the others. Keep watching."

It was the sensible way to do it.

I nodded, and put the glasses back to my eyes. Incredibly, the Shrinemen were arranging themselves in their evening ritual position, as calmly as though it were any sundown; they formed their semicircle in front of the Window, and brought forth the shining silver-tipped quills

41

that were their badge of office, held them up like dart-throwers, as they always did, and began their sundown chant!

Perhaps the Window had not closed before. If it had, it had opened again. My first thought was that the Guardian Figure had fallen. But it was not a Figure. It was alive.

It was blue and glistening, and it sprang down to the ground, crouched, alert, so clearly menacing in its intentions it was not necessary to see the face to understand the inherent malice. It had barely touched ground when a quill—a *dart,* rather—from the first Shrineman in the semicircle caught it in the face. (The eye, I have always assumed—the same left eye that must be the key to the Shrine?)

By that time, another had leaped out—and the next dart brought it down. It went so almost-casually, so rhythmically, so soundlessly, and with such economy of motion on both sides, that it seemed unreal. There were ten of the blue things altogether; at the sixth, I took my eyes from the glasses, blinked, shook my head, and looked back, unbelieving. I saw the same thing.

But remember—I did have that moment of doubt.

Without any break in the rhythm, the eleventh figure came out of the Shrine. It was not blue, or crouching or perilous; it was brown-gold of skin, and leaped like a dancer, and as it landed the Shrinemen who still held their darts poised, dropped them, and the whole semicircle burst into a chant of overwhelming joy and welcoming.

They faltered just once—when, still in the same timing, the twelfth creature came forth: then it rang out again, louder and more joyous.

But those who had dropped unused darts retrieved them.

They finished the song, the two Lives of the Shrine standing inside their circle, apart from the heap of lifeless blue bodies. Then—the Window must have closed meantime; they clearly knew the Rebirth was completed—four of them walked to the two shining creatures, bowed to them (in the islanders' bow of courtesy—not one of reverence), and led them into the House. The others

42

approached the dead entities, picked them up, and carried them off, around the House, out of sight.

My stage was empty. I waited till dark, but saw no more. Not till I started down to the camp did I even wonder what had become of Henry and the others, who should have had time to arrive at the scene before the chant began. I found out when they joined me a few minutes after I got back to camp: the gates of the Shrine courtyard had been closed and barred; they had knocked and called out and waited—also till dark—without answer. They had heard the chant of rejoicing; they had seen nothing.

I told them what I had seen. I told it hesitantly; I did not completely believe my own memory. When, next day, and days after that, all our questions and probings produced only mildly startled or baffled replies from villagers and Shrinemen alike, we decided I had been the victim of some extraordinarily powerful hypnotic illusion.

We felt fairly sure of what part of it Henry and I had seen together; and this was further supported by the presence of a strange ship in the forest, with no passengers —and by Lucky's disappearance.

We left the island a few weeks later. Our supplies might have lasted another month, but we all felt restless, and we missed Lucky, both personally and in our work. We knew there were answers we could not get from anyone, about what had happened. But we saw no likelihood of getting them by staying longer. And we had to report the strange ship.

We agreed that as far as we knew—as far as four so-called scientists could claim to know anything—four people had entered the Shrine; a watcher on the hilltop (Henry's article so describes me) experienced an extraordinarily vivid hallucination of hypnotic illusion afterwards, during the ritual chant.

For the others, that agreement was sufficient. *They* hadn't had the "hallucination."

I went back. And of course, we had left too soon.

43

Our questions had been, naturally, *oklall*. The life of the Shrine is never revealed until the next Rites . . .

This time it was a tremendous revelation; never before had twin Lives occurred.

I stayed two full seasons on the island, that second trip. This time, I lived, in a special visitor's capacity, with Lallayall's family. I learned to speak their language much better, and I spent many hours in talk with the Shrinemen and with the Lives.

The Lives told me about Lucky's meeting with the strange Pinkies; they told me how he felt when he fell on his knees before the Lifegiver; they told me they were reborn of him in the Shrine.

They told me how it felt, but could not tell me how or why it happened. They did not know. We all speculated —the Lives, the Shrinemen, and I—on what the Shrine itself might be, and what sort of force could produce ten glistening blue demons from three evil humans, and two golden angels from one lucky boy.

With all the speculation, and all I was told, I came back with not one shred of scientific evidence that anything of the sort happened. For all I know, the Lives may still be a hypnotic illusion produced by the Shrinemen; they may be some sort of periodic mutation. They may be Lucky Reborn.

They do not know, any more than I, how the Shrine came to be there, or what happened inside a chamber which they describe only as "filled with great light."

I tried approaching the Lifegiver, as Lucky had. The Shrinemen gave full permission, clearly amused. Nothing happened, though I tried it often, with minute variations of head and hand positions.

I may have missed the exact pressure points; I may have had the wrong attitude. I believe, myself, that I simply do not have the kind of unconsciousness Lucky had.

My own tendency, also, is to believe that the Shrine is a sort of outpost of some other planet—but why this should feel any more "scientific" to me than the Shrinemen's belief in an ancient lost magic, I don't know.

The Shrinemen, by the way, are still worried over

some things. The weight of the entering bodies was never ascertained, they point out. If there was unused mass left inside the Shrine, they cannot say what may come forth the next time a pure innocent embraces goodness for her own sake.

These things must be done by the formulae, they say. (They feel this Rebirth was most unscientific, you see.) The embracer is not supposed to enter the Shrine. A fawn of so-and-so much weight, precisely, is the only proper sacrifice.

But these minor worries are unimportant, beside the double miracle of two Lives of the Shrine at one Rebirth. The islanders generally feel they are alive at a time of great good luck. They are creating dozens of songs and stories and paintings and dances about Lallayall, the lucky one who brought luck to his people.

I present this account of what I saw, what I heard, what I know, of the Shrine and its Rebirth Recurrence. I have no evidence to prove its validity.

The idea was Campbell's: love as a weapon. Friend Mark Clifton supplied the key anecdote. Startling Stories—*December, 1952.*

Whoever You Are

This is a love story. That is to say, it is a story of the greatest need and greatest fear men know. It is also a story of conquest and defeat, of courage and cowardice, and the heroism that is a product of both of them. It begins in security and isolation; it ends in victory and desecration. Whoever you are, this story has happened to you already, and will again. Whoever you are, however you live, you are writing the ending to the story with every breath you take, with every move you make.

In the cabin of the Service rocket, Scanliter Six, Sergeant Bolster and his new crewman, Pfc. Joe Fromm, were playing checkers. It was the bored third day of a routine one-week tour of duty on the Web, checking the activities of the scanner-satellites that held the tight-woven mesh of e-m-g in a hollow sphere of protective power cast around the System.

Fromm studied the board soberly, sighed, and moved a man into unavoidable trouble. Bolster smiled, and both of them looked up momentarily as they heard the click of the keys cutting tape on the receiver.

The sergeant returned his attention to the checkerboard and jumped two men before he bothered to look up at the viewer. He saw a streak of light move upward and across the screen in a wide expected curve, from right to left, reached over to inspect the fresh-cut tape, and grunted approval.

"BB-3, coming in at 26° 13', 37", all correct," he said. "Check 'em off, Joe. That's nine, thirty-eight, and one-oh-seven at the point of entry. All in correlation. Transmission clear. It's your move."

Fromm picked up the clipboard with the scanlite-station checkoff chart, and marked three tiny squares with his initials, almost without looking. He was still staring at the view-screen, empty now of everything but the distant specks of light that were the stars.

"Hey," Bolster said again. "It's your move."

Joe Fromm didn't even hear him. The scanner outside completed its revolution around the small ship, and . . . *there it was again!* The flaring trail of rockets traveled across the screen, independent of the up-and-down motion of the revolving scanner.

The sergeant grunted again. "What's the matter? Didn't you ever see one home before?"

"That's the first," Fromm said without turning. "Shouldn't we be recording the tape?"

"Not yet." Bolster surveyed the checkerboard sadly; he'd have a king on the next move . . . if Fromm ever made another move. "All we got now is radar-recog. Then . . . there you are . . ." He nodded at the renewed clacking of the keys. "That'll be the code-dope coming in. Then we wait till after it hits detection, and we get the last okay, before we send the tape to the Post."

He explained it all dutifully just the same. It used to be when they sent a new man out, they at least took him on a practice tour first. "Look, make a move, will you? You got a whole year to sit and look at 'em come in."

With difficulty, the Pfc. took his eyes off the viewer, touched a piece on the board at random, and pushed it forward, leaving Bolster with the choice of a three-man jump to nowhere, or the one-man jump that would net him his king. The private leaned forward to finger the tape as it emerged from the receiver, reading off the replies to

48

code-dope demands, and signal responses, with a certain reverent intensity. "Did you ever see an illegal entry?" he asked. "I mean an attempt? Somebody told me there was one on this sect—"

At that instant the BB-3 hit the detector field awaiting it at the point of entry on the Web, and generated mechanical panic in an entire sequence of scanlite instruments. Synchronized pulses from the three scanlite stations circling the point of entry transmitted their frustration in the face of the unprecedented and unpredicted, and the tape in the cabin of Scanliter Six vibrated out of the recorder under the furious impact of the chattering keys.

Alarm bells began to shrill; first in the small cabin directly over the sergeant's head; then in similar cabins on four other Scanliter rockets within range; finally, about two minutes later; in the Exec Office at Phobos Post, which was the nearest Solar Defense base to the point of entry at the time.

Pfc. Joe Fromm stopped his hesitant query in mid-word, feeling vaguely guilty for having brought the subject up. Sergeant Bolster knocked over the checkerboard reaching for the tape. He read it, paled visibly, passed it across to the private, and started transmitting to the Post almost at the same instant.

On Phobos, a Signal Tech. depressed three levers on his switchboard before he stopped to wonder what was wrong. Green alarm meant emergency calls to the O.D., Psychofficer, and P.R. Chief. The Tech. sent out the summons, then stopped to read the tape.

DYTEKTR FYLD RYPORT: BB-3 EM RADASHNZ INDKAT ALYN LIF—RYPYT ALYN LIF UBORD. RYPT: DYTEKTR FYLD RYPORT VIA SKANLITS 9-38-107 TU SKANLITR 6 SHOZ NO UMN LIF UBORD BB-3.

                              BOLSTER, SGT/SKNR 6

By the time the Phobos Post Commander got up from his dinner table, the Psychofficer put down the kitten he was playing with, and the Public Relations Deputy pushed back the stool at her dressing table, the crews of all five Scanliters within range of the point of entry, as well as the

Signals Tech. on Phobos, knew all the pertinent details of what had occurred.

The *Baby Byrd III,* a five-man starscout, under command of Captain James Malcolm, due back after almost a full year out of System, had approached a point of entry just outside the orbit of Saturn on the electro-magneto-gravitic Web of force that surrounded the Solar System. It had signalled the correct radar recognition pattern, and replied to the challenge of the scanlite stations circling the point of entry with the anticipated code responses. Accordingly, the point had been softened to permit entry of the ship, and a standard detector set up around the soft spot.

Thus far, it was routine homecoming for a starscout. It was only when the BB-3 entered the detector field that the automatics on the scanner-satellite stations began to shrill the alarms for human help. The field registered no human electromagnetic emanations on board the BB-3. The e-m pattern it got was undoubtedly alive . . . and just as undeniably alien.

For the third time in the history of the Web, an attempt at entry had been made by unauthorized aliens; and those aliens were apparently in sole possession of a Solar starscout. The third attempt . . . and the third failure: the BB-3 was already secured in a slightly intensified smaller sphere of the same e-m-g mesh that made up the Web, suspended at midpoint between the three circling scanilte stations.

Eternal vigilance is most assuredly the price of the peace of the womb. The membrane of force that guarded the System from intrusion had, in turn, to be guarded and maintained by the men who lived within it. The scanner-satellites were as nearly infallible as a machine can be; they might have run effectively for centuries on their own very slowly diminishing feedback-power systems. But man's security was too precious a thing to trust entirely to the products of man's ingenuity. Each year a new group of the System's youth was called to Service, and at the end of the year, a few were chosen from among the volunteers to man the Scanliters that serviced the satellite stations which comprised the Web.

For even the most adventurous of youths, one further year of Scanliting was usually enough; they came back from their fifty tours Outside prepared to keep their feet on solid ground and to forget the brief experience of facing the unknown. But each year, too, there were a few of them who learned to crave the intoxication of danger, who could no longer be content to settle back into the warm security of the System. It was these warped veterans of the Web who became Byrdmen.

Secure within the womb-enclosure of the Web, five billion Solar citizens could wreak their wills upon their little worlds and carry on the ever more complex design for nourishment of all the intra-System castes and categories.

Outside, the emissaries of mankind streaked through the heavens on their chariots of fire, spreading the Solar culture through galactic space, spawning the seeds of men between the stars. First went the Baby Byrds, to scout new lands beyond the farthest outposts; then the Byrds, with their full complements of scientists, and giant laboratories, to test the promise of the newly-charted planets; and after them, the giant one-way starships went.

Somehow there were always just enough bold, desperate souls, yearning for danger and ready to die for a dream, to fill the human cargo-couches of the colony ships: the *Mayflowers* and *Livingstons* and *Columbos* that left the safety of the Web forever to fix new germ-cells of humanity on far-flung planets in the speckled skies.

Inside the Web, on four inhabited planets and half a thousand habitable asteroids, men lived in the light of the sun by day and drew their warmth and power from it. By night, they turned to rest at peace; each one under his own sector of the high-domed sky, the hollow sphere of force through which no alien source of light could penetrate and still retain identity.

The Web glowed always with the mingled and diffracted energy of all the universe Outside; no photon passed its portals, no smallest particle of energy came through without the necessary pause for hail-and-password that maintained the calm security of the Web's inner light.

Scanliter Six was already proceeding at full speed toward the trapped BB, acting on normal emergency procedures, when the keys taped out the order from Commander Harston on Phobos post to do just that. No stars showed on the viewer; they had stopped the rotation of the scanner and the screen held a steady picture of the three Scanlite stations with a fuzzy hump in the center that was too bright to look at comfortably. Scanner rays could not possibly penetrate the thick field that held the BB-3 suspended in the Web.

"Well," Bolster said sourly. "Here's your chance to be a hero, kid."

Joe Fromm knew it was childish of him to be excited. He tried not to look interested. "Yeah?" he said.

"Yeah. What happens now is, we get there and code in that the situation is as reported. Then the brass has a conference and they decide somebody has got to investigate, so they ask for volunteers. We're the laddies on the spot. The other boys are all on Stand-by according to this . . ."

He waved the orders tape at Fromm, who caught it and read it through carefully.

"And if we were on Stand-by instead of Proceed, you know what we'd be doing right now?" the sergeant went on, enjoying his own discomfort as loudly as possible. "I'll tell you what. We'd be standing all right, right smack where we were when the tape came in. Not one second closer."

"Stand-by is supposed to mean that you get into the best position for observation," the Pfc. recited.

"Sure. The best position for observation, kid, is in-scan and out of blowup range. So you take your choice: you stay where you are when the tape comes in, or you back out as far as you can and stay in-scan. Anyhow, we're the boys on the spot, see? They're going to want a volunteer to board the Beebee, and I got a hunch," he finished with a faint note of hope, "that I might come out of this in one piece just on account of you are probably going to want to be a hero."

"Could be," Fromm said nonchalantly. "You're senior; after all, it's your privilege."

He was delighted that he managed to keep a poker face throughout the statement.

Joe Fromm stepped out of the airlock into space and let himself float free, orienting, for a slow count of five. He had done it a hundred times and more in drill, but it felt different now. As in the drill, he made a routine extra check of his equipment: tank, jetter, axe, welder, magnograpple, mechitape, recorder (no radio in an insulsuit), knife, gun, signal mirror, medikit. All OK.

He set the jet at gentle and squirted off toward the glowing ball of force that held the starscout. Two more squirts, and he was as close as he could get. He flashed the mirror twice at Bolster in the Scanliter, to start the passageway in the sphere opening. This was the last contact till he came out again. If he . . .

If I come out again . . . He thought the whole phrase through deliberately, and was surprised at the way his mind accepted the possibility and dismissed it. He felt tremendously alive, almost as if each separate cell was tingling with some special vigor and awareness. And in the center of it all, in some hidden part of himself, he was dead calm, almost amused. Was this what they called courage?

He flashed the mirror again. Bolster was certainly taking his time. All he had to do was throw a switch. Fromm began flashing angry code with the mirror and kept it up, knowing Bolster couldn't answer and rejoicing in the knowledge, until he saw the opening appear in the ball of force and begin to expand.

Then he realized it wasn't simply throwing a switch. Once the passageway-mechanism was put into operation, it had to keep going on its own, opening and closing at intervals so as to permit him egress, and still not let enough e-m-g through in either direction to disturb the power-stasis inside. It took only a little bit of computer work . . . but quite a bit more intricate checking of the relays, to make certain the automatics would not fail.

He had to hold himself back to keep from diving through as soon as the hole was as big as his suit . . . but he waited, as he had been trained to do, until it

53

stopped enlarging. The computer knew better than he did how much space he needed.

Then he squirted forward and through. The BB looked strange, hanging there in the middle of nothing, with an air of polite impatience, waiting to finish its passage into the System.

Joe grinned and duly spoke his thought out loud for the record. "Every single thing that passes through your head," they'd said over and over again in school. "When you're on any kind of solo operation, you want to be sure the guy who takes over knows everything you did, no matter how crazy it seems. An idea that doesn't connect for you could make sense to him."

So Joe Fromm told the mechitape attachment on his suit that the starscout looked impatient. He kept talking, describing his actions and thoughts and emotions, as he approached the ship cautiously and opened the outer lock door. More waiting, and he informed the tape that the airlock was in operating condition.

Then he was in the ship and omitted to mention in his running commentary that he was scared silly. Down the corridor . . . open the cabin doors one at a time . . . empty, empty . . . *not* empty. *Go on in, Joe; he's out cold; couldn't hurt a fly.*

"One of the aliens is in this cabin. This is the third door I have opened, second cabin to the right going down the corridor from the lock to Control . . . he's either dead or unconscious . . . hope they're all like that . . . he's *big* . . . hope they're not all like that. Maybe ten feet tall, sort of curled up on the bunk, might have been asleep." *Might still be, might wake up.*

He gulped and decided he'd better put it on record. "Might still . . ." No, that was foolish. These characters had registered e-m radiations on the instruments in the stations. They couldn't stay conscious inside the e-m-g field without insul-suits. Anything strong enough to stop a BB in its tracks would stop a man too.

But it's not a man; it's . . . "It's definitely humanoid . . . hard to believe any alien creatures could evolve so much like humans. No tentacles, nothing like that. Arms and hands look like ours . . . fingers, too. He's wearing some kind of robe . . . hard to get it loose with these gloves on, can't see the legs for sure, but the arms are human, all right. Face is different, something funny about the mouth, sort of pursed-up-looking. Closed, can't see the inside . . . guess I can try and open it . . . no, later, maybe. I better take a look around. Anyhow, this guy is a lot like you and me only almost twice as big. Not very hairy, dark skin, big black eyes . . . how can anything that's not human have eyes that look at you like that, even when he's out cold? I don't know . . . going out now, next cabin, second door on the left . . .

"Here's another one . . . on the floor this time, kind of crumpled up . . . must have been standing when the field hit, and fell down. Nothing new here . . . wait a minute, this fella must have cut his hand on something when he fell . . . yeah, there's an open locker door, with an edge. Blood is dried, looks like it's a lot darker than ours, but it's crazy how human it looks anyhow . . . Going out again now . . . in the corridor, no more doors here . . ."

There were two more of them in the control room: one strapped in the pilot's seat, squeezed in, really; he just about could make it. The other was slumped over the solar analog computer.

"Looks like he was checking the landing data," Fromm reported. "These guys sure were confident. Two of 'em off shift when they were coming in, and everything set for a normal landing. Didn't they figure on any trouble at all? They should have realized they couldn't just sit down on one of our planets. Hell, they knew about the Web; they gave the code-dope straight, and they decelerated to approach, and had the correct angle . . . I don't get it . . . Here goes once around the room now. I will check all instruments.

"Starting from the door, and turning right: Star-chart microviewer intact and operating, films filed properly, I think. Won't take time to check them all now, but they look right . . . Radio desk appears in normal condition for use, can't test . . . Space suit locker is full of strange stuff, will come back to examine . . . analog comps come next; this guy is sprawled all over them. . ."

He followed his nose around the cylindrical room, till he came back to the door again. Everything was, or

55

seemed to be, in good working order. A few adjustments had been made in levers and handholds, to fit the aliens' larger hands; otherwise, virtually nothing had been touched except for normal use.

"Okay, I guess I better start on the locker now . . ." But he didn't want to; he felt suddenly tired. Not scared any more . . . maybe that was it. Now he knew he was safe, and there weren't any booby traps or anything seriously wrong, he was feeling the strain. *Let Bolster do some work too,* he thought angrily, and almost said it out loud for the tape. Then he realized that his sudden pique was really just weariness, and at the same time he became acutely aware of hunger and an even more pressing biological urge. *Time to go home, Joe. Always leave the party early, that's how to stay popular.*

He ought at least to get the robe off one of the creatures first, and make sure about their anatomy, but he had an odd reluctance to do it. They were too human . . . it seemed as if it wasn't *fair* somehow to go poking around under their clothes.

Hell! Let Bolster do it! He left the ship.

Alone in the Scanliter, Joe Fromm played his mechi-tape into the permanent recorder, and turned up the volume so he could hear it himself and get everything clear for his report to Phobos. Some of the stuff sounded crazy, but he could tell what part was fact and what was just his own imagination. He chewed on a pencil end and occasionally noted down something he should be sure to remember.

Altogether, composing the report was more painful than visiting the ship had been. He had just started putting it onto the transmitter when he saw the indicator for the outer lock light up. Bolster sure hadn't stayed on that ship long! He felt better now about coming back himself.

The sergeant came inside shedding his insul-suit and bursting with excitement.

"You should of looked in that locker, kid!" He was triumphant. "Anyway, it's a good thing for me you didn't. This is the kind of luck bonuses are made of." He removed an envelope carefully from the storage pocket on the outside of the suit. "Got your stuff in yet? I want to shoot this to them fast!"

"I just started . . ." Fromm said.

"Well, we'll flash this, and you can finish up afterwards."

He handed the envelope to the younger man and started climbing out of the leg pieces of the suit. "Go on! Read it, man!"

Fromm opened the flap and unfolded a piece of official Service stationary. *To whom it may concern,* it said on top, and then right underneath, *To the Staff Officers of Solar Defense:*

"The other men have asked me to write this message, and I guess I can do it all right, but I'm afraid I'll have to be pretty informal. I've tried to write it up in military report style, only it's just not the kind of thing that Service language fits.

"For one thing, the very first line of the report form stopped me, because we don't know where we are. Only the Captain knew our orders and he's dead now, and we couldn't find his log, or any of his papers, anywhere in the ship.

"We've set a course for the big fellas by backtracking on the analog comps. That means it will take them almost as long to get back as it took us to get there, but that's just as well, because it will bring them in about the time our tour is due up, and maybe that'll make it easier for them to get in.

"We've done our best to explain to them all the dangers involved—not being sure of the course, even, and being pretty sure you folk won't let them through. But we can't talk to them as easy as they talk to us. We can get over general ideas all right, and any kind of thought that has a solid object nearby to attach to, but the idea of people, of humans, that is, not wanting to let them into the System—well, even if we talked the same language . . . that is, if they talked a language at all that we could learn . . . I don't think they could understand that idea.

"I'm not going to try to tell you anything about them because if they get far enough to show you this, they can explain everything themselves. This message is just to let you know that the four of us are here, safe and

57

sound, and staying behind of our own free will. Since Captain Malcolm's suicide, there's nobody to order us home, and we like it here. Besides, there isn't room enough in the BB for more than five people—humans, I mean—or four of them (they need more food). And they want to send four along on the trip; I think they picked out their leading scientists in different fields so they can get as much information as possible and be able to answer your questions.

"I don't know. Probably a Psychoffice or some of our scientists will be able to communicate better with them on this kind of thing. We get along fine for everyday purposes, but you see, I'm not even sure what kind of scientists they're sending.

"The only thing the others and I are sure of, and that's what this message is for, is that you can trust these big fellas up to the limit. They've treated us fine, and they . . . well, it's a funny way to put it, but 'like' isn't strong enough . . . they just seem to love everybody, humans as well as their own kind.

"We will wait here for further orders. You can probably figure out where we are from the analog comp records.

"Respectfully yours,
"George Gentile, Byrdman 1st Class,
and on behalf of
Johann Grauber By/2
Tsin Lao-Li, By/2
Arne Carlsen, By/3."

"I did a tour of duty with Jim Malcolm once," the Commander said slowly. "He was a pretty good guy. I . . . liked him. It's hard to think of him committing suicide. I wish this Gentile had been a little more specific."

Lucille Ardin, Public Relations Deputy at Phobos Post, skimmed the message tape rapidly and passed it along to the Psychoffice. She cocked one feathery eyebrow cynically. "These boys just don't make sense," she said. "They've been sold something, all right . . . but what?"

The Commander shook his head, waiting for Dr. Schwartz to finish reading. "Well, Bob?" he said, as soon as the Psychoffice looked up. "What do you think?"

"I'd like to see that log," Schwartz said thoughtfully.

"So would I!" Commander William Hartson had earned his position as Assistant Chief of Staff for Solar Defense. He was that rare thing: an officer admired equally by the general public and by the men who worked under him. At sixty-eight years of age, he was still in the prime of health and vitality—but old enough to have seen his fill of violence, danger, and death. He was decisive in action, but a decision involving the lives of others would be made with care.

Bob Schwartz had worked with Hartson long enough to understand these things. "This Captain . . . ? he asked, "Malcolm? Would you say he *was* . . . well, a fairly typical line officer?"

The Commander permitted himself a faint smile. "Trying to figure the 'military mind' again, Bob? As a matter of fact, I think Jim Malcolm is—*was* one of the few officers who'd fit your picture pretty well. Courage, devotion, precision—a stubborn s.o.b. who went by the rule book himself and figured everybody else could do at least as much . . . but the kind who'd lay down his life for his Service without thinking twice. It's just suicide that doesn't make sense. . ."

Hartson's voice broke off, and for a moment the only sound in the room was the shuffling of paper. Schwartz still held the message tape, running it through his fingers as if the feel of it would somehow help him to understand its meaning better. Lucy Ardin pushed away the pad on which she'd been scribbling Hartson's explanation of the forcesphere that was holding the BB-3 captive and its alien crew unconscious.

"God, what a story!" she whispered reverently into the silence. She ground out a half-smoked cigarette in the Commander's big ashtray and stood up; the silver-sequinned dinner gown in which she'd answered the alarm glittered painfully under the overhead light. It was entirely typical of Lucy that when the call-bell rang in her bedroom, she had pushed back the stool from her dressing table without taking even the extra instant's time to complete the slash of crimson on her lips. Then picking up the portfolio that was always ready for use, she had arrived at the Exec Office, with the lipsticking finished en route, within seconds after the two men who lived on the Post.

"All right," she said briskly. "What happens now? We stitch up some six-tentacled straitjackets and make our visitors nice and safe, then we take the field off and haul 'em down? Where to? What do we do with them afterwards? Who gets to interview them?"

The Psychofficer looked up sharply, and Hartson chuckled. "Relax, Bob. I'm afraid it's our baby all the way down the line. I wish I was looking forward to it like you two are. I have a hunch it may turn out to be something of a mess . . . The aliens, by the way, are humanoid, Miss Ardin. Perhaps you'd like to see the tape again? I believe there's a detailed description . . . hey, Bob? You're done with it, aren't you?"

"Sorry." Schwartz handed it to the girl and snapped out of his abstracted mood. "Is it safe to leave them in the stasis a little longer, Bill?" he asked.

"Can't say for sure. With humans, twelve hours doesn't do any harm. These fellas may be dead already for all we know. Best we can do is assume they react like us."

"It seems to me that log must be somewhere on the ship," the Psychofficer said. "If there's time, I think it might be a good idea to try and find it before we decide anything. A man like Malcolm would have made sure the papers were safe, if he had any way to do it at all."

"You're right." Hartson, too, came up from his reflections and sprang into action. "You're damned right! If it's there, we can find it. And if we can't—well, that's an answer, too!"

Joe Fromm went back to the BB-3 with two other men from the stand-in Scanliters that had now been ordered up to assist. Between them, they searched the *Byrd* from nose to nozzles, and behind a panel in the electrical repair cabinet they found the ship's papers: charts, orders, and the missing log.

Fromm took time to open the log and look at the last page: he hardly had to struggle with his conscience at all over it. Under the dateline, in neat typing, it said:

"Carlsen should have been back an hour ago. Under the circumstances, that means they've got him too. My error was in not leaving after I talked to Tsin last week. Three of us could have brought the ship back. Alone, I don't believe I can do it.

"I have considered taking off anyhow, simply in order to make certain the natives do not gain any further knowledge of the ship. My only choices now are betrayal or self-destruction, and between these two, I am afraid I have no real choice. I must therefore pick the most effective means of suicide, and after giving the matter careful thought, have determined that a systematic destruction of the control room is a wiser procedure than the complete removal of the ship from the planet.

"This evening, I shall have my last supper in style. Tomorrow, I shall finish the dismantling of the controls and hide this book, together with the more important of the ship's papers . . . and may God have mercy on my soul!"

Below that, in almost equally neat and legible script, were two paragraphs.

"Once more I have delayed too long. Gentile, my first-classman, is at the outer lock now, and he has three of the natives with him. Apparently they now have him sufficiently under control so that he will do for them what they have not dared to do for themselves. They are coming into the ship.

"I expect they are coming for me, and I cannot risk exposing myself to their control. I know too much that they can use. The work of dismantling the controls is barely started; I'm afraid the enlisted men can still repair it readily, but none of them, after all, even know where we are; the star-charts and orders will be hidden with this log. I can only hope the papers remain hidden until the right people come to find them."

Underneath, there was a careful signature: "James Malcolm, Captain. Solar Byrd Service, in command *Baby Byrd III*," and in parenthesis below that, one word of macabre humor, "(deceased)."

They ordered Scanliter Six down to Phobos Post to bring in the papers of the BB-3. There was too much material to transmit by radio.

Bolster grinned and slapped his Pfc. on the back. "We're both a couple of bloomin' heroes," he said. "Just the kind of a hero I like to be. Some other guys'll be around when they decide to blast that *Baby,* and you and me can watch it all from the Post."

"Blast it?" Joe looked up from the log, holding his finger in the page. "You're kidding. Why would they . . ."

"Brother, you got the reason wrapped around your finger. One look at that, and they'll blow those babies clear back to where they come from! You can take a chance on a guy who fights fair, but these fellas—"

"How do you know they're fighting us?" Fromm demanded. "You saw the Byrdman's note, the one you brought in . . . This guy Malcolm was off his rocker!"

"Well, I'll buy that one, too. You can't tell with brass when they get an idea in their heads. But look, kid, you gotta grow up some. That note I brought in—it's pretty easy to get a guy to write something like that if you got him hypnotized to start with, and you're twice his size anyhow—not to mention there being a whole planetful of your kind and only four of his. I can tell you, anyhow, that's how the brass'll see it. Solar Defense doesn't take chances."

"Did you read what it says here?" Fromm insisted. "The part where Malcolm tells us about talking to Tsin? It just doesn't make sense to take it the way he did. He was space-happy, that's all. The Commander isn't going to swallow this stuff."

"You wait and see," the sergeant said again. "And when you do, you're gonna be awful glad you're down there instead of here."

"I . . . look, I know this sounds crazy . . ." Fromm put the log down, finally, and blurted out the rest of it. "I'd like to stick around. If anybody goes back out there, I want a chance to take another look at those guys. You think you could take somebody from one of the other ships down with you, and leave me here?"

"It not only sounds crazy," Bolster said. "It is crazy. But it's your body, son. You want to stick around, you can bet nobody else does." He shook his head uncomprehendingly and began punching out a message to Scanliter Twelve, where Chan Lal would jump at the chance to change spots with his weak-witted Pfc.

"I ordered him to return to ship immediately. He refused. His exact words, insofar as I recall them, were, 'Captain, I wish I could do as you desire me to—or even better that I could convince you to come with me and visit our friends. They are our friends. If you would give them a chance to talk with you, I think you might understand better. It is hard to explain with just words. But I simply *cannot* go back now. (Emphasis is mine . . . JM) You are a married man, sir. Perhaps I might feel differently if there were some love waiting for me at home, too. But I am young and not yet married, and . . .'

"I broke in here, thinking that I might be able to use persuasion, where authority had failed. I pointed out that there was very little likelihood he would ever be married, if I decided to take up the ship, abandoning him and Gentile on the planet—as of course, I have every right to do in view of their outright insubordination. The natives here, for all their startlingly humanoid appearance, are twice our size, and are almost certainly not suitable for breeding, from a purely biologic viewpoint.

"He replied quite earnestly that he hoped I would not take that drastic step . . . that he did not wish to remain permanently among the natives, but that he felt he 'had to' stay long enough to become fully acquainted with them and with their way of life, and to 'be healed of all the hurts and scars of a lifetime in the System.'

"The conversation went on for some time, but the parts I have already recorded contain the gist of it. There was one thing Tsin said, however, that I feel should be included here, along with the train of thought that followed it. If anything should happen to me or to my ship, I suspect it will in some way be connected with my low susceptibility to the emotional point he seemed to be trying to make.

"Tsin reminded me, during the conversation, of a story I have always considered rather bathetic: that of the little orphan girl, in the days before the creches, who threw a note over the high wall of the 'orphanage' saying: 'Whoever you are, I love you.'

"This anecdote, I gathered, was supposed to define for me the nature of the emotional 'healing' he was receiving at the hands—or I suppose I should say the minds—of the natives.

63

"This particular bit of bathos has been annoying me for years. I have had the story related to me at least three times previously, always to illustrate some similarly obscure emotional point. And I have always wondered afterwards what the end of the story might have been.

"Now it seems very important to be able to foresee the results of the child's action. What happened when the note was picked up and read? And *why* did the child write it?

"It is this last question, I think that bothers me the most. A sentimentalist might answer that she meant it, but I find this unlikely. At best, I believe, she meant that she hoped whoever found it would love her; and that is the very best interpretation I can put on it. It seems even more likely that her motive was even more specific: if she threw such *billet doux* over the wall regularly, I should think eventually one of the sentimentalists would have found it, made some response, and provided the means for her to get over the orphanage wall into the world outside.

"The natives here have a fairly highly-developed technology, and quite obviously a very highly-developed psychology or mental science of some sort. They are telepaths, after all. And they have taken no pains to conceal from us their interest in acquiring a means of space travel.

"There is nothing to pin down, no way to make certain of their real attitudes towards us. They have greeted us warmly and have done nothing to indicate any hostility or to harm us in any way—nothing but walk off with two of my crew in an apparently friendly fashion.

"Perhaps the wisest course of action would be to leave now, while I still have two men on board. But it is a hard decision to make—to maroon two of my men on an alien planet.

"If I believed for a moment that Gentile and Tsin were responsible for their own actions, I should not hesitate to make that decision. But their behavior is so entirely 'out of character' that I can see no explanation except that they are acting under some form of hypnotic control. As I see it, my duty is to make every effort, including main force, to return them to the ship before I leave."

Hartson read it for the fourth time and slapped the typescript down the desk. "I . . . hell, Jim Malcolm was a friend of mine! How can I tell? It sounds like him . . . sure! It sounds like every report he ever wrote, except where it sounds like him being pie-eyed in a bull session."

He sat down and let the blank bewilderment he felt show in his eyes as he faced the Psychofficer. "Well, what do you say? I can't decide this one by myself."

Courtesy turned him, halfway through the question, to face the PR Deputy on the other side of the desk. Courtesy and common sense, both. Officially, Lucy's job was just to get out the news—or to keep it in, as seemed wisest. The catch was in that last phrase. In practice, she was both public censor and interpreter-at-large for the Post: and her Civil Service appointment made her the only authority on Phobos who was independent of the Service.

The Commander had been dealing with the P.R. Bureau long enough so that in six months at the Post, Lucy had never yet had any cause to remove her velvet glove. It was easy to forget sometimes about the iron beneath it; one might almost think that she forgot herself.

"I'll check to Doctor Schwartz," she demurred now.

Schwartz managed a smile. "Will you please stop being polite?" he asked. "You've got an opinion. Let's hear it." She hesitated, and he added, "I don't even like what I'm thinking. I better think it a little more before I say it."

"All right." Her voice was controlled, but her eyes gleamed with excitement. She was talking at Schwartz, almost ignoring the Commander. "I think these fellas have the biggest thing since e-m-g. It's the one thing we haven't been able to crack at all; you know it as well as I do. They've got the unbeatable weapon—the psychological weapon. You can't fight 'em, because you don't want to. People call modern P.R. mass hypnotism, but the techniques we've got are child's play compared to what these guys can do. They've got the real thing. The question is, can we get it away from them? Has Psych Section got any way of handling something this hot?"

"I take it," Hartson put in drily, "that you are convinced of the accuracy of Captain Malcolm's interpretation of the events?"

She looked puzzled. "Why . . . yes. How else can you explain it? Has there ever been a case of desertion like that before?"

"Never," he said crisply, and turned to the Psychofficer again. "All right, Bob. You've had some time now."

"Let me start this way" Schwartz said hesitantly. "I think Lucy is right in one respect, anyway . . . what they've got is an irresistible weapon. If it is a weapon. But to accept that idea, we'd have to presuppose the existence of a war, or at least hostility between them and us. There's a verse that's been running through my head for the last hour. I'm sorry, Bill, to be so roundabout. Just try to put up with me a few minutes, will you? I can't quite remember the whole thing, but it's about an 'enemy' who 'drew a circle to keep me out.' Then there's a line I remember clearly: 'But love and I knew better. We drew a circle to bring him in.' You see what I'm driving at? Certainly our basic attitude toward any alien is potentially hostile. They are guilty until proven innocent."

"We've been all over that ground, Bob," Hartson broke in. "I know your opinion, and you ought to know mine by now. I don't like it, either, but it's the reason why we have been consistently successful in such contacts."

"Consistently victorious, I'd say. All right, let's just put it that I am emotionally more inclined to accept Gentile's attitude than Malcolm's. I see no evidence to support the view that these people are using a hypnotic weapon; it is at least as likely that the feeling they projected at our men was honest and uncalculated. Why not assume for a moment that the occupants of that ship really are four of their leading scientists, sent here to exchange knowledge with us?"

"You've got a point there," Lucy Ardin said unexpectedly. "An act of aggression against these four could make trouble if they were on the level to start with. I think it gets down to a good old-fashioned problem in shielding. Has Psych Section got any way of handling these boys if we bring them in, Doc?"

He considered for a moment.

"That depends. We've got anti-hypnotics, and we've got

personnel specially trained against susceptibility to hypnosis. But the Beebee had the same drugs, and should have had some trained personnel, too. There's a point, Bill. I'd like to see the basic psych ratings on all five of those men, if you can get 'em. Especially Malcolm's. I could get the papers myself," he added, smiling weakly. "Through channels, it wouldn't take more than three or four weeks. Can you get 'em fast?"

"I can try." Hartson jumped at the chance for concrete action. He rang for an aide and scribbled an order to Records in his own handwriting. "Put this on the facscan," he said briskly, "and give it a top-rush priority. I think I see what you're getting at, Bob," he said, as the door closed behind the uniformed girl. "I remember I was kind of surprised myself when I heard Jim had gone into the Byrd Service. Couldn't imagine him going Outside voluntarily. He was an Earthman all the way through. Why, he didn't even believe Marsmen were really human. Is that what you wanted to know?"

"Part of it. That much was pretty clear in his report. I want to know the comparative resistance of the crew members to hypnosis and what the other men's attitudes were toward alien life—things like that."

"I thought all Byrdmen had to pass standardized tests for that," the PR Deputy said, just a little sharply.

"They do. At least, the enlisted men do. But there's still a range of individual variation. And officers . . . well, they have a tough time getting enough men to command the Beebees. I think just about any regular line officer who volunteered would pass the test. . ."

He looked to Hartson for confirmation and got a reluctant nod; then he went on. "Even with the men, it depends where they took their tests. That'll show on the papers. Psych Section isn't too—efficient—in some spots."

"I'll bear that in mind," Lucy said tautly. "But I'd still like to know just how much Psych Section right here is equipped to do. You say you've got the drugs and the personnel, Doctor. All right, then, if the Commander brings these fellows in alive, can you handle them? If you can't . . ." She shrugged.

"That depends." The Psychofficer declined the challenge

of her tone and went on deliberately: "We can handle it all right . . . if it's as simple a thing as hypnosis. It happens that I don't believe Captain Malcolm was right about that. I can tell better after I see his psych ratings . . . ."

"All right! Then I take it we're going to sit around here for the next few hours waiting to see what the tests say? That gives you a little more time to make up your mind. Well, if I'm going to spend the night here, I'd like to be a little more comfortable. Do you mind if I run home for a change of clothes while we're waiting, Commander?"

Hartson eyed the shimmering stiffness of her dinner gown unhappily. "I'm sorry, Miss Ardin, I hope you'll understand. This qualifies as a Major Policy decision, and I'm afraid I'll have to ask you not to leave until we are finished with whatever we decide."

She shrugged again and sat down. "Could I have a typer then? I could be getting some of my story into shape."

Schwartz laughed. From the vantage point of the smoking jacket and carpet slippers in which he'd answered the emergency call, he said easily, "Bill, couldn't you order something from Supply for the lady? S.I. coveralls, or something like that? It might make a difference in our decision if she could be more comfortable."

"I can do that," Hartson said shortly. "And of course you may have any equipment you wish, Miss Ardin."

"Thank you, Commander," she said, too sweetly. "I'm sure it will help. I wonder if perhaps we could facilitate matters by sending for the doctor's uniform, too? If I'm to be made more flexible, I suspect a change of clothes might make him more decisive."

Hartson grinned. "She's got a point there, Bob," he said mildly.

"All right!" The Psychofficer stood up abruptly, paced the length of the small room, and wheeled to face them. "All right, I'll tell you what I think. I think the human race is too damn scared and too damn hungry to be able to face this thing. Hungry for security, for reassurance, for comfort—for love. And scared! Scared of anything different, anything Outside, anything one degree more intense than the rules allow.

"Also—pardon my bluntness, Bill—I think Captain Malcolm's reaction was typical of all that's sickest in our System. The very fact that we are seriously sitting here considering how much of a menace these four individuals represent—four humanoid beings, who come armed with nothing but a message of love! That very fact—that we sit and stew over it, I mean—makes them dangerous.

"You want to know what I think? I think what they've got—whether it's a weapon or a natural way of life, whether it's hypnotism or open-hearted honesty, or anything else, is—not unbeatable, not ultimate, not any of the other adjectives that've been thrown around here tonight, but, specifically, irresistible.

"I think all of us—you, Bill, wanting to do the 'blameless' thing—and you, suffering through hours of torment in those ridiculous clothes because they're supposed to make you 'attractive'—and maybe me most of all, hating to say what I know because it's brutal—all of us and the rest of the System, too, have one crying need that the lousy culture we've made for ourselves can't possibly fulfill.

"We want love. We need love. Every poor blessed damned soul among us. And we need it so much, it can be used as a weapon against us!

"Understand, please, just because it's important for me to have it on the record, that I don't for a moment believe it's hypnotism they're using. I think they mean it. But . . ."

"Well, at last!" Lucy Ardin sighed and moved a tense finger for the first time since he'd started talking. "Then you think you can handle it?"

Schwartz stared at her in amazement. "Didn't you hear anything I said? No. No, I don't think I can handle it, or that anybody else can. I don't believe it's hypnosis, but I can't see that that matters. Or rather, I might feel more at ease about it if I could believe that.

"Damn it, Bill, I hate this! I want you to understand clearly that the advice I am giving you is against my own inclinations and instincts. Now look: if it is to be regarded

69

as a weapon—and I see no other way we may regard it from the point of view of Solar Defense—then it is irresistible. There is no way to tie or bind the minds of these—people—except by keeping them unconscious, which would automatically defeat any purpose of investigation."

He picked up his copy of the summary and excerpts from the log, riffled through the pages, and threw it down again, sadly. "Bill, I'd give all my ratings and ten years off my life for the chance to talk to those guys myself and find out . . . but my advice as an officer of Solar Defense is that we have no choice but to destroy the aliens before they regain consciousness."

Both the others were on their feet as he finished.

"God damn it, Bob!" Hartson shouted. "You can't just—"

"Don't you see?" Lucy Ardin's crisp voice cut in. "All he's saying is he doesn't know! None of us know, and I want to find out! I'm not scared of it. Maybe you need love that bad, Psychofficer, but I don't!" She sat down again, triumphant and breathless.

The Commander ignored her. "Is that your last word, Bob? Shall I take that as your decision?"

"I'm afraid so, Bill. You heard Lucy just now. Remember what Malcolm was wondering, about the end of the story of the little orphan girl? That's one answer. In terms of the little girl, it would mean that whoever found the note took it back inside and told the authorities that one of their children was writing dirty notes—so the kid could be investigated. That's just one ending. There are lots of others, but don't forget the one he was afraid of. Don't forget all the sentimentalists—like me, for instance. If I were to forget my duty as an officer of the Service, I would want nothing more than to get the little girl out of the orphanage, just so she could love them.

"And don't forget, either, that there would be any number of different answers besides. And that everyone would feel strongly about his own solution. You have your choice, Commander. You can destroy them in the name of Security and Safety—or you can risk a System-wide civil war, and total 'conquest' by an alien race. What'll you have?"

70

Commander Hartson smiled wryly. "I'll take vanilla," he said distinctly, and rang for an aide. The uniformed girl appeared in the doorway. "Jenny," he said, "I want orders typed up for countersigning to arrange all details for the moving of the *Baby Byrd III* to Deimos Isolation Post immediately. The ship will be piloted by Pfc. Joseph Fromm, now aboard the Scanliter Twelve. We will want a continuous radio report from the pilot starting with his entry into the ship.

"Separate orders are to go to Scanliters Seventeen and Twenty-two to follow the BB-3 in with all artillery on the ready. They are to maintain radio silence, with vocal reception open. Private Fromm is to know nothing of the ready-fire orders. The word "apple" will be the signal to fire, if I decide it is necessary to destroy the ship. Is that all clear?"

"Yes, sir."

The door closed quietly behind her, and Bob Schwartz stood up and walked around the desk to shake the Commander's hand.

"They say you're a great man, Bill," he said gently. "I'm beginning to think you are. Now, I'd like to ask a favor I'm not entitled to. I did my duty as I saw it and gave you my advice as an officer of the S.D. Now I'm asking for a privilege as an old friend. If you're going to try bringing that ship in, I'd like to be aboard her on the way. I want to be there when they come to. I'm a qualified observer, and it shouldn't take more than an hour to get me up there. It won't be much of a delay."

The Commander's voice was icy. "I think you know that's impossible, Bob. Certainly you're qualified—too qualified. We have to have a man on that ship, but we only need one man, and he has to be expendable. The only qualifications he needs are to know how to pilot the ship and to be able to talk continuously. We already have a volunteer for the job, and he's acceptable. If you want to give him any instructions about what to look for or what to talk about, you have five minutes to prepare them. After that, the action will start. You understand, I am taking your advice. But I feel I must first prove to myself that your premises are correct. I want to see just how irresistible they are."

He turned to the P.R. Deputy and went on as coldly: "You are free to leave now, Miss Ardin. You'll want to hear the reports as they come in, I imagine. It should be about twenty minutes before the ship is actually under way."

Pfc. Joe Fromm walked through the inner airlock into the BB-3, climbed out of his space suit, and made a quick examination of the cabins. Three of the aliens, still unconscious, were bound ankle to ankle and wrist to wrist on the floor of one cabin. That door was to be locked. The other cabin was empty, as it was supposed to be.

"Cabins okay as planned," he muttered into the mouth-piece strapped to his chest. "Corridor and cabinets clear." He entered the control room and tested the manacles restraining the outside limbs of the alien who had formerly occupied the pilot's seat, and who was now secured in a specially built chair. "Alien in control room unconscious and I'd say pretty safe, the way he's tied down. Instrument check: electronic controls, okay; radar, okay; rocket controls . . . ."

He went down the list, cheerful with the familiar routine, talking easily, untroubled by the need for extra breaths between words that had plagued his inspection of the aliens.

"I am now strapping myself into the pilot-seat and preparing for takeoff. Ready to leave as soon as I am signalled free . . . signal received, blasting off now . . . utilizing minimum acceleration, coming in at Diemos on direct approach . . . the fella in the control room here seems to be wriggling his toes . . . you wouldn't think they'd have toes just like us, would you? . . . he's coming to, all right . . . I am on direct course to Deimos at minax still . . . I think maybe everything'll work out okay . . ."

He had to watch the instruments with one eye and the alien with the other. The—whatever he was—didn't seem to be trying to bust loose at all.

"He's moving his head now and looking around . . . looking at his handcuffs, and the chair, trying to turn his head around to see where his legs are cuffed underneath, but he isn't struggling at all . . . looking me over now . . . I caught his eye for a minute just then, or he caught mine. I think he wants me to look at him again, but I'll try not to. He has to be able to fasten my attention on something to hypnotize me, doesn't he? I am moving my eyes around checking instruments and thinking as many different thoughts as I can . . . .

"We are now approaching an orbit around Mars, decelerating. My radar screen shows two Scanliters following us . . . should they be so close inside range in case it is necessary to fire on us? . . . Please don't . . . *that's not my thought!*

"It . . . he's thinking at me . . . they are telepaths, all right. He doesn't seem to . . . I don't know, the first thought I was sure wasn't mine was, please don't fire on us, we are friends. It seemed so natural I started to say it. His thoughts aren't in clear words now . . . I heard once that to 'receive' stuff like this you have to not concentrate . . . something like that. Maybe I'm trying too hard . . . No. *I'm too tense* . . . that was his thought, not mine, he was telling me not to be so tense and I'd understand . . .

"He says—you can call it 'says'; it's enough like talking —he says they're friends, they like us. They want to be friends. He keeps saying it different ways, but it's the same feeling all the time, with different—pictures, I guess to go with it . . . ."

Pictures! Hey, stay out of there!

"He wants me to . . . to *love* him. That's what he says. He . . . men don't feel that way about each other . . . no! . . . love me, he loves all—not men, some kind of thought for his own people, and all—living creatures— those are on his home planet. He loves all men, this time he means men."

That was silly of me . . . he wasn't being nasty . . . he just meant love . . . that picture was mine . . .

"He says the pictures I get for meanings are all my own, so I might get his meaning wrong sometimes. He makes a picture in his mind, the way he'd visualize a thought on his world, but I see it the way it would be on mine. . . .

"Listen, Captain Malcolm just didn't understand. This *is important* . . . they don't mean the kind of things we

73

do when they say 'love.' They mean liking and sharing and . . . we haven't got the right words for it, but it's all right. It's not a *grabby* feeling, or taking anything, or hurting anybody. There's nothing to be afraid of. The only thing that Captain got right was that story about the kid. . . ."

On Phobos Base, Lucy Ardin's typer clacked eagerly, while Bill Hartson and Bob Schwartz turned from the viewer together. Hartson was a soldier; his face was stern and set as he reached for the mike. The only emotion he showed was the single flash from his eyes to his friend's when he looked at Schwartz and saw the tears of frustration rolling unashamed down the psychofficer's face.

". . . the one who threw the note over the wall. That is the way they feel. He's telling me now, to tell all of you, he's agreeing, he says I understand now, it's the way human beings love when they're kids, like the note the girl wrote: Whoever you are . . ."

The Commander spoke one word. "Apple."

". . . I love you."

John Ciardi edited the Twayne Triplet, "The Petrified Planet," in which the novella first appeared in 1953. It ran later in New Worlds *(1966) in England.*

Daughters of Earth

I

Martha begat Joan, and Joan begat Ariadne. Ariadne lived and died at home on Pluto, but her daughter, Emma, took the long trip out to a distant planet of an alien sun.

Emma begat Leah, and Leah begat Carla, who was the first to make her bridal voyage through sub-space, a long journey faster than the speed of light itself.

Six women in direct descent—some brave, some beautiful, some brilliant: smug or simple, willful or compliant, all different, all daughters of Earth, though half of them never set foot on the Old Planet.

This story could have started anywhere. It began with unspoken prayer, before there were words, when an unnamed man and woman looked upward to a point of distant light and wondered. Started again with a pointing pyramid; once more with the naming of a constellation; and once again with the casting of a horoscope.

One of its beginnings was in the squalid centuries of churchly darkness, when Brahe and Bruno, Kepler, Copernicus, and Galileo ripped off the veils of godly ignorance so men could see the stars again. Then in another age of madness, a scant two centuries ago, it began with the pioneer cranks, Goddard and Tsiolkovsky, and the compulsive evangelism of Ley and Gernsback and Clarke. It is beginning again now, here on Uller. But in this narrative, it starts with Martha:

Martha was born on Earth, in the worst of the black decades of the 20th century, in the year 1941. She lived out her time and died of miserable old age at less than eighty years at home on Earth. Once in her life, she went to the Moon.

She had two children. Her son, Richard, was a good and dutiful young man, a loving son, and a sober husband when he married. He watched his mother age and weaken with worry and fear after the Pluto expedition left and could never bring himself to hurt her again as his sister had done.

Joan was the one who got away.

II

. . . centure easegone manlookttuthe stahzanprade eeee maythem hizgozzenn izz gahahdenno thawthen izzgole . . .

"It's—beautiful!"

Martha nodded automatically, but she heard the catch in the boy's voice, the sudden sharp inhalation of awe and envy, and she shivered and reached for his hand.

Beautiful, yes: beautiful, brazen, deadly, and triumphant. Martha stared at the wickedly gleaming flanks of the great rocket resting majestically on its bed of steel and hated it with all the stored and unspent venom of her life.

She had not planned to come. She had produced a headache, claimed illness, ignored the amused understanding in her husband's eyes.

Even more, she dreaded having Richard go. But his father voiced one rarely used impatient word, and she knew there was no arguing about the boy.

In the end she had to do it, too: go and be witness at disaster for herself. The three of them took their

76

places in the Moon rocket—suddenly safe-seeming and familiar—and now they stood together in the shadow of that rocket's monstrous spawn under the clear plastic skin of Moondome.

. . . rodwee havetrav uldsolo lee beyewere eeyanway stfulmen zzz . . .

The silvery span of runway that would send it off *today* stretched out of sight up the crater wall, the diminishing curve beyond the bloated belly already lost in the distance it was made to rule. Cameras ground steadily; TV commentators, perched on platforms stilted high like lifeguard chairs, filled in a chattering counterpoint against the drone from the loudspeakers of the well-worn words that had launched the first Moondome expedition, how long back?

Sixteen years? Impossible. Much longer. How many children had painfully memorized those tired words since? But here was George, listening as though he'd never heard a word of it before, and Richard between them, his face shimmering with reflections of some private glory, and the adolescent fervor of his voice—"It's *beautiful!*"—drawing a baritone-to-tremolo screech across the hypnosoporific of the loudspeakers' drone.

She shivered. "Yes, dear, it is," and took his hand, held it too tightly, and had to feel him pull away. A camera pointed at them, and she tried to fix her face to look the way the commentator would be saying all these mothers here today were feeling.

She looked for the first time at the woman next to her and caught an echo of her own effort at transformation. All around her, she saw with gratitude and dismay, were the faint strained lines at lips and eyes, the same tensed fingers grasping for a hand, or just at air.

Back on Earth, perhaps among the millions crowded around TV sets, there could be honest pride and pleasure at this spectacle. But here—?

The cameras stopped roaming, and a man stood up on the raised central dais.

"The President of United Earth," the speakers boomed sepulchrally.

An instant's hush, then:

"Today we are sending forth two hundred of our sons

77

and daughters to the last outpost of the solar world—the far room from which we hope they may open an exit to the vistas of space itself. Before they go, it is proper that we pause . . ."

She stopped listening. The words were different, but it was still the same. No doubt the children would have to memorize this one, too.

Did they *feel this way?*

It was a frightening, and then a cooling, thought. There was no other way they could have felt, the other mothers who watched that first Moondome rocket leaving Earth.

". . . for their children's children, who will reach to the unknown stars." Silence. That was the end, then.

The silence was broken by the rolling syllables of the two hundred names, as each straight neat white uniform went up to take the hand of the President and complete the ritual. Then it was over and Joan was standing before her: her daughter, a stranger behind a mask of glory. Seven months ago—seven short and stormy months—a schoolgirl still. Now—what did the President say?—an "emissary to the farthest new frontiers."

Martha reached out a hand, but George was before her, folding the slender girl in a wide embrace, laughing proudly into her eyes, chucking her inanely under the chin. Then Richard, still too young not to spurn sentimentality, shaking Joan's hand, suffering her kiss on his forehead, saying thickly, "You show 'em, sis!"

It was her turn now. Martha leaned forward, coolly kissed the smiling face above the white jacket and felt the untamed tears press up behind her eyes.

"Joan," she cried wildly. "Joan, baby, aren't you *afraid?*"

What a *stupid* thing to say! She wiped hastily at her eyes and saw that the shine in Joan's eyes was moisture, too.

Joan took her mother's hands and held them tight.

"I'm petrified," she said, slowly, gravely, and very low. No one else heard it. Then she turned with her brave smile to Alex, standing at her side.

"Pluto or bust!" she giggled.

Martha kissed Alex, and George shook his hand. Then

the two of them went off, in their white uniforms, to join the other couples, all in line.

Martha felt proud.

(Parenthesis to Carla: i)

Josetown, Uller, 3/9/52

Dear Carla . . .

Forgive me my somewhat dramatic opening. Both the sections that preceded this were written years ago, at rather widely separated times, and of course the one about Martha's farewell to Joan involved a good bit of imaginative assumption—though less of it than you may think at this point.

Frankly, I hesitated for some time before I decided it was proper to include such bits in what is primarily intended to be an informational account. But information is not to be confused with statistics and when I found myself uncertain, later, whether it was all right to include these explanatory asides, I made up my mind that if I were to write the story at all, it would have to be done my own way, with whatever idiosyncratic eccentricities or godlike presumptions of comprehension might be involved.

As you already know if you are reading this, I am putting this together for you as a sort of goodbye present for your trip. There is little you will be able to take with you, and when you leave, there will be no way to foresee the likelihood of our ever meeting again; even if your trip is entirely successful and you return from it safely, we both know how uncertain the time-transformation equations are. You may be back, twenty years older, five minutes after you leave; more probably, it may be many years after my own death that you return—perhaps only a year or two older than you are now.

But however we learn to juggle our bodies through space *or* time, we live our lives on a subjective time scale. Thus, though I was born in 2026, and the *Newhope* landed on Uller in 2091, *I* was then, roughly, 27 years old—including two subjective years, overall, for the trip. And although the sixty-one years I have lived here would be counted as closer to sixty-seven on Earth, or on Pluto,

I think that the body—and I *know* that the mind—pays more attention to the rhythm of planetary seasons, the alternations of heat and cold and radiation intensities, than to the ticking of some cosmic metronome counting off whatever Absolute Time might be. So I call myself 88 years old—and I digress, but not as far as it may seem.

I said, for instance, that Martha died "of miserable old age" at less than eighty, and this would seem to contradict my talk of seasons-and-subjectivity here. I am not exactly senile, and can look forward to another forty years, in all likelihood, of moderately useful life. We do learn something as we go along: a hundred years before Martha's time (indeed, even at her time, on some parts of Earth) few people lived to see sixty. (You, at twenty-eight, would have been entering middle age.) Yet the essential *rhythms* of their lives were remarkably similar to our own. The advances of biophysics have enlarged our scope: we have more time for learning and living both; but we have correspondingly more to learn and live. We still progress through adolescence and education (which once ended at 14, then 18, 21, 25 . . .) to youth, marriage, procreation, maturity, middle age, senescence, and death. And in a similar way, I think, there are certain rhythms of human history which recur in (widening, perhaps enriched, but increasingly discernible) moderately predictable patterns of motion and emotion both.

A recognition of this sort of rhythm is implicit, I think, in the joke that would not go away, which finally made the official name of the—ship?—in which you will depart *The Ark* (for *Archaic?*). In any case, this story is, on its most basic levels, an exposition of such rhythms: among them is the curious business of the generations, and their alternations: at least it was that thought (or rationale) that finally permitted me to indulge myself with my dramatic opening.

On an equally important, though more superficial, level, my purpose in putting this together is to provide you with —this is embarrassing—a "heritage." I had something of this sort from Joan Thurman, and found it valuable; whether this will be equally so for you, I do not know. I do know I have only two months left in which to put this together and that is little enough for an inexperienced story-teller like myself. (And glory be! there *is* something I am inexperienced at. Many things, actually—but the writing of this is the first reminder I have had in a while. It feels *good* to be doing something new and difficult.)

My parenthesis seems to be full of parentheses. Well, I never was what you'd call a straight-line thinker: the side trails are often more productive, anyhow . . .

And there I go again. What I set out to tell you here, Carla, is that this story was lived over many years, and written over a shorter period, but still a long one. There are the odd bits (like the one about Martha preceding this) which I did a long time ago, as a sort of "therapy-writing" and kept, till now, to myself. Other parts, like what follows here, are adapted from Joan Thurman's papers. Some parts are new. And then there is this matter of rhythms again—

Some things in life remain vivid in minute detail till the day you die; others are of interest only as background. Some things are very personal and immediate, no matter how remote in time; others seem almost to be happening to another person, even as they occur. Thus, you will find this narrative full of sudden changes of pace and style. I find, for instance, that it is almost impossible in some sections to write about myself as "Emma" in the third person; and other places equally difficult to say "I" and "me," but I do not think you will have too much trouble following.

III

I WAS BORN on Pluto in the Earth-year 2026, and I grew up there. I was twenty-two years old when we boarded the *Newhope* to come to Uller. But that was such a long time ago, and so much has happened since, that the words themselves have lost all personal meaning to me. They are statistics. I am Emma Tarbell now, and have been for many years. My home is on Uller. A little girl named Emma Malook grew up on Pluto. Her mother's name was Ariadne, and her father's name was Bob. Her grandmother, Joan Thurman, was a famous pioneer, one of the first-ship colonists.

In the normal course of events, Joan would have taken her degree that spring and gone to work as a biophysicist until she found a husband. The prospect appalled her. Nineteen months earlier she'd started the accelerated studies, without mentioning it at home; her mother thought she was busy with the usual run of extracurricular self-expression at school. She'd had a year of avid learning before she passed the prelims and was ready for advanced special training. That meant a different school, and the beginning of the psych conferences and background inquiries. She had to tell her family then.

The school was too near home for her to live in the already crowded dorms. She had to stick it out at home for six months of battle and persuasion, sleepless nights and stormy mornings. And all the time studying to be done.

She wasn't the only one. Even the dorm residents got it; letters and telegrams and phone calls, and frantic unannounced visitations. Two thousand of them entered final training together; less than seven hundred lasted the full six months, and most of those who left did so of their own accord.

Joan stuck it out, and she met Alex, and added to her fears and doubts: if one of them was chosen, and not the other . . . ?

Cautiously, they held back from commitments till the end. And then, in spite of any heaven or earth Martha could move, the decision was made. Joan had her one last month on Earth of joy and triumph: graduation, marriage, four weeks of honeymoon and fame; the planning, the packing, the round of farewells.

Now with her hand in Alex's, she followed the others, all in their gleaming white uniforms, up the ramp to the airlock, and into the third of a waiting line of moon-buggies. Ten buggies, ten passengers to each, two trips apiece, and the gaping hole in the side of the giant rocket had swallowed them all.

The rocket was not really large, not from the inside. So much fuel, so much freight, so many passengers; the proportions were flexible only within narrow limits. Each couple passed through the airlock hand in hand and edged along the corridor, crabwise, to their own cubicle.

Inside, they stripped off the white snowy uniforms, folded them neatly, and piled them in the doorway for collection. Stripped to the skin, they checked their equipment for the last time and settled themselves side by side, in the grooves and contours carefully molded to their bodies.

In perfect drilled coordination, almost ritualistically, they closed down the compartmented upper sections, starting at the feet, and leaned across each other to fasten the complex fastenings. When they were enclosed up to the armpits, they laid their heads into the fitted hollow facing each other at one-quarter-view, and strapped down the forehead bands and chin pads. Alex pushed the button that brought down the glassine air-dome over their upper bodies, and both of them set to work testing the supplier tubes and nozzles inside, making certain for one last extra time that everything reached as far as it should. Then, in perfect unison, as if this too were part of the ritual they had learned, each one extended a hand for a last touch, grasped and held tight, and let loose in haste.

Someone came down the hall—they could still see through the open doorway—collecting the uniforms to be dumped before takeoff.

They wriggled their arms down into the cushioned spaces along their sides; later, the arms could be freed again, to manipulate the supplier tubes, but during acceleration, every part of the body was enwombed, protected from shock and pressure, cold and heat, nauseous fear and killing radiations.

A gong went off inside the head-dome; that meant they were sealed in now. The loudspeaker began to tick off seconds. Frantically, foolishly, Joan tried to move her hips, suddenly certain that a necessary opening in the nest had been misplaced. She never remembered to feel glorious. There was a rending blast of soundless vibration, and a pushing, squeezing pain within the flesh, and brief relief about the placing of the opening, before the blackout came.

IV

PLUTO, PLANET OF MYSTERY

". . . frozen dark wastes, forever uninhabitable to man? Or will our pioneering sons and daughters find a new world to live upon? No one can foretell what they will find. Our best astronomers are in dispute. Our largest and most piercing telescopes give us daily—or nightly—new information, which only contradicts the hypotheses of the night before . . .

"We literally do not know, even today—and it is now three quarters of a century since Clyde Tombaugh confirmed the existence of the planet—what the size, the mass, or the true temperature of Pluto are . . . whether it has a frozen atmosphere or none . . . what composes its dark surface . . . or whether it is a native of our solar system at all!"

The newspapers and broadcasters of the time speculated loudly on the likelihood that the bright remote planet was a visitor from the stars, a wandering planet caught at the very fringe of the sun's gravitation, or even a watchful outpost of some alien race, a conscious visitant, swinging in distant orbit around this star against the day when men propelled themselves beyond the boundaries of their own system.

They even mentioned, but less often, the great likelihood that the confusing data on the planet merely meant it was composed entirely of very heavy metals. Uranium, for instance . . .

But for the far-sighted, for the world planners, the politicians and promoters who had made the trip possible, the near certainty of heavy metals was second only to one other goal: a starship.

The basic design of the *Newhope* was even then under government lock and key, a full forty years before the first step was taken in its construction. The fuel was in development. Astronomers, sociologists, metallurgists, psychologists, thousands of technicians and researchers on

Earth and Mars and the Moon were tackling the thousand and one problems of development. And the entire line of work hinged on one combination: there had to be a source of heavy metals near the building site: and the building site had to be at the outer edges of the System.

But Pluto was on the way *out*: a step to the stars.

They lived in the rocket at first; it was specially designed for that. The fuel tanks had been built for conversion to living quarters, because nobody knew for sure when they set out whether they'd ever be able to live on the surface. So they swung the ship into a steady orbit around the planet and got to work on the conversion. The designs were good; it was only a short time before the living quarters were set up and they could turn their attention to their new world.

What they found is by now so obvious and so familiar it is hard to conceive of the excitement of the discovery to *them*. But the simple discoveries of that first month could never have been made from Earth, or from Mars. For years astronomers had puzzled over the discrepancy between Pluto's reflective powers and its otherwise extrapolated size and mass. There had never been a valid planetary theory to account for its unique inclination to the ecliptic or the eccentricities of its orbit. Two years of observation by the Ganymede Expedition had added barely enough to what was already known to weigh the balance in favor of the completion of Project Pluto.

But from the vantage point of an orbit around the planet itself, the facts became self-evident. A whole new theory of planetary formation come into being almost overnight—and with it the final justification for the construction of the *Newhope*. There was no longer any doubt that other planetary systems existed; and in a surprisingly short time, the techniques for determining the nature of such planets were worked out as well.

Three months after arrival, the Pluto colonists began ferrying down the material for construction of a dome. Altogether, they lived in the rocket for thirteen Earth-months, before their surface settlement was habitable. But long before that, every one of them had at one time or another been down to the planet, and mining operations had begun.

Message rockets carried the progress reports back to Earth, and financial gears shifted everywhere. The government of the world poured all its power into the energizing of space travel industries. A new ship was built in a tenth the time the first had taken, and a crew of three piloted urgently needed supplies to the colonists.

Still, it was a one-way trip. Still, and for years to come, the supply rockets were designed for dismantling on arrival. Every part of a rocket-ship, after all, has an equivalent use on the ground; by building the ships themselves out of needed materials, the effective cargo space could be quadrupled.

From the beginning, every plan was made with one objective in view: the starhop. Nobody knew at first where the ship would go; no one understood *why* it had to go. But go it must, and Pluto was a way station.

Joan Thurman died young; she was barely sixty-seven when the accumulated strains of the early Pluto years wore her out. At that, she outlasted all but three of her fellow-passengers on that first Pluto rocket; and she outlived her husband, Alex, by 28 years.

Alex Thurman died in '06 in the Dome Collapse at what was to have been Threetown. Joan had been working before that on the theory for open-air cities; but it was after the crash that she turned her whole being to a concentrated effort. The result was TAP: the Thurman Atmosphere Process. Or that was *one* of the results.

When Alex died, Joan had three small children: Ariadne was ten years old, one of the very first Pluto babies; just exactly old enough to be able to take on most of the care of Thomas and John, who were four and three respectively.

Adne was born into pioneer hardship and pioneer cheerfulness. Then at the age of ten, the cheerfulness abruptly departed. Her father's seemingly indestructible strength betrayed her; her mother's watchful care was turned elsewhere. From the premature beginnings of her adolescence through its duration, she was effectively mother and housekeeper and wielder of authority to two growing vigorous boys.

When she was nineteen the first "passenger ships" were established between Pluto and Earth—round-trip transports—and a new kind of colonist began to arrive. The Malooks, who landed in '17, were typical, and Robert, their son and heir, was Ariadne's romantic ideal. When she was twenty they were married, despite everything that was done in either family to avert the expected disaster. For her, it was paradise . . . for a while. She read Bob's Earth-microfilms, and learned to imitate his Earth-accent. She never had to do a day's hard work from that time on, and still she had the handling of a charming irresponsible boy-child—as well as his money—until he grew up.

Bob was a year younger, you see . . . and till he did grow up, he loved having Adne's sweetly feminine domination exerted on his behalf. She showed him how to spend his money, how to live comfortably under dome conditions, how to adapt his Earth education to Pluto's circumstances.

The disaster Joan and the Malooks had anticipated did not occur. Adne and Bob simply drifted apart, eventually, after a few assertive acts on his part and several unpleasant quarrels. My birth may have precipitated things somewhat: they had managed well enough for ten years before colonial social pressures pushed Ariadne into pregnancy. Perhaps, once I was born, she found an infant daughter more interesting than a full-grown son. I don't know. I knew surprisingly little about either of them at the time; it is only in retrospect—in parallel, perhaps I should say—that I understand Ariadne at all. (If there had been any relatives on hand when Leah was growing up, I expect they'd have said she "took after" her grandmother.)

As for Bob, I hardly knew him at all until after they separated, when I was five or six; after that, he took me out on holidays and excursions, and he was beyond a doubt the most charming, exciting, fascinating man who ever lived—until I got old enough to be awkward for him. I never knew for sure, but I think he was some sort of professional gambler, or high-class con man, later on.

One way or another, I can see why Joe Prell looked good to Ariadne after Bob. I was nine, then.

V

JOE PRELL was a brash newcomer, as social standing went on Pluto: a passenger, not a pioneer. But he was energetic and smart. Two years after he landed, he and Ariadne were married.

It made very little difference to Em at first. If anything, she was happier after the divorce, because when she saw Bob, she had him all to herself. Anyhow, Joan was still alive then; her death, a year later, was a more serious matter.

By that time, though, Emma had begun to find a life of her own. She already knew that she wanted to be a doctor. She had learned chemistry and biology from her grandmother as easily and inevitably as she'd learned to eat with a spoon or later, to do a picture puzzle. She was still too young to start specializing in school, but she had Joan's library to work with. Joan's personal effects came to Emma, too, but the box of papers and letter-tapes didn't begin to interest her till much later. She spent most of her time, the next few years, bent over a micro-reader unrolling reel after reel of fascinating fact and speculation, absorbing all of it and understanding little, just letting it accumulate in her mind for later use.

Adne disapproved. She thought Emma should play more, and spend more time with other children. But Adne was too busy to disapprove very forcibly. Joe Prell was not a tyrannical man; he was a demanding one. And somewhere in there the twins came along: two baby sisters called Teenie and Tess. Emma was briefly interested in the phenomena of birth and baby care, but her "cold-blooded" and "unnatural" experimental attitudes succeeded in horrifying Ariadne so thoroughly that she returned without much regret, and no further restraint, to the library.

By that time, too, Pluto was becoming a pleasant place

88

to live. The first open-air city, built on the TAP principles, was completed when Emma was fourteen. Of course, only the richest people could afford it. The Prells could. Joe was a man who knew how to make the most out of a growing planet.

His financial operations were typical of his personality: he had a finger in real estate, and a finger in transport, but of course the big thing on Pluto was mining, and he had the other eight fingers firmly clamped on that.

Until they started building the *Newhope*. Or really, when they started talking seriously about it. Prell wised up fast. He let the real estate go and cut down on mining and wound up with Pluto Transport neatly tied up in a bundle just right for his left hand. From that time on, Prell's right hand sold his left everything that was needed to build the starship Prell was publicly promoting.

It was a really big deal to him. To Emma it was a dream, a goal, the meaning of everything. Joe didn't understand any part of the significance of that ship . . . but with his uncanny feel for such things, he was right in the middle of all the important projects. He was in on the actual construction job; he knew about the new designs, and the fuel specs . . . knew at least as much as Emma did, or most of the others actually in the expedition. But he and Emma had very different notions of what that fuel meant, and they argued about it right up to the last minute.

Or, rather, *she* argued. Joe Prell never argued with anybody. If he couldn't find a basis for agreement, he just turned the discussion into a joke.

Nothing could have been better calculated to infuriate Emma. She was twenty-four then, and very intense. Life was exciting, but more than that, life was terribly *important*. (As indeed it is, Carla; though I think you now see—or feel—the importance more clearly than I.) Prell wouldn't—couldn't—understand that; he never understood why anyone was willing to make the trip at all . . . to take a dangerous voyage to a distant unknown star!

Oh, he *could* see part of it: the challenge, the adventure. These are common enough stimuli, and the response to them not so different in nature from his own kind of adventurousness. It wasn't just wealth and power Joe was after; it was the getting of them, and he played the game as an artist. Patiently, over and over again (quite clearly feeling his responsibility *in loco*) he explained to Emma, and later to Ken, how little chance there was that the ship would ever reach Uller . . . how the voyagers were almost certainly doomed from the start . . . and how many other ways there were for restless, bright young people to satisfy their craving for excitement.

Emma sputtered and stammered trying to make him understand, but she succeeded only in making herself ludicrous. Actually, she didn't believe any more than he did that the ship had much chance of getting here. There were so *many* hazards, so many unknown factors; it was almost certain that somewhere in the plans some vital defense, some basic need, had been overlooked.

But the Project itself was important, whatever happened to those who were engaged in it. Just *building* the starship was what mattered: new problems to conquer, new knowledge to gain, new skills to acquire. And beyond that, the dream itself: "Centuries gone, man looked to the stars and prayed . . . He made them his gods, then his garden of thought, then his goals . . ."

Emma quoted the speech of a long-dead man, and thought Joe Prell would understand. She even brought him, hesitantly, Joan Thurman's diary to read; that, if anything, should have made him understand.

Prell was amazed, but unconvinced. He expressed at some length, and with considerable wit, his astonishment that the girl who wrote that diary could later have done the painstaking practical work that developed TAP. He couldn't see that all of it was part of the same dream.

He listened a little more respectfully when Ken tried to explain. Curiously enough, the two men got along. Prell liked Tarbell, and Ken at least could understand the other man. (I think, too, Joe was much impressed by Ken's audacity in marrying me; it had been firmly concluded at home some time before that I was doomed to single bliss. Too direct, too determined, too intellectual, too *strong*; no man would feel up to it, said Ariadne, and her husband agreed.) Ken spoke more calmly than Emma had, with fewer words, and much less argument, but what he said amounted to the same thing, and Joe Prell couldn't see it. He was too busy making money.

And he made it. He made enough, among other things, to fulfill Ariadne's greatest dream: before she died, she had her trip to Earth; she saw the sights and institutions and museums, made all the tourist stops, brought home souvenirs enough to keep her content for her remaining years.

But before that, she saw her daughter Emma off for Uller.

Ariadne was present when the tender took off from Pluto Port to deliver the lambs to the slaughter, carry them off to the starship that had hovered for months like a giant moon around the planet.

"It's . . . beautiful," someone standing beside her said, looking up, and Ariadne nodded automatically. It *was* beautiful; the most beautiful, most dangerous, most triumphant enemy she'd ever known, and she hated it with all the stored-up passion of her life.

"Emma!" she cried involuntarily in her farewell, "Emma, aren't you *afraid?*"

I tried to look at her, to let her look *into* me, but there was an unexpected veil of moisture on my eyes.

"I'm scared stiff," I said, and it was true, and then I smiled to let her know it didn't matter.

Then Ken had come up from somewhere, and was right beside me. He hadn't heard; at least I hoped he hadn't. I flashed the same smile up at him and looked away quickly, blinking the tear mist out of my eyes, and trying to send a wordless warning to my mother. If she said anything now . . .

She didn't have a chance.

"Come on, kid," Ken said. "They're waiting." He took my hand in one of his while he was still shaking hands with Joe Prell, and I blew a last kiss each to Tess and Teenie; then we turned and ran to the tender. I can remember being very conscious of our importance at the moment, how we must look to all the people there: two tall slim citizens of the universe, shining symbols of glamor and excitement.

Then we were in the tender, the whole bunch of us

91

on our way up to the giant ship. All the familiar faces looked just a bit more formal and self-conscious than usual, in spite of being jammed into the inadequate space and doubled up on the seats.

Somewhere in a corner, a group started singing, but no one else took it up, and it faded out. There wasn't much talk. We just sat there two by two . . . men and women, boys and girls, really—and tried to visualize what lay ahead.

Somewhere out there, beyond the spatial comprehension of a system-bound being, was a star. They called it Beta Hydri, and a group of strange men in a learned university said it had a planet. They called the planet Uller and credited it with mass and gravity and atmosphere tolerable to humans.

They could be wrong, of course. In thirty years of star-searching from the Pluto Observatory, it was the only one so credited. The professors weren't sure, but . . .

But someone had to go find out, and we were lucky. Out of the thousands upon thousands who applied for the privilege, we had been chosen. And even before we knew we were both to go, we'd found and chosen each other. We weren't cautious and careful the way Joan and Alex had been . . . the way most of the others in training were. The first time we met, we knew how it *had* to be for us. And though we worried, sometimes, that one of us would be picked, and the other left behind, it never seemed very likely; it just wouldn't *happen* that way.

But now we had chosen and been chosen in turn, and we had come to the end of the choosing.

When we left the tender, we knew what to do. We'd all done it dozens of times before in practice drill. We filed behind the couple in front to the ice trays, and took our places, lying down. We got our shots. When the crane lowered us into the hold, we still had our hands firmly intertwined. I know I shivered once, and thought I felt a tremor in Ken's hand and . . .

VI

AND WOKE UP slowly, still shivering, tingling in her toes

92

and fingertips and nose and ears, as her body warmed. Her hand was still in Ken's, and he was grinning at her.

"We made it, kid."

"So far," she said.

Somebody handed her a bowl of soup. That seemed outlandish, for some reason, and then she realized why. They weren't back on Pluto now; they were in space . . . far out . . . how far? Her hand shook, and the spoon with it, spilling hot soup on her leg, and there was no reason after all why they shouldn't have soup on a spaceship. *How* far?

She managed to get a spoonful to her mouth and became curious. Somebody had given it to her; who? She looked up.

Thad Levine was leaning over her, slipping a tray under the bowl for balance. He looked anxious. Em remembered him and now consciously remembered everything.

"Where's Sally?" she asked, and found her voice sounded normal.

"Instrument check," Thad said. The phrase was meaningful within seconds after she heard it, and then, as if a key had been turned in her mind, a whole set of meaning and concepts fell into place, and she was oriented.

Thad was looking down at her, smiling. "Feels funny, doesn't it?" he said. "Coming out, I mean." Of course; he'd been through it all already.

"A lot better than it felt going down!" Ken said explosively.

Em nodded. "Only I didn't really feel anything then," she said, "Did you? I was just . . ."

"*Scared!*" Ken picked up promptly on her hesitation. "You and me, and all the rest of 'em, too, baby."

"The freeze is too fast for you to feel . . ." Thad started mechanically, and grinned and let it drop. They'd all heard it over and over, said it to each other again and again, during the months of training. They'd had their practice-freeze periods and come out to reassure each other once more. "It's too fast to feel anything." The phrase was drummed into all of them before they went aboard for the last time. They all knew it.

But *cold* was not the only way it might make you feel; they all knew that by now. *Scared* was a feeling, too.

In training, you went into a room, and lay down in the tray, and you came to again in the same room, with the same people standing around, just a few hours, or even minutes, later. This time . . .

This time, they'd all gone under *not knowing*: not knowing whether they'd ever come out of it alive . . . whether their bodies could withstand year after year of frozen suspension, instead of the brief testing period . . . whether they'd wake up in the ship, or wind up as floating particles in space, or smashed on the surface of some unknown planet.

The Tarbells, Em and Ken, were just about halfway down the list; their shift of duty was timed for the twenty-fourth year of the voyage. And no one knew for sure that day they left whether the ship would really still be on its way in a quarter of a century.

Sally came in, bustling a little, as always. She was so familiar, she made Em realize for the first time how long it was. *On Pluto we'd be past forty now!*

"Em!" Sally rushed over to kiss her, and Ken must have realized at the same time Emma did that they'd hardly touched each other.

"Hey, she's *mine*," he said. And with his arms around her, everything was perfectly normal again.

(Parenthesis to Carla: ii)

27/9/52

It is a curious phenomenon of the human mind—or at least of mine—that past pain is painless in recall, but pleasure past and lost is excruciating to remember. I have found that for the purposes of telling this story I can readily undergo Recall Process for almost any desired period. The "Pluto Planet of Mystery" article came up intact from a batch of Joan Thurman's papers that I looked at more than a hundred years ago. And I went back to remember what Joe Prell looked like, and how he laughed at me. That didn't hurt in memory: it made me angry, both at his stupidity and at his unkindness, but it didn't hurt.

Carla, I tried to do Recall on the eighteen months I

spent in space with Ken, and with the four other couples who at one time or other were shift-partners. I know it was the *happiest* time I ever spent, but the one little part I remembered in detail, the section you have already read, was so packed with poignant pleasure that it almost stopped this work entirely.

I shall not attempt again to recall my days and nights with Ken. As much as I remember, through a rosy blur, is all I feel competent to talk of. It took years after his death to adjust to the loss. I do not know that I could make that adjustment again, and I will not subject myself to it.

As for the details of the trip . . . they are interesting, but I'm afraid they're all laid over with the sentimental mist that emanates from my happiness. It must have been vastly uncomfortable in the tiny cubicle we had as home. Certainly, we fought claustrophobia every minute of the time. We worked very hard, I know, and we were never quite without fear.

The starship *Newhope* had accommodation for five hundred passengers in the deep freeze, but only six in the living quarters. Three tiny cubicles surrounded three beds, and the walls were lined with overhead storage space.

The ship had been carefully designed to be run in routine circumstances by a crew of six, and a cautious and fore-sighted psychologist had arranged for overlapping shifts. When we woke up, the Levines were ending their shift: it was their last night out. We shared the first six months with Ray and Veda Toglio and the Gorevitches. Six months later, another couple replaced the Toglios, and six months after that it rotated again. Shift-change nights were big events. Later, the new couple would read the Log, and catch up on everything, but that first night everything would come out in a jumble of incident and anecdote, gossip and laughter: the no-doubt grossly exaggerated story of the error Jommy Bacon made three shifts back, before the Levines came out . . . a joke written into the log by Tom Kielty, fourteen years ago, but still fresh and funny . . . the harrowing account of a meeting with a comet in the third year out.

It is difficult to picture the situation. Next month you

95

are going to a planet infinitely farther away than Uller was from Earth, and yet you know with great exactness what you will find there. We had no such instruments in our day as now exist. All we knew when we set out was that this star appeared to have planets composed of terrestrial elements in quantities and proportions similar to those of the habitable solar planets.

We did not know whether we would find a place with breathable atmosphere, or bearable gravity, or water, or . . . or whether we'd find a planet at all. When our shift ended, and we went back into the freeze, it would be with almost as much uncertainty as the first time.

There was nothing to be certain of except the difficulties we had yet to face: if everything else worked out, if we completed the trip, and found a suitable planet, we would still be presented with almost insuperable obstacles. It was atomic fuel, after all, that made the starhop possible; it also made unthinkable any such doubling in space as had been designed for the Pluto ship. Our fuel tanks would be too hot for human habitation twenty years after we landed.

We weren't going to be able to live in an orbit; we were going to have to land and establish ourselves— wherever we were going—as quickly as we could.

VII

I DIDN'T GET out of the ship at all in the first thirty-six hours. There were twelve of us medics specially trained for the job of defrosting, and we had equipment to do only three couples at a time. Three medics to a unit, we worked over the humming machinery and the still bodies, testing, checking, adjusting, and checking again. You don't save seconds when the use of a limb or the functioning of an organ is involved.

Every delicate part of the human beings we worked over had to receive the same minute attentions: quick-thaw, circulator, oiler, hydrator . . . and then, when they began to come out of it, some familiar face to watch over them, to say the right things, to bring food at the right time.

But that part wasn't our job. Jose Cabrini was in charge in the awakening room. They came into our section frozen and motionless; they went out thawed, still motionless. It was weird and unreal and disheartening. We kept doing it because it was the thing to do, six hours on, three hours off to catnap in one of the cubicles, and back again to the waxen-stiff shapes of human bodies.

Ken was outside all that time. He was in the first batch of defrosts: a construction expert, he was also a third-generation Marsman. He was born in Taptown on Mars —the first TAP settlement—and had grown up under primitive open-air frontier conditions: a big-chested hawk-nosed man, wiry-muscled, steel-boned and almost literally leather-skinned. All the Marsmen we had were sent out in the first groups.

There were fifteen men altogether in his construction gang. In haste and near-total silence, still orienting to consciousness, they ate their bowls of fortified soup, drew their tools from Supply, and filed into the air space between the flimsy backwall of the tanks and the alumalloy sheets of the inner hull.

There was just space enough to stand and work while they pried the first plates loose. After that, they had more space: another twelve inches to the mid-plates.

Here they could begin to see space damage, the dents and warps of imploding matter from outside—even an occasional rent in the metal fabric.

Five of the big plates to make a shelter. Each one went a little more quickly. In twenty minutes they were ready to go Outside.

They knew it was safe. Other people were out there already. But each of them had lived through eighteen months of that voyage, consciously: eighteen months of smooth plates underfoot and glowing indirect lighting, of cramped quarters enclosed by walls, and cutting corners to save space—eighteen months closed in *from* Space . . .

They stood in the lock, and hesitated. Eyes met, and looked away.

Then somebody said:

"What the hell are we waiting for?"

"Sure, let's go out and take a walk."

"Come on out, the air is fine," someone else said shrilly.

Ken was Mars-born, and tough; he couldn't remember ever feeling this way before. He noticed it was an Earther who finally laid hand on the lever to open the door.

They left the plates in the lock while they got their footing on the terrain and blinked back the light of the sun.

Some of the others were cold, but Ken had chased sand devils on Mars at 10 below. He let the strange sun hit his head, drew the strange breath into his lungs, and exultation exploded inside him.

He wanted to shout; he wanted to run; he wanted to kiss the ground beneath his feet, embrace the man next to him. He wanted to get Emma and pull her out of the ship. He turned to the others.

"Come on!" he shouted. "Let's go!"

They dragged the heavy plates over the ground to a spot already marked out, and started building.

It was almost too easy.

Everything went according to schedule. The plans for re-use of the inner plates turned out to be sound. The temporary shelters were up and ready for use before the sun went down, and by the next day they were even moderately comfortable inside. Every bit of material that had gone into the construction of the starship, save the fuel areas and the outer hull, had been designed to serve a double purpose, and almost every design was satisfactory and practicable.

Oh, it wasn't easy in terms of work. Every man and woman of the five hundred worked till they dropped, those first two days. It wasn't just construction and renovation. There was an infinite amount of testing and retesting to be done, checking and rechecking. Round-the-clock shifts were stationed in the labs and at the instruments for the accumulation of data about the new planet, its star and system, its chemistry and geology and biology.

And through all the furious activity, data continued to accumulate. Almost-continuous broadcasts over the loudspeaker system relayed information to workers in and out of ship.

We heard the story of the landing: how the crew had

tested the planets, one by one, with routine spectroscopy and boomer-rocket samplers: the tenth at a distance vastly greater than Pluto's from the sun; the eighth, fifth, fourth (the missing ones were on the other side of the sun); and each time found rock-ribbed wastes, without air, without warmth, without hope of hospitality.

The third could have been made habitable, if necessary. To create an atmosphere is possible, when you have a base from which to work. But to have moved out of our ship into domes would have been difficult. We didn't have to. The second planet was Uller.

To those of us who were still in ship, the reports were probably more impressive than to those outside. If you could *see* the earth and feel it underfoot, if you were actually *breathing* the air, and lifting and carrying against the pull of gravity, the facts and figures wouldn't mean so much.

To me, each new item of information was overwhelming.

Atmosphere almost Earth-normal (closer than Mars's; as good as the best open-air city on Pluto).

Gravity almost Earth-normal (closer than any other *solar* planet).

Temperature outside, 8 degrees C. at the equator, where we'd landed. (Warmer than Mars; infinitely warmer than Pluto. *Livable!*)

First chemical analyses showed a scarcity of calcium, a scarcity of chlorine, an abundance of silicon.

Water: *drinkable!*

That floored me completely. To travel across the void, to an unknown planet, and find good drinking water! Well, not really *good*; the water here is actually a dilute solution of what we used to call "water glass" back on Pluto. It didn't *taste* right, but it wasn't harmful. (And in the early days in Josetown I got used to the taste, too. We didn't take the trouble to Precipitate it half the time.)

Uller was simply, unbelievably, Earth-like. With the single exception of the silicon change in chemistry, it might almost have been Earth.

These things are easy to remember and record. Speeches and announcements, and the impact of thoughts and words

. . . but I find it almost impossible to visualize again the way Uller looked to me when I first saw it. It all seems natural and familiar now; I know how strange and beautiful and frightening it was then, but I cannot quite place what was strange, or what was terrifying, or what seemed so lovely. What a foreign place has become home.

And if I could remember clearly, how could I describe it to people who have grown here?

I can only describe it as it looked to Emma, who grew up on Pluto, when it was her turn at last to stand with a group of medics in the airlock, and hesitate.

Sound, sight, smell, sensation . . . a whole new world, a strange world, a fairyland fantasy world of gem-encrusted trees and opalescent plants, of granular smooth ground laid out in shimmering changeable striae of color . . .

And all of it the stranger for the incredibly Earth-like sunset. She'd seen that sunset thirty times on Earth, and marveled every time. Here it was again, the same in every way, except for the sparkling reflections it struck from the impossible tree trunks and flowers.

Around it all the smell of growing things, subtly familiar, tangy, hard to identify, but undeniably the scent of life.

The double row of alumalloy structures looked dull and ugly in this stage setting of iridescence.

And it was cool . . . cold, even, but that didn't matter. *Where's Ken?*

For thirty-six hours she had been awake, and she had not yet touched him or talked with him.

She stood there, feeling the gritty granular *earth* beneath her feet, through her boots, not really looking at things, not trying to see or hear or taste or smell, but letting everything impinge on her, soak in as it would, while her eyes moved urgently, seeking one person in the weaving patterns around the street of houses, listening for just one voice in the murmuring welter of sound. Thirty-six hours one way, but literally *years,* in another sense . . .

"Em!"

He charged across the open space, big and bony and

beautiful, grimy, unshaven, hollow-eyed, his coveralls flapping around his legs, his arms reaching out for her long before he got there.

"Em!"

His arms went around her, pulling her against him, lifting her clear off the ground. The bristly hair on his face scratched her cheek, and the dirt of the new planet rubbed off his coveralls onto her spotless white jacket, and she smiled and opened her lips to his.

"You're cold," he said, after a while.

"Cold?" They found each other again, with hands, with eyes, with lips, and they stood close in a warmth of their own while the wind went around them.

Cold?

She laughed against his shoulder, opened her eyes sidewise to a flash of brilliant color, and backed off to look at *him* instead.

"Break it u-u-p!"

Someone was shouting at them, teasing, and someone else took her arm, and there was a whole crowd of people talking at once; she never remembered who they were, but friends, all of them, familiar faces. Hands to shake and cheeks to kiss, and excited words and gestures. And then more work to do.

Ten couples to a household; that was the plan for the temporary settlement. The outer walls and roofs were finished, but inside partitioning was still going on. Everyone helped; they all wanted their own rooms finished for the night.

Someone came around distributing mattress sacks, and Ken went off with Thad Levine to find an air pump. There was wild hilarity and a strange admixture of hysteria with relief, as one couple after another finished off their partitions and joined the others in the central hall.

Ken and Em stood a little apart from the others, watching, very much aware of the special and extraordinary quality of their own happiness.

Out of a picked group of five hundred healthy, eager young men and women, it is not difficult to select two hundred and fifty well-matched couples. Yet, when it is *necessary* to couple off, and all five hundred know it, a true marriage is the exception. Ken and Em were lucky, and they knew it. Em, watching the others, with Ken's arm around her, wanted somehow to share with all of them the flood of emotion in which she herself was caught up. They were all so impoverished by comparison . . .

The one unbearable thought ran fleeting across her mind, and left with it a chill track of envy for those other poor ones:

If anything happens to him . . .

Her hand tightened on his, and he looked down to her, not smiling, knowing what she felt. Together, they moved away from the group. They went into their empty room and closed the new-hung door behind them.

A body is a solitary thing. You live with it, live in it, use its parts as best you can. But always it is alone, a thing apart, your own unique and individual portion of space.

It stands alone while the mind flicks out to make contact with the surrounding world; while the brain receives images from the eyes, the nose, the ears; while the mouth tastes and the fingers touch: and even while food is swallowed and ingested. All this time the body, as a whole, is lonely.

At points in time, infinitely far apart from the viewpoint of the cell-components of this body, two people may find unity, complete and perfect, with each other. In the act of procreation confluence occurs—or more often in the mimicry of the act.

Many bodies never know anything but solitude. The motions of procreation are gone through again and yet again, without awareness. But Kenneth and Emma Tarbell were fortunate in their bodies. Loneliness called to desperate isolation, and they came together from the first with ease and understanding.

They kissed. That was all, for the time being: mouth to mouth, sealed together, while the breath sweetened between them, his hand on her shoulder, hers against his back, merged to a single entity. They kissed, endlessly, and without reserve.

Then they lay back on the floor together, close and content, relaxed and knowledgeable in their unity with each other.

After a while Ken moved. He lifted himself on an elbow, looked down on her peaceful face, and traced her smile with a fingertip. Her eyes opened, welcoming his touch, and she stretched luxuriously, with great contentment, then turned to meet his hunger with her own.

When Sally came banging on the door, yelling about dinner, they realized they were both starved. They went out and sat in a circle with the others, in the central hall, eating the landing meal of roast beef and corn and fruit that had left with them and traveled with them in the freezer across the years. And with it they drank, most ceremoniously, coffee made with Uller water. The vinegar-precipitation gave it an odd taste, but from that day on the taste of vinegar was good to all of them.

Little by little, the realization was sinking in. They were, thus, easily, and without obstacles, established on a planet twenty-one light years from home!

None of them stayed long after dinner. Two by two, they went off to their small separate cubicles, dragging their mattresses with them.

Leah Tarbell was not the only baby conceived that night.

VIII

THEY WOKE UP to brilliant sunlight, chill still air, and a hubbub of human activity. The big project now was exploration. The observations made by the landing crew indicated that the near-equatorial spot where they had landed was probably the most favorable location for a settlement. But we wanted closer ground observation before any further effort was made to establish the colony on a permanent basis.

Conditions over the surface of the planet varied widely —or *wildly* would be a better word, from the point of view of a solar meteorologist. This was the first human contact with a planet whose axis of rotation lay in the plane of its orbit of revolution. All the solar planets have axes more or less perpendicular to their orbits. On Earth, for instance, there is a shorter winter-night and corresponding summer-day at either pole: but only at the poles.

It took a good deal of readjustment in thinking habits to calculate Uller conditions with any degree of realistic accuracy.

The most obvious activity that day was the beginning of the construction of light aircraft for exploratory trips. Ken, of course, stayed on construction work, salvaging parts from the bowels of the big ship to build the smaller ones.

Meantime, scouting parties were being briefed and trained for their work, absorbing new information about what they were likely to find just as fast as it came out of the labs, still operating in ship around the clock. And everyone not directly concerned with the big project, or working in the labs, was assigned to one of the local scouting groups or specimen-collecting squads. Em found herself safety-monitoring a batch of wide-eyed collectors under the direction of a botanist, Eric Karga.

There were seven of them in the party, the others loaded down with sample cases and preservatives, Emma with a battery of micro-instruments strapped about her waist, a radiophone suspended in front of her face, and a kit of testing tongs and chemical reactors flapping against her leg. Nothing was to be touched bare-handed, smelled, or sampled, until the monitor's instruments had analyzed it and a verbal report on procedure had been made to the ship. With these precautions, it became evident almost as soon as they entered the forest that there were too many collectors and not enough instruments. Karga himself would have thrown all discretion to the winds . . . if there had been any wind, that is.

That was the first thing Emma became aware of when they were out of range of the bustling activity of the settlement: the literally unearthly silence. Emma had grown up in this kind of background silence, under domes. Later, she'd lived in a TAP open-air city filled with "natural" noises: leaves rustling in a made breeze; birds singing; small animals squeaking and creeping; an uninterrupted and infinitely inventive symphony of sound, behind and around the machines and voices and activities of men.

Here, in a *natural* open-air world, there was nothing to hear but the excited busyness of the small group of people: Karga rushing recklessly from horny-tipped plants to opalescent trees; the monitor-instruments clicking off their messages; the steady murmur of my own voice into the radiphone; and the awed exclamation of the collectors as novelty after unexpected novelty was uncovered in the fairyland fantasy of a forest.

The first two-hour period went by almost before they realized it. None of them wanted to go back, and the prearranged return for a complete checkup in medicenter seemed foolish even to Em, considering how careful on-the-spot precautions had been. But they really needed another monitor, or at least another phone. And even more to the point: the rule had been established; therefore it must be obeyed. Regularity and conformity are the materials of which caution is formed, and caution was the order of the day.

Five hundred people seemed like a lot when they were all crowded into the tender that took them up to the *Newhope* orbit around Pluto; or when they were being processed through defrost, the first two days on Uller; or when shelter had to be provided, and fast, for all of them. Now, looking outward from a double row of thin metal-walled huts at an unknown planet, five hundred humans seemed very few indeed. One death would leave a hole that could not be filled.

They griped about unnecessary precautions all the way back, but back they went, and through the careful psychophysical that Jose Cabrini and Basil Dooley had worked out together.

Over a quick cup of coffee, they picked up some fresh data on the morning's discoveries. Evidence so far showed no signs of a dominant civilized, or even intelligent, natural species. Some small carapaced insect-like creatures had been found, one or two varieties in abundance. And the river from which they had drawn and purified their water was teeming with microscopic life. But nothing larger than a healthy Earth-type cockroach had turned up yet, and nothing any more dangerous, either.

The small fauna, like the plant life, appeared to be almost entirely constructed along the lines of the silicate exoskeleton, carbon metabolism variety. Some of the smallest amoebas lacked the skeleton, but everything

just smart enough not to want to show their faces? On a planet this size, a *small* species could have a completely material civilization, if that's what you're looking for—they could even make noise, by their own standards—and we'd have a hell of a time finding out about it."

"Well, they'd have some kind of effect on the ecology of the planet, wouldn't they?"

"We wouldn't know that yet, either," Emma said slowly. She was excited now, turning over the possibilities Jo was suggesting, but she knew better than to display her excitement in the discussion. People always seemed to mistrust enthusiasm. "TAP is honest ecology," she pointed out. "An alien coming to Pluto would have a rough time finding out that the open-air cities are all artificial."

Intelligent life! Non-human, non-solar intelligent life! And it was possible! This world had every prerequisite for it.

"Well, if they're that small, you're going to have some trouble talking to them."

"Might *never* find out," someone else suggested, "if they didn't find some way to communicate with humans. That's your real problem, Jo. Suppose you find these critters? How are you going to talk to them? And turn it around: if they live in what looks like natural circumstances to us, how will we know which ones to try and talk to?"

"Which sums up neatly," Jo answered him, "the problems to which I shall probably devote the rest of my life."

There was an intensity in his tone that silenced the table for a moment.

"Then whatever they are, let's hope you don't find 'em. We can't afford to lose your services, Jo." It was Ken. He slid his long legs over the bench next to Emma and squeezed her hand. "What goes on?"

Everybody began talking at once again; everyone except Emma, who was surprised at the irritation she felt. He had no business stepping on Jo that way, she thought, and she didn't want to talk about it any more.

"Aren't you eating?" she asked.

"Ate before; they said you were getting a checkup, so I had lunch and left my coffee to have with you."

He smiled at her and reached for her hand again, and

the irritation vanished. Even when the argument resumed, and she found that the two of them were tending to opposite extremes of attitude, she wasn't annoyed any more. They didn't have to agree about everything, after all. They had disagreed before. But this was such an *important* thing—the way you'd feel about an alien creature.

Still, she could understand it better in Ken than in Basil. Ken was a construction man. His work was in materials, in parts and pieces to fit together. He didn't think in terms of the living organism, or the subtle and marvelous interplay of functions between organs, organism, individuals, species. Basil was a medic, and a good one; he should have understood.

Karga was at her shoulder, politely restraining himself from urging her, but too anxious to keep himself from a silent display of impatience. She stood up and threw off the whole foolish mood. Ken would understand when they had more time to talk. And there would be plenty of time later . . .

IX

IT MIGHT HAVE been a segment of petrified log. But it had legs, and the tapered bulbous end was a head. It might have been a cross between a pig and a dachshund, painted in streaky silver, and speckled with sequins. But it had *six* legs, and the head was too shapeless; there was no visible mouth, and there were no ears at all.

And when you looked more closely, it wasn't actually walking. It was skating; six-legged tandem skating, with the sharp-runnered feet never lifting out of the ground, leaving an even double row of lines incised in the granular ground behind it. And the squat barrel body glided forward with unexpected grace.

It moved into the street of huts, its head set rigidly right in front of its body, while the bulging dull black eyes darted and danced in all directions.

The first man who saw it shouted, and it froze in midglide. Then the man's comrade silenced him, and the creature started forward again. A crowd began to gather, and after the manner of a crowd, a murmuring noise grew from it. The creature froze once more, and veered off in another direction.

Someone in the crowd had a gun. He raised it and took careful aim, but someone else reached out to lower the barrel before the fool could shoot.

"It hasn't hurt anything!"

"Why wait till it does?"

"How do you know . . . ?"

"Here's Jose."

"Hey, Jo, here's your native. Look smart to you?"

Laughter. Comments and wonder and more and more uncontrollable laughter, while the creature skated directly away from the crowd and edged up against an alumalloy hut.

"Think we can catch it?"

"The projector . . . are they getting it?"

Jose sent a whisper running back, and it only increased the volume of the sound. Better one noise than the hubbub, he thought, and spoke sharply above the crowd.

"Quiet!" Then in the momentary silence he spoke more softly. "I don't think it likes noise."

After that, he left the group and stepped forward steadily, slowly, toward the shadow of the hut where the creature stood.

He tried to curb his own eagerness and make his advance without hurry and without menace. He tried, too, to ignore the slowly swelling hum of the crowd behind him. All his thoughts were on the animal, all his attention focused.

If it had intelligence, there had to be a way, *some* way, to make contact with it.

He was close enough now to touch it if he would, but he held back. It was looking at him, and from that moment on, he never once doubted that the animal was rational, impressionable, capable of communication. It was there in the eyes, in the way the eyes studied him, in something he *felt* in his own mind, hazily and without comprehension, examination-and-greeting was exchanged between them.

The creature turned to the hut, and there was a questioning feeling in Jose's mind. He did not want to speak aloud. Telepathy? Something of the sort. He thought the idea of a dwelling place, a shelter; all animals understood the concept. He thought it as hard as he could, and knew he had failed, because the animal's next act was one of deliberate destruction.

Jose was the only one close enough to see exactly what was happening, but by that time they had cameras running from three different angles. Everybody saw the details, blown up, later: the people in the crowd, and those who, like Ken, were in ship, or like Em, out of the settlement.

It glided forward smoothly once again, edging toward the house, and gradually its body tilted sideways at an angle to the ground, without bending except at a concealed joint between the barrel-trunk and the righthand set of legs.

The lefthand set described a perfect clean curve up the side of the building and down to the ground again. Then it reversed, and moving backwards, once more standing upright, edged the lefthand front runner slightly sideways and sheared a neat chord out of the wall.

The crowd saw the piece of metal fall away, and gasped, in unison, and then, for the first time, fell completely silent. What had just happened was virtually impossible. Alumalloy was *tough*. An oxy torch would cut it . . . in a matter of hours. This creature had sliced it like a piece of meat.

The man with the gun took aim again, and nobody stopped him, but he couldn't fire. Jose was too close to the beast.

"Jo!" he called, and then a woman's voice said loudly, "Shhh!" as the animal froze again. Jose looked around and smiled and waved another silencing motion at them.

He looked back just in time to see the tuskongs coming out. Two parallel needle-edged blades, curved like a set of parentheses, they descended slowly from underneath the head, and went through the metal like tongues of fire through straw. The creature glided forward, and a long thin strip was sliced from the center of the chord. The blades were hinged, somehow, and they seemed to be sticky inside. The needle edges met under the strip of metal, and the strip was carried up inside the tusks—

110

or tongs—as they retracted slowly into whatever opening (a mouth?) they came from.

"Jo, get outa there! I'm gonna shoot!"

There was no doubting that tone of voice. Jose held up a pleading hand, and stepping softly, walked backwards toward the crowd. Until he turned around, he knew, the man would hold fire. He waited till he was too close for his turned back to matter any more, then asked quietly, with all the command he could put into a low tone. "Wait."

"Why?" The man whispered in reply; then he would wait to shoot.

"We might as well see what it's going to do."

"Ruined a wall already. Why wait for more?"

The words were passed back through the crowd, and the murmuring swelled again. The creature seemed to have adjusted to the noise. Calmly, it sliced another strip of the virtually impregnable alloy and drew the metal into its interior.

Then, while they watched, it turned again to the wall, and, folding its legs under it, slanted forward to edge its snub-ended snout inside.

The gun came up once more, and Jose knew he couldn't stop it: the beast had poked its head inside a sacrosanct human habitation. But: "Higher!" he whispered piercingly, "Over its head!" The barrel jerked upward imperceptibly just as the gun fired.

It couldn't have hit; Jose was sure of that. But a sunburst of cracks appeared on the surface of the animal's hide, for all the world like the impact of a projectile on bulletproof glass. And at the same instant a jagged lightning-streak arced from the center of the "wound" to the side of the hut.

The gunner drew his breath in sharply. "It's a goddam walkin' dynamo!"

And the crowd talk started up once more.

"Quartz . . . crystals . . . piezo-electric . . *generates!*"

It's scared, Jose thought—but now the animal had shown what power it had, so was the man. The gun came up again.

"*Stop!*" Jose shouted. "Can't you see it's scared?"

It worked: not on the man, but as Jose had hoped,

111

on the beast, and the man hesitated. The creature backed away from the wall and started forward past the hut, away from the crowd and the street. It was leaning to one side, the good side, and lurching a little, going very slowly. Now its trail was a deep indentation on one side, and a barely marked line on the other, and in between a grayish ooze of something that didn't seem to be coming from the injured side. Perhaps from the "mouth" or whatever those tusks went into? It was hard to tell.

The gunner still stood with his weapon half-raised.

"The field projector," Jose whispered to him, and the man handed his gun to his neighbor, and ran for the rocket.

The Ullern animal had progressed perhaps fifty meters when he came out of the airlock again, a dozen others tumbling after him, with bulky pieces of equipment that took rapid shape on the ground.

There was grim speed in the way they worked. Jose, watching them, understood their fear, and could not share it; felt the pain of the hurt animal and grieved for it; fervently hoped the creature's piezo-electric properties would not make it unduly vulnerable to the projector.

There was a crackling, blinding flash of electricity as the field hit it.

Ken Tarbell answered the alarm bell reflexively, absorbed the data, and fell into drilled pattern responses with the projector team, getting it out of the airlock, setting it up, aiming, firing.

It should have trapped the animal in an invisible miniature dome through which no physical object could pass. Instead there was a small-scale electric storm over the creature, and when the glare was gone, it was lurching along just as slowly as before, with an odd look of urgency, but apparently none the worse for wear.

There was total silence in the camp, and then a shot shattered the quiet. Ken saw it hit; he saw the bullet *bounce* off the creature's hide, and saw the ragged black cracks radiate from the point of impact on the glittering surface of the skin. And he saw the *thing* keep moving, a little slower, maybe, but still making progress. It was heading towards the forest where Emma was.

Had anyone warned them?

Em had a radiphone; Ken turned and raced back to the ship, fear moving his feet while completely separate thoughts went through his head. The thing could fight off an electromagnetic field, but it was vulnerable to shock; he knew how to stop it.

In ship, he clambered up the ladder to Supply, grabbed the two things he needed, and leaped down again ignoring the footholds. Outside, he realized the others were on the same track, but their weapon was not strong enough. The crowd had separated into three groups, surrounding the thing, and they were shouting at it, screaming, singing, yelling, stomping, first from one side, then the other.

Each time it responded more feebly than before, moving away from the new source of noise. Someone ran past Ken, headed for the ship, and he caught from somewhere a few words of questioning conversation. They thought they could head it into a trap; but what kind of trap would *hold* it?

Ken had the phone ready at his mouth, and the weapon in his hand. His eyes were on the beast, and he saw that each time the direction of the noises changed, it seemed a little less frightened, a little less anxious to change its path. Any animal learns what to fear, and what is safe. The shouting wouldn't hold it long, he thought, and as he thought it, saw the creature head straight for the group that stood between it and the forest edge, undeterred by stamping, screaming cacophony.

"Emma! Em!" He spoke urgently, low-voiced, into the phone. "There's an animal here. Headed your way. *Watch out!*"

He didn't realize for the first instant what had happened. The Ullern wasn't limping out toward the forest any more. It was moving fast now, as if something had galvanized it into action, somehow summoned its last resources of strength and speed. It was gliding fast and smooth and with a purpose in its direction . . . back into camp, back toward the rocket, *straight at Ken*.

It was coming too fast to stop or fight or escape. There was only one thing to do, and Ken did it. He threw the hand grenade he'd brought from the ship.

Let me through now, everybody out of the way, I'm a doctor, let me through. There's a man hurt in there, I'm a doctor.

Ken, oh Ken . . .

Come on now, everybody out of the way, this door is in the way. Oh, Ken!

"I'm sorry, Emma. You know we can't let you in. We're doing everything we can . . ."

"Oh, Basil, don't be silly. I have a *right* to help."

"Em, I think we can manage better than you could. He's . . . he's pretty badly cut up. You'd be bound to . . ."

"What do you think I am, Dooley? Somebody's sniveling wife? I'm *a doctor!*" *And this is how they feel when we tell them they have to wait, now I'm not a doctor, he's right, I'm a sniveling wife, I'm even sniveling, I can hear it. But I'm a doctor, if I act like one they'll have to let me in . . .* "What . . . what do you . . . What are his chances, Doctor?"

"They'll be better if we let Basil get back in there, Em."

Oh, it's you, is it? The nice careful semantic psychologist, the happy little word-weigher, the fellow who wanted to see some native life! "Leave me alone, Jose. Please, go away! Basil . . ."

Basil is gone, he went back to Ken, you can't go to Ken, they won't let you, they're going to let him die, and they won't let you help, they've got the door locked, too, you tried that before, and they're all in there and they'll let him die.

"Em . . ."

"I said go away. Leave me *alone,* won't you?"

"Em . . . it's me, Thad."

And she collapsed gratefully, childishly, in familiar, friendly arms, abandoning the effort to be calm, to be convincing, to be reasonable and professional. They weren't going to let her into that room, whatever she did, so she sobbed in Thad's arms, until he said:

"Go, on, Emmy, cry all you want to," And then she stopped.

The door opened and closed again, and she looked up at Thad, and saw the news there, and all the confused emotion was gone. Now she was calm enough, and tired.

"He's . . ."

"Dead," Thad said out loud; one of them had to.

"They never let me say goodbye."

"He wasn't conscious, Em."

"He would have known!"

Thad didn't try to answer.

X

TWO DAYS LATER, the entire settlement was fenced in with a vibration-field. No other animals showed up in the time it took to get the fence operating, and the occasional creature that came in sight afterwards turned quickly away. We knew, from that first experience, that vibration was not necessarily fatal to the beasts, but that they could be frightened and/or hurt by anything along the line, in or out of the human sonic range.

I think now that most of us rather overestimated, at the time, the danger that vibration represented to them; it was natural enough, because we were all attributing the creature's obvious difficulty when it left the hut to the cracks the first shot had left on its surface. Actually, it took a shock as severe as the bomb that was finally exploded almost underneath it, to damage the brittle armor enough to stop it in its tracks.

It was interesting, too, that when they tested the bullets in the ballistics lab, it turned out the first hadn't touched the animal, and the second had hit squarely, been flattened by the impact of the super-hard hide, and *bounced* off. Yet the cracks from the second had been hardly more severe than from the first. It was difficult to visualize a living creature, a mobile animal, going about with a skin as brittle as glass, as easily shattered by shock waves and vibration as by actual impact; yet that was obviously the case.

The bullet cracks, we decided during the autopsy, were just about as serious, and as painful, as whip-welts might be to a human. That is, there was no loss of "blood" and no real impairment of function; there was, instead, a state of potential damage, in which any ill-considered motion might result in a serious tissue break. However, if you cover a man's *entire* body with welts, no matter how carefully you place them so as not to break the skin, you

115

can incapacitate him completely, and possibly even kill him, by reducing skin function. This was, apparently, the net effect of the bomb: simply to destroy the animal's exterior mechanism for reacting to stimulus.

There was some doubt, too, as to whether the bomb had actually killed the thing. Possibly it wasn't entirely dead at first, but just immobilized. We didn't get close enough the first few hours to know for sure whether it was still breathing. We did, with instruments, check on temperature and response to various stimuli, and all the results, *in human terms,* indicated an absence of life. But it appears that the creature may have continued to ooze out that curious gel for some time after it fell. At least, when it was moved, there was a largish puddle underneath it; this might, of course, have been ejected at the time of the fall.

It took several days of fine and fancy improvization at dissection (we had only the one sample, and we didn't want to spoil it) to find out just what that ooze was. Of course, we got a chemanalysis right away, but that only gave us an idea. The stuff was a mixture of alumalloy compounds and body fluids of a high Ph, containing short-chain silicones and some quartz. The analysis presented a variety of interesting possibilities, but it needed the completion of the dissection to be certain.

When we knew, it was funny, in a way. The visiting beastie had got itself a bellyache from eating our house. All we could figure was that it ordinarily subsisted on the native plant life, hard-shelled and soft-interiored, silicone outside the silicarb inside. It had identified, with whatever sense organs it used for the purpose, the discernible trace of silicate in the alumalloy, and the presence of carbon in the interior, and had mistaken the house for an extra-large new variety of plant life. The aluminum, in compound with more tidbits of this and that than I can now remember, had reacted to the additional jolt of silicones in the animal's stomach by turning into a mess of indigestible (even for *it*) gelatinous-metallic stuff. The oozing trail it left behind as it tried to leave the settlement was nothing more or less than the trickling regurgitation of an animal with an inflexible outer hide and an extreme vulnerability to the shock of sudden motion.

This much we knew after we had traced the thing's alimentary canal with an oxy-torch, a hacksaw, and (when we got inside) more ordinary surgical implements. The inner tissues were more familiar-looking than the outside, of about the same composition and consistency one would find in an Earth animal, differing only in the replacement of the carbon chain compounds by silicon chains. Perhaps the most curious and interesting phenomenon, from a medical viewpoint, was the way the soft inner tissues changed gradually to tough fibrous stuff, somewhat similar to silicon-rubber, and then, still gradually, so that it was almost impossible to determine at what point the actual "skin" began, to the pure amorphous quartz of the hide-armor. The vicious-looking tuskongs were a natural enough adaptation for a creature that had to chomp up horn-hard surfaces with a minimum of vibration.

All this, and a good deal more of no especial interest except to a medic, we learned in the dissecting room and in reports from the chem lab during the two days it took to get the fence operating. Meanwhile, all exploration was stopped; a guard was maintained around the camp at all times until the field was in force, and a smaller lookout-guard afterwards. Work on the light aircraft went on, and construction of freight transport planes began immediately. We had already determined that we would move the settlement, if any habitable part of the planet could be found where these creatures did not exist. And all further investigation, as well as transport, would proceed by air.

The move was made exactly forty days after the Ullern came into the camp. If you've read the old Bible, there's a certain quaint symbolism in that figure. The date, of course, was 12/7—Firstown Day. And it is curious to note, in passing, the odd sentimentalities that were applied to this business of dates and calendars.

One of the most impressive similarities between Earth and Uller was in the matter of time. An Earth-hour is a few minutes shorter than an hour here; the Uller-day, according to the Earth-setting of the chronos when we arrived, was about 26 hours long. And the year on Earth —the actual period of revolution around the sun—is slightly more than 365 days, instead of our 400.

Logically, when we arrived, we should have established a new metrical calendar and time-scale. Ten months of forty days, or forty weeks of ten days each—either one—would have been simple and efficient. A day divided into ten or twenty hours would have been sensible. But either one would have had the same effect: to make us stop and think when we spoke of time.

Humans—set apart from all other indigenous species of Earth by their ability to think—have a long-bred habit of avoiding mental strain. And the similarities to Earth-time were too noticeable and too tempting. We simply fixed our clocks and chronos to run slower and so saved ourselves from adjustment to the difference. The day here is still twenty-four hours, and the year has twelve months still. It didn't bother us to have 36 days each month, that part of the calendar had always been flexible. And the interim Fourday at year's end was an old Earth custom, too, I've since found out. Our only real departure was the six-day week.

(Parenthesis to Carla: iii)

2/10/.52

I'M AFRAID I have been, in these last pages, rather drily concerned with facts as familiar to you as to anyone who has grown up side by side with the Ullerns. This was partly in an effort to get across to you some of the feeling we had then: how new all this information was to us and how difficult to assimilate. Also, the jump out of emotion into preoccupation with data was typical of my own reactions at the time.

I had one emotion that I was willing to identify, and that was hate. I worked in the dissection lab whenever I was awake, and took my meals there too, watching the work as it proceeded, and enjoying every slice and sliver that was carved out of that beast. That much I *felt*; for the rest, I had ceased to be aware of any feelings at all. I had an overwhelming thirst for knowledge about the animal that had killed Ken; but Ken himself, and what his death meant to me . . . this I refused to think about at all.

118

When I realized I was pregnant, I was still sleepwalking as the true love of a dead man. I was gloriously happy, and terribly depressed. Ken's baby would be Ken-continuing, and so not-quite-dead. But Ken *was* dead! I had no husband, and my child would have no father to grow up with.

Most of the time, the first few months, I just forgot I was pregnant. I mean that, literally. Someone would say something about it, and I'd have to collect my wits and remember, consciously, what they were talking about. Maybe I didn't want to have the baby, and was trying to lose it by behaving as if I weren't pregnant, working long hours at tough jobs . . . but I don't think so. I think I was determined not to be happy about anything, and afraid of being depressed. I was, in short, determined not to *feel* anything.

You can't grow a child inside you without feeling it: feeling it physically, as your body changes, and feeling the subtle complex of emotions that accompanies the changes. But I tried, and for a short time I succeeded.

I remember that Jose fell into step with me one time, as I was going from my room to the lab, and tried to talk to me; it didn't occur to me that he was taking a professional interest. I thought I had myself completely under control and was rather proud of the way I was behaving. I didn't even listen to what he said, but took for granted that he still considered me his ally in the stupid argument of the first day of exploration.

"How are you feeling, Emma?" I guess he said . . . some such thing, because it gave me an opening to turn on him and demand:

"How do *you* feel? Now you've got your *intelligent* life, how do you like it?"

I can remember thinking I'd said something witty as I stalked away. The unforgivable thing that Jose had done to me, you see, was not that he had convinced me of an erroneous attitude, but that he had convinced me of something about which I argued with Ken the last time I saw him . . . and that I had continued to question Ken, and to cling to Jo's attitude, right up to the moment Ken proved his point with his own death.

I do not now apologize for these reactions, or even

comment on them, but simply state them here as honestly as possible. Perhaps it was healthy, after all, that I reacted as I did. Hate kept me going where grief would have, literally, prostrated me. And I did not mourn Ken, then; I just hated: everything and everyone that had contributed in any way to his death.

It occurs to me only now that perhaps that curious business of our time-reckoning system, as well as many other apparently irrational things we did, was done in part to save our faculties of adaptation for necessities. I still don't know whether it was inherent weakness or instinctive wisdom. It doesn't matter, really, and I see I'm digressing again. I *am* getting older. But I can still remember being very scornful of the same sentimental clinging to a calendar when I was a child on Pluto—and there they'd had more excuse. Pluto doesn't rotate at all; it has no natural day. And its year is hundreds of Earth-years long. So for a system of time-reckoning that applied to human values, the old one was as good as any other there, except in terms of arithmetical efficiency.

Here it was another matter altogether: we *forced* an old system to fit new circumstance; why? Because we were human, and each of us had grown up somewhere. Because we had been children back there, and some part of each of us was still a child *there*, and needed a safe familiar handle of some sort to cling to. In space, we were completely set apart from "home." Time was our handle.

XI

THE NIGHTS WERE already long when the colony moved south. Firstown was located just below the 47th parallel, close enough to the pole so that few of the Ullern animals cared to brave the scorching summers or freezing winters; still far enough so that humans could hope to survive them.

They had just about nine weeks of steadily shortening days in which to prepare for the winter night; and at that latitude, it would be fourteen weeks after the last sunset before it would rise again for a few minutes of semi-day-

120

light. The temperature, in Fourmonth, was already below freezing, and Meteorology predicted cheerfully that the winter-night low would be somewhere about −50 degrees.

To some of the others, the long stretch of cold and darkness was frightening. To the Plutonians and Marsmen the cold meant nothing, and for the former, artificial light was as natural as sun. Emma, had she stopped to think about it, would have been grateful for even the few months each year of Earth-normal temperate weather and sunlight.

She didn't think about it. She worked, with grim preoccupation, all through those early months. When she no longer had the body of the beast to cut up, she threw herself into the conquest of the *planet* that had killed Ken . . . which was, too, the fulfillment of their joint dream. She was alone now, but somehow if she worked twice as hard, she could still make the dream come true for *both* of them.

She was lucky, too, because throughout that fall and winter there was always more work to be done than there were hands to do it. When her own shift at Medicenter was done each day, she went out and found more work; filled in on the auxiliary power plant construction when people were sick; helped build the nursery and furnish it; spent long hours in the library, as she had done in her youth. Now she was studying chemistry, silicon chemistry. *Organic* silicon chemistry, working it out where it didn't exist, from what little the films recorded of solar knowledge.

She worked alongside other people, but made little contact with any of them, and she was happiest in the hours she spent alone, studying. She did not join the others in the big social hall, when they met on 18/5 to spend the last full hour of sunlight under the U.V. glass dome; she barely noticed when the long night set in. Almost, she might have been Emma Malook again, living under the Pluto dome, moving through artificial light and air, such as she'd known since birth, between Joan Thurman's library and Joe Prell's home, living all the time, wherever she was, in a fantasy of being grownup and a doctor. Only now she *was* a doctor, and the fantasy was being Emma Malook. She was Emma Tarbell, and

121

she was going to have a baby, by which she knew indisputably that she was full-grown now.

The days went by, one like the last, and all of them almost painless. In her sleep, she would reach out across the bed to emptiness and withdraw her hand before she woke to know her own loneliness. But once awake, she followed the pattern of work and study rigorously, tended her body and the new body growing inside it, and when she was tired enough not to lie awake, went back to bed again.

The single event that stirred her immediate interest that winter was the Ullern they caught. One of the regular weekly scouting parties brought it back, along with their charts and statistics on conditions outside. They'd thought it was dead at first, then they discovered it was living, but too weak to resist capture. In the lab, they found out quickly enough that the animal was simply half-starved. They fed it on specimens of local flora, and it flourished.

Then why, outside, surrounded by the same plants in abundance, had it almost died of starvation? That took a little longer to find out. Cabrini tried a specimen from outside on it when the next scouting squad returned and found it refused the frozen food. After that, they tried a range of temperatures and discovered it would eat nothing below the freezing point of carbon dioxide. That made sense, too, when you thought about the problems of eliminating solid CO_2.

Jo was tremendously excited. "If they had fire, they could use the whole planet!" he pointed out, and met a circle of questioning eyes.

"Planning to teach this one?" Basil asked, too quietly. Jose joined the general laughter, and let the matter slide. It was encouraging to know that at least half the year the colony was completely safe from the beasts . . . and to have some kind of clue to a method of attack.

They kept the animal in a sort of one-man zoo, an island of Uller-earth and Uller-plants surrounded by a five-foot moat of gluey fluid through which its runners could not penetrate. And Jo, apparently through sheer stubborn conviction that it was possible to do so, actually managed to make "friends" with the creature, at least, he was the only one who could approach it when it regained its strength, without some display of hostility.

The first sun rose again on 6/8, and by the beginning of Ninemonth, the days were already nine hours long. By then, too, Emma was far enough along to have to slow her pace; she had just twelve more weeks—two months—to term.

It was a sad and lovely springtime. In the last weeks of waiting, Emma gave up everything except her regular work at Medicenter. Studying no longer interested her; instead she would go out and sit for hours in the crisp fresh air and Tenmonth sunshine, intensely conscious of the life within her, impatient for its birth, and yet somehow fearful of letting it loose. It would be a boy, of course, it had to be a boy, and she would name it Kenneth.

Leah was born on 36/10, right in the middle of Medicenter's first and biggest baby boom. There were twenty-three new infants in the colony in two weeks' time.

Inevitably, Emma spent much of her time the next month with the other young mothers, all of them learning and sharing the care of their babies. After the first—not disappointment, but surprise—she didn't mind Lee being a girl; and she was surprised, too, to discover how much pleasure she could find in the simple routine of feeding and cleaning a tiny infant. Her own infant.

She was busy and useful again, because the other mothers came to her for advice and opinions at every turn. She was a medic, after all, and had *some* previous experience with babies.

Under the best of circumstances, it is likely to be eight or ten weeks after birth before the mother is once again quite convinced of her own existence as a separate and individual person. Emma had little desire to return to that conviction. She was stirred by occasional questioning curiosities about the details of the refrigerating system, as the heat outside mounted through the summer day. She began to pick up some of the chemistry films a little more often, and went, from time to time, to the zoo-in-a-lab where the Ullern was still kept, to find out what they had learned about it. But on the whole, she was more than content with the narrow slice of reality in which she found herself. Even her work at Medicenter, as she resumed it, somehow concerned itself primarily with babies: those already born, and those that were still expected.

The first New Year's Eve on Uller came in midsummer, just long enough after Lee's birth for Em to have gone to the celebration comfortably if she wished. She preferred to stay in the nursery and let the other mothers go, with their husbands. Two months later, when the early fall nights were beginning to be long enough to cool the air a little, she found her first real pleasure in contact with the new environment.

In the hour before dawn, it was possible to go outside without frig-suits; and every day, from that time, Em adjusted her sleeping so that she would be awake at that time of day. First, when the nights were still short, she would leave the sleeping baby in the nursery; later, when dawn began to coincide with the chrono-morning, she would take Lee with her.

Alone, or with the baby at her side in a basket on the ground, she would sit by the edge of the dry riverbed and watch the world wake up. The first sun's rays, felt before they were seen, brought a swarm of near microscopic life out of the moist earth of the riverbed, and started an almost imperceptible stirring in the trees. Emma would sit and watch while the budded branches snaked up and out of the sparkling columns of their trunks, turned their tender new greenery up to the sun for a brief time, and then melted back into the safety of the cool trunk shells.

Day after day, she tried to remember why the flexible tree trunks were so fondly familiar. It was *silly,* somehow; and then at last the memory came. A little ball of stuff that bounced, and broke off clean when you stretched it . . . that molded to any shape, and dropped back slowly to a formless mass again when you left it alone . . . a childhood toy, that someone had called *silly putty*. Some kind of silicon compound, she supposed, and told little Lee, who did not understand: "See? See the silly-putty trees?"

On another level of interest, the phenomenon of twice-yearly budding fascinated her, as well as the marvelous apparatus offered by the flexible branches to protect the leaves against too much sun as well as against the winter cold. Each day, too, as the sun rose farther in the north, the branches turned their budded sides to catch its rays aslant: like the sunflower on Earth, but these trees turned to face the source of life throughout the year, instead of by the day.

When the tree trunks began to crawl back in their shells, it was time to go inside. Minutes later, the sun would be too hot to take. But for the hour before that, it was a cool and peaceful world on the riverbank.

By the time Lee was six months old, the weather outside had passed its brief month of perfection and was once again too cold for pleasure. By that time, too, the first epidemic of parenthood was dying down. Emma was back at general medic work; the world was achieving a sort of normalcy. She had her baby. She had her work. And she was beginning to be aware of the fact that she was terribly lonely.

By that time, too, there were some unattached men. A good many of those early marriages broke up in the first year. In spite of the growing emphasis on typically frontier-puritan monogamous family patterns, divorce was, of necessity, kept easy: simply a matter of mutual decision and registration. For that matter, the morality in the early years was more that of the huddled commune than of the pioneer farmland.

Emma saw a lot of men that winter. Lee was a convenient age . . . old enough not to need hovering attention, young enough still to be asleep a large part of the time. Emma was a romantic figure, too, by virtue of her widowhood; her long grief for Ken established her as a better marriage risk than those who had made an error the first time and had had to admit it. The dawning recognition of these facts provided her at first with amusement, and later with a certain degree of satisfaction. She had been an intellectual adolescent, after all. Now, for the first time, she found out what it was like to be a popular girl. She discovered a new kind of pleasure in human relationships: the casual contact.

She found out that friends could be loved without being *the* beloved; that men could be friends without intensity;

that affection came in varying degrees, and that she could have many different kinds of affection from many different people . . . even though Ken was dead.

Yes, she found out too that Ken *was* dead. Perhaps it was fortunate that Lee was a girl; a boy named Kenneth might have helped her keep the truth from herself a while longer. And the inescapable violence of the seasonal changes made a difference. Life was determined to continue, and to do so it was constantly in a state of change. Even the silly-putty trees told her that much.

There was an impulse toward gaiety throughout the colony generally during the second winter night. The first one had been too full of work and worry. Now, they felt established and moderately secure. They had survived a full year of what troubles the planet could offer, and Ken's death was still their only loss. A new science of chemistry and physics in the labs and a new technology beginning to appear. Perhaps a new biology as well: Jo now had two Ullerns in his zoo, and there was some reason to believe that the creatures were capable of mating.

There was a warm sense of security in the colony, and when they had to take to the underground corridors again to keep their warmth, it added a womb-like complacency. It was a winter of parties and celebrations and increasing complexities of human relations. It merged into a springtime of renewed activity and interest for everyone, and most of all for Emma.

Now, when she went to the riverbank at dusk, instead of dawn, she had to watch the toddling one-year-old baby and keep her from the rushing waters of the river. Everything, all around, was full of motion and excitement, even the intellectual life that was hesitantly picking up once more.

There was *so* much to learn: she started going to the library again, after Lee was in bed for the night, and scanning the recorded knowledge there for clues to the new facts of life. She spent hours, sometimes, in the zoo-lab, watching the two Ullerns, and in spite of her open amusement at Jo's undiminished belief in their intelligence as a species, she listened eagerly while he talked about their habits. He had been watching them for months. She did not have to accept his interpretation of the data he'd

126

acquired, but the observations themselves were fascinating.

The zoo became something of a center of debate throughout the colony. It was now firmly established that one of the creatures was, in human terms, female. Medicenter wanted the male for dissection now that a new generation was assured. Jose wouldn't hear of it. There was a good deal of humor at his expense, and an increasing amount of discussion and argument, too, on both sides. Emma couldn't take it too seriously; the birth of her child had given her a new attitude toward time. There were years ahead of them. If Jo wanted his pet alive, why kill it? They'd catch more . . .

The days were constantly longer and fuller. Now sunset came too late to take Lee with her when she went down to the riverbank, and the water was beginning to move more thinly and slowly, low between the sides. The half-hour out there before bed was the only part of the day now that was quiet and unoccupied. It was a time for feeling, instead of thinking or doing, for a renewal of the loneliness she refused, quite, to surrender.

Refused, that is, until the evening Bart Heimrich met her there, and in the cool of twilight, just as the sun went down, took her in his arms. It shouldn't have made that much difference; they were two grown people, and one kiss by the side of the slow-moving water could hardly have mattered so much.

Emma was frightened. For two weeks after that, she stayed away from the river, and she wouldn't see Bart, either. She'd been in love once, and once was enough. There were plenty of men around. This kind of thing was more than she wanted. As she had done a year ago, she threw herself into study and work.

There was still plenty to do. As unofficial specialist in obstetrics, she had been somehow selected to watch over the Ullern creature's pregnancy. She spent more time at the zoo, now, trying to weed out the facts and theories Jo threw at her. He was so sure of his conclusions about the Ullerns that it was almost impossible for him to separate observations from hypotheses, and Emma was alternately amused and infuriated by the problem of working with him. He was a first-rate psychologist, after all, and a careful semanticist . . . where other people's attitudes were concerned. Even about himself, she decided on reflection—except in this one area of most-intense belief.

Was that true for everyone? Was there, for each person, a space where one's own judgment *could not* be trusted? How about herself, and Bart?

Jo was a good psychologist, almost all the time. They were talking, for the thousandth time, about the fate of the male Ullern. Jo had achieved a reprieve for the beast, till after the young ones were born, with the argument that they should at least wait and make sure they had another male to replace it. Emma approved the argument; it suited her tendency to temporize.

"Emmy," Jo asked in a sudden silence, "has it occurred to you yet that *you* have a long time to live, too?"

Her first impulse was to laugh. "Never thought about it much," she said lightly.

"Well, why don't you?"

"I don't know." She was decidedly uncomfortable. "What's that got to do with the price of baby Ullerns?"

"Nothing at all. I was just wondering, most intrusively, about you and Bart."

"Me and . . . what are you talking about?"

"I told you I was being intrusive. It's none of my business. Would you rather not talk about it?"

"I'd much rather . . ." She changed her sentence halfway through. "Much rather talk about it, I guess."

"All right, then. What's the matter, Emmy? Don't you like him?"

"*Like* him? I . . ." Then she saw he was smiling, and grinned ruefully herself. "All right, so I'm wild about him. But . . ." There was no way to explain it.

"But what?"

"Well . . . it's not the *same*. I can't feel the same way about him that I did about . . . Ken. I don't think I'll ever feel that way about anybody again. It wouldn't be fair . . ."

"Come off it, Emmy. What are you afraid of? If you're sure you'll never feel the same way, what's there to worry about?"

She looked up, startled, and waited a moment to answer, while she admitted to herself that it wasn't Bart she was afraid of hurting at all.

"I don't know. Look, things are all right the way they are. I don't need him; he doesn't need me. Why should we get all tangled up so we *do* need each other? What for? Oh, Jo, don't you see I can't take a chance on anything like that again? I . . . this is a crazy thing to say, but I think if he was married, I'd be more willing to . . . that's not very nice, is it?"

"Nice?" He shrugged. "It's pretty normal. Understandable, anyhow. And just what I was talking about. You've got a long time to live yet, Emmy. You going to stick it out alone?"

She nodded slowly. "Yes," she said. "I am." And with the words spoken aloud, the impossible loneliness of the future struck her for the first time fully. She hadn't cried since the day Ken died; now a slow tear came to one eye, and she didn't try to stop it. There was another, and another, and she was sobbing, great gasping sobs, against Jo's comforting shoulder.

He *was* a good psychologist. He didn't tell her it was all right to cry; he didn't tell her anything, except to murmur an occasional word of sympathy and affection. He stroked her hair and patted her shoulder, and waited till she was done. Then he grinned and said, "You look like hell. Better wash up here before you go see him."

For a year and more, Bart and Emma spent most of what free time they had together. They had fun, and they had tender happy moments. They understood and enjoyed each other. They might have married, but marriage was a sacred cow still; no matter how much she loved Bart, or liked being with him, Emma steadfastly refused to sign the vows. It wasn't the same as it had been with Ken; she was both relieved and disappointed to discover that. But if she married him, it might get to be the same—or it might not. Which prospect was the worse she hardly knew.

When, occasionally, she still felt frightened about caring as much as she did, there was always Jose to talk it over with, and talking to him always made her feel better. She might have resolved the ambivalence entirely through therapy. Jose hinted at the notion from time to time, but she didn't want to, and he knew better than to push it.

More and more, too, Emma and Jo were working so closely together in the zoo-lab that a therapy relationship between them would have been hard to establish. And Jo was the only really qualified therapist in the colony. The techniques were familiar to all the people in Medicenter, but psychotherapy is not a skill to be acquired in rapid training. Jo had a natural aptitude for it, that was all.

Jo was good to work with as Bart was to love. The important factor in each case was enthusiasm, the ability to participate completely. Emma's interest in the Ullerns differed from Jo's in all respects but one, and that was intensity. She listened to his theories both patiently and painstakingly, believing little and using much to further her own knowledge of the weird biology of the creatures. She was quite content to discard the largest part of what he said, and select the most workable of his ideas for followup. By the end of that year, she had begun to recognize, reluctantly, that she was getting good results surprisingly often when she worked along the lines suggested by his thinking. But it took a major incident to make her look back and count the trials and errors, before she would admit how consistent the pattern of predictability had been.

The Ullern babies had been born in the fall of '92. There were three of them, but it wasn't until early spring that it was possible to determine with any degree of certainty that two of them were female and one a male. Perhaps it could have been determined a little sooner; Jose had managed to get a postponement of the father Ullern's death sentence once again, until the sex of the young ones was known, and there was some feeling that he, at least, knew for quite a while before he told anyone.

Once the announcement was made, however, there was no further question of delaying the opportunity for an autopsy. The only question now was whether it might not be best to take the older female and gain some additional information about the reproductive system.

130

Discussion and debate went round and about for some ten days. It was terminated by the incredible information that the adult male had escaped.

The talk stopped then, because nobody wanted to say out loud what everybody was thinking. You see, it was simply not possible for the creature to make his way unaided through that gluey moat.

If there was any doubt at all in the public mind about what had happened, there was none in Emma's. She was shocked and angry, and she saw to it that she had no further talks with Jo in which he might be tempted to confide anything she didn't want to know.

XII

THE ANNOUNCEMENT, POSTED two days after the Ullern's escape, said simply:

LECTURE
In the Small Hall, 19/5/93, at 20.00 hours.
A report by Jose Cabrini on
the possibilities for direct communication
with the native inhabitants of Uller.

I read it, and couldn't help feeling relieved on Jo's behalf. I might have known he wouldn't risk anything so unpopular as letting that animal get away unless he had something else up his sleeve. What it was, I didn't know; Jose had never discussed with me any clues he had to the problem of direct communication.

He should have known the Small Hall wouldn't hold the crowd that turned out. Maybe he did know; if so, it was effective staging, when the early arrivals had to move to the Main Hall and latecomers found a sign directing them there.

Jose began his speech very informally, joking about the size of his audience, with some very hoary gags about being unaccustomed to such *very* public speaking. Then his tone changed.

"I'm afraid the news I have for you tonight is more dramatic than it is useful . . . so far. I think what has

131

already been learned will eventually enable us to communicate directly with the natives of this planet, and perhaps—if my estimate of their capacities is accurate—to live on a cooperative basis with them. For the present time, however, my information does little more than answer a question that has baffled a good many of us."

I had no idea what was coming.

"If you will all think back to our first contact with an Ullern," he said slowly and distinctly, "You may recall that there was one particularly puzzling piece of behavior on the part of the animal—one question that was never answered in the autopsy."

Thinking back was still too vivid. I shuddered in the warm room and missed the next few words.

". . . attack Ken Tarbell? What gave it the renewed energy to make such a fierce charge, when it was already badly hurt, and was seeking nothing but escape? My own theory at the time was that the Ullern was reacting with what would be, in the human metabolism, an adrenal release, to the telepathically received information that Tarbell had found a means of attacking it fatally.

"That theory was inadequate. If you think of telepathy as a mystic or metaphysical power, my analysis was *entirely* incorrect. But if you will try to think of it, for the moment, as an emanation similar in nature to radio or electromagnetic waves, I was close to the truth.

"You are all familiar with the piezo-electric properties of the Ullern physiology. You can see it for yourselves in the zoo; even the babies react electrically to certain irritations. Analogizing pretty broadly, one might say that the electrical reaction to stimulus in an Ullern *is* similar to the adrenal reaction in humans: that is, it is produced by just such irritations as might reasonably be expected to provoke the emotion of fear or anger.

"Now, in a human, the application of such a stimulus can have differing results. An unkind word, the semiserious threat of a blow, anything on that order, will produce enough of an adrenal release so that the person affected may express his reaction rapidly in expletive, or door-slamming, or some similarly mild expenditure of energy. A slightly greater threat will produce a cocked fist; a little more will make a man strike out. But a really

132

strong stimulus, ordinarily, will not produce a direct counteraction. If a man threatens your life by holding a gun at your head . . . or if you are knocked over by a blow to the belly . . . you will conserve the extra energy of the resulting adrenal release for an all-out effort against the attacker.

"This is, essentially, what the Ullern did. The many irritations to which is was subjected produced a variety of reactions, most of them in the fear spectrum. The first shot, which failed to hit it, but shattered a part of its armor with shock vibrations, angered it only within the fast-reaction range, and it responded, without conscious 'planning,' by an emission of 'lightning.' Apparently it was unable to place the source of the shot, and believed the shock to have come from the building; so the electrical 'punch' was aimed at the wall.

"Subsequent irritations made it aware of some consciousness on the part of large lumps of carbon which it had previously ignored as being, in all past experience, most likely inorganic, or at least inedible, entities. The idea was devastatingly new and at least as frightening as the actual vibrations the carbon creatures then commenced to 'hit' it with . . ."

There was a murmur of noise through the hall; some laughter, some coughing, much shuffling.

"All right," Jo said, smiling, "I'll get to the point now. So far it's all been theorizing and analogy. Briefly, my information is this: the Ullerns contain, in their quartzhide armor, crystals capable of sending and receiving radio waves . . . by which I mean specifically that they can exchange information on the same frequency bands on which our radiphones operate."

The sentence was delivered so quietly it took a moment to penetrate. Then the hall was in an uproar. Jose couldn't go on with the speech until he had answered a hailstorm of questions from the audience.

"What's that got to do with Tarbell?" somebody wanted to know first.

"Emma," Jo said from the stand, "maybe you can explain that best?"

I was a little confused myself. I got to my feet, and said hesitantly, "Ken tried to warn me . . . he phoned me about the Ullern heading our way . . . that's why we came back . . ."

"I suppose the gooks understand English!" somebody roared from the back of the room, and someone else added:

"Suppose they did? Wouldn't even an Uller-beast give a man the right to warn his wife?"

Laughter, and foot-stamping, and gradual quiet as I continued to stand in my place. "Maybe it's funny to the rest of you," I said, "but *I'd* like to know just what Jo meant. So far, what he's said has made sense. If anybody who isn't interested will leave, perhaps the rest of us can learn something."

I was just angry enough, and just intense enough, I guess, to get an effect. There was prompt and total silence. Jo went on.

There is no point in reproducing the rest of the speech here. It was, like most important discoveries, only very briefly incredible. After even the smallest amount of reflection, we could all see how logical the explanation was. The wonder was that we hadn't thought of it before. The same explanation can be found, almost word for word, in the basic biology text on Ullerns. Cabrini said simply, that when Ken used the phone, on a frequency just a little off the personal-broadcast wavelength that particular Ullern was tuned to, the heterodyning effect was the equivalent to it, in pain, of the belly-punch he'd mentioned earlier. It was immobilized momentarily, and the next immediate reaction was to utilize the energy thus generated in a life-or-death charge at locating the source; a radio beam is easier to track than a bullet, if your senses happen to include a direction-finder.

I didn't listen to most of the discussion that followed the speech. I was busy readjusting, or admitting to readjustments. I had stopped hating the Ullerns a long time back, and now at last I had a rationale on which to hang what had seemed like a betrayal.

The attack on Ken was not irrational or unprovoked. In Ullern terms, Ken had attacked first. A silly difference, a piece of nonsense, really, but important to me at the time. It was no longer necessary to keep hating, even on a conscious verbal level.

As soon as I got that much clear in my mind, I wanted to leave.

"You stay if you want to," I told Bart. "I just want to get out of here and do some thinking."

"Would you rather be alone?" He was a very sweet guy. I knew he meant just that; he'd let me go alone if I preferred it, or come along if I wanted him to.

I shook my head. "No, I wouldn't. If you don't mind missing this, I'd like to have someone to talk to, a little bit."

He took my arm and saw to it that we got out without interference; stopped people who wanted to question me, and pushed through the knots of conversationalists who were too absorbed or excited to notice us.

Outside, it was hot. So close to summertime it was always hot, but the sun was down when we left the hall, and it was possible to stay outdoors.

We walked down to the riverbank in silence and stood there and I looked around me and let myself know, for the first time, fully, how much I loved this place. It was mine; I had paid for it with the greatest loss I was ever to know. And now the loss was complete, because I understood it.

Bart saw the tears in my eyes.

"That son-of-a-bitch!" he said. "Didn't he even *warn* you?"

"Who?" I didn't know what he was talking about.

"Cabrini. He had no business . . . look, darling, never mind about him. The big thing is, we've got the know-how now. We've got a way to fight them! We can . . ."

"What?" I was sure I still didn't understand. "What are you talking about, Bart?"

"Don't you see, dear? Naturally, Cabrini didn't put it that way, but this thing is a weapon . . . a *real* weapon! We can live anyplace on the planet now. If radio waves hurt the things that much, they'll kill 'em too. We can . . ."

"Bart," I begged. "Don't you understand? Can't you see what it means? They're intelligent! We can learn to talk to them. We can make *friends* with them."

I searched his face for some signs of comprehension and found only indulgence there. "Emma, you are just

135

too good to be true," he said. "And you need some sleep. Come on, I'll take you back now, and we can talk about it tomorrow." He put his arm around me.

He meant well. I have no doubt at all that he meant well.

"Will you please get the hell out of here?" I said, as quietly as possible. I would have said much more, but he went.

When he was gone, I lay down on the riverbank and pressed my face against the dirt of my planet and cried. That was the third time I cried, and now it was for the loss of Bart as well as Ken.

(Parenthesis to Carla: iv)

Josetown, Uller, 1/11/52

Dear Child:

I am, frankly, annoyed. This story was supposed to be about the generations of women who came before you, and about the early years on Uller. Looking back, I find it is almost entirely about one small portion of my own life.

I think I know what happened. Somewhat earlier in this narrative, I made a statement about the oddity of reversed pain and pleasure in Recall. I suspect that I enjoyed the reliving of those early months on Uller far more in the telling than I ever did in the experience. From the day Ken died till the day when I wept out my sorrows on the riverbank, I was never entirely happy. There was much isolated pleasure during that period: delight in my baby, and fun with Bart, and satisfaction in my work . . . and certainly much more pleasure in knowing Jose than I realized. But all through those two years, life had no meaning beyond the moment. I did not, would not, believe in any kind of future, without Ken.

In the years that followed, there were many hardships and moments of unhappiness and despair, but from that time on, I had a growing purpose in existence. Apparently, I have less need to re-experience the productive years than the others. And of course, there is really very little more that I can tell you. Thad Levine wrote the story of the bitter three years' quarrel in the colony, and wrote it far better than I could. You have heard from me, and probably from a dozen others, too, the woe-filled history of the establishment of Josetown. Jo himself wrote a painstaking account of the tortuous methodology by which the Ullern code was worked out, and I know you have read that, too.

(I am sternly repressing the inclination to excuse my many omissions by pointing to the date above, and referring to the page number. Time is short now, and the story too long. But neither of these is an honest reason for my failure to do what I planned . . . no more than are my excuses in the paragraph immediately above.)

I had hoped, when I started this, to give you some clue to my own mistakes, so that you might avoid them. There are such striking similarities, Carla dear, between Joan Thurman and myself, between me and you! And on the other side, there is such a pattern of identity between Martha and Adne and Lee. It seems to me there should be some way of braking the pendulum swing . . . of producing, sometime, a child who is neither rebelliously "idealistic" nor possessively demanding of security in its most obvious forms.

It was at least partly in the hope that the history of those who went before you might teach you how to achieve this goal of impossible perfection with your children, when you have them, that I undertook this journal. I hope I have managed to include more helpful information in it than it now seems to me I have done.

In any case, I see little purpose in carrying the story further. I have mulled over it for weeks now, and have written several chapters about what came after the day of Jo's lecture, and have decided, each time, to leave them out.

There are many things I wanted to say that I've left out . . . little things, mostly, for which I could not find a proper spot in the narration. I could ramble on here, filling them in, but again there is no real purpose in it, except to satisfy myself.

But reading what I have just written, I realize that there is still much unresolved conflict in my own attitudes. Yes (I tell myself), I should like to see you rear your children to be perfect little happy mediums—and yet I am so pleased, Carla, to see you playing out the rôle I know so well myself.

Perhaps the others—Leah and Ariadne and Martha—perhaps they knew some happiness I never understood; but I am certain that they never knew the kind of total purpose in living that has been my great joy. I had a dream . . . I learned it from Joan Thurman. That dream is yours, too, and I'm quite irrationally pleased to think that you acquired it, in part, from me.

Tomorrow you will leave, Carla, and I will give you this film to take with you. When you leave, it will be as a part of the first great experiment with time . . . and like the fuel for the *Newhope,* which has made over the whole life of man, the mastery of time has come as an adjunct to a commercial venture. Joe Prell, if he were here today, would laugh at the implications I see in your voyage . . . but *not* at the possible profits. I . . . *I* think it is more risk than merited to go to Nifleheim for new and more uranium. But to go in profitable comradeship with the Ullerns—this is the fulfillment of my own life's dream. And to go as the advance guard of a whole new science—this is the beginning of yours.

If it takes uranium to make the Prells pay for a time machine (did you know that's what you have?—at least the beginnings of one), why, let us have enough of the stuff to blow us all sky-high!

(Epilogue)

I HAVE JUST come back from the ceremonies of the take-off, and I am more annoyed than ever. Now that I have handed over my imperfect gift, I have found out what it was lacking. There is no way of knowing, as I write, whether Carla has reached . . . will reach . . . her destination safely, or whether, if she does, she will arrive (has arrived?) there in a time-conjunction through which she can communicate with us. I can only wait, and hope there is some word.

But I shall assume, as I must, that she is safe, and that some time these words will reach her. The story is yet to be finished, and I found out today why I was

138

unable to finish it before. (I suppose I thought I was too old and too objective to carry any more scars of hurt or hatred from Lee!)

Leah Tarbell was born on Uller, and grew up there. She was too young to understand the fury of the debate that preceded her mother's move from Firstown to Josetown; but she was not too young at all to resent the loss of her Uncle Bart's company a scant few weeks after she had learned to pronounce his name.

Over the next three years, she understood well enough that her mother was somehow in disrepute with the parents of most of her playmates. And at five years of age, she was quite old enough to blame her mother for the almost complete loss of those playmates. Only four other children accompanied the group of sixty-seven "Josites" when they betook themselves, their pet Ullerns, their special knowledge, and their apportioned share of the human colony's possessions to the new location on the 20th parallel that became known as Josetown.

Only one of the other children was near her own age; that was Hannah Levine, and she was only four, really. The two little girls, of necessity, became friends. They played and ate and often slept together. At bedtime, they were lonely together, too, while their parents went off to conferences and lab sessions. And late at night, sometimes, they would wake up and be frightened together, remembering the stories they'd heard in the nursery at home about the Ullerns who lived at the foot of the hill.

She tried to cry about leaving her mother when she was sent back to Firstown a year and a half later, with Alice Cabrini and the two Cabrini children, to go to school. But she didn't really expect to miss Emma; Em was always working, anyhow. Back home, the grownups had more time to pay attention to kids.

From that time till she was fourteen, she lived with Alice in Firstown, and she was happy there. When Alice decided it was safe to rejoin Jose in the smaller settlement, Leah desperately did not want to go. She tried every device an adolescent mind could contrive to keep Alice at home. But when it came down to a choice of going with them, or being left behind, she couldn't quite face the desertion of the family she loved as her own.

She went along, and her adolescent imagination seized on a whisper here and a word there to find real cause to hate her mother. She was not blind, as the adults seemed to be, to the fact that Emma and Jo had worked together day after day through the years, while Alice endured long nights of loneliness for the sake of the three children who needed her care.

Lee watched the three grownups closely. She heard the inflexion of every word they spoke to each other and noticed each small gesture that passed between them. In the end, she satisfied herself that Emma and Jose were not lovers (as indeed we had not been since Alice's return). Then she felt something amounting almost to compassion for her mother. She had not failed to observe the flush of enthusiasm with which Emma listened to Jo's ideas and poured out ideas of her own to command his attention. At the same time she saw how Alice, sitting quietly in the background, pretending interest in nothing but Jo himself, and his home and the children, succeeded in drawing his attention.

She did not understand how her mother could be so stupid as to try to attract a man by being *bright*. She did not even begin to understand the further fact that she could not help observing: Emma seemed to be perfectly happy sharing Jo's work, and letting Alice share his home and his bed. As long as it was true, however, Lee was willing to let Emma go her own strange way.

She was less willing to accept any of the belated affection her mother tried to give her. And Emma's ludicrous attempts to convince her of the importance of the work they were doing in Josetown did not succeed even in antagonizing her. Lee had lived long enough in Firstown to know how little it mattered whether the code was ever completed. She knew the plans the other colony had already laid down for an equatorial settlement—a settlement which was to follow the extinction of the Ullerns. The agreement between the larger group and the small one had given Jose ten years to make a go of his project. Eight of those years had passed now, and he

140

could hardly claim that making friends with a local group of Ullerns constituted proof of their intelligence. Any animal may be domesticated by one means or another.

All these things Lee knew, and she was not interested in learning any part of the foolishness in which her mother was engaged. After a while, Emma stopped trying to interest her in the work at Josetown, and for a while they got along together.

Lee never thought of the Josetown period as anything more than an enforced hiatus in her life. If by some miracle the settlement continued after the ten years were up, she for one had no intention of remaining in it. When she was seventeen, she knew, she would have the right to live by herself if she chose, and she had already chosen. She would live in Firstown, where her friends and loyalties were.

She stuck to her resolve, even after the message from Earth. Not even the dramatic opening of subspace communication between Uller and the mother system disturbed her tight little plans. Nor did her private opinion of the foolishness of the Josetown project change when popular opinion shifted to favor it. Earth's problems were no concern of hers, and she saw no reason to give up her hopes or hatreds, either one, just because Jose Cabrini had somehow turned out to be right.

Her strongest reaction to the news from Earth was irritation, because it meant that Josetown would continue beyond the ten-year period after all, and that she herself would have to spend a full year more there than she had expected.

She made use of the time. She started learning the code, and even studied a little Ullern biology. She helped Jo prepare his lab notes for printing in the form in which they are now available, and learned the history of the project while she did it. By the time she was old enough to go back to Firstown and take up residence in the single girls' dorm, she knew enough about the Josetown work to take a really intelligent part in discussions with the men back home.

As it turned out, Lee was our best ambassador. She had picked up, from Jo's notes, one item of information we had not intended to release just yet. Fortunately, as it turned out, she felt no ties of loyalty to us. That was how the news got out that Jose actually *had* taught Ullerns the use of fire, and it was that news that led to the Conference of 2108.

Fifteen of us went back to Firstown for the Conference, armed with notes and speeches and films to document our defense. We were somewhat taken aback to find that no defense was necessary; Firstown was way ahead of us in recognizing the implications of the Ullerns' use of fire. I suppose we had grown so accustomed to defensiveness by then, we simply couldn't see beyond the necessity of protecting next year's work. The people at Firstown were used to thinking in terms of expansion and utilization of knowledge; they had the engineering minds to put our research to use.

Lee was only seventeen, but her greatest ability, even then, was the tactful manipulation of other people. It was her carefully developed friendship with Louis Dooley that made it possible for Basil and Jose to meet privately before the Conference started and hash out their ideas. And it was in that private meeting that the mutual advantages of humans-Ullern cooperation in the Nifleheim venture were recognized.

When we went back to Josetown, it was with the long-range plan already worked out: the further development of the code to the point where we could communicate with Ullerns in the abstractions we were certain they were capable of understanding; they continued work on Ullern biochemistry to determine whether the quartz-to-teflon adaptation would actually take place, as we believed, in the atmosphere of Nifleheim; and the long, long process of persuading the Ullerns that other humans besides our own small group now wanted friendship with them.

That was our part of the job. Back in Firstown, they worked, in communication with Earth, on the other end of the problem: the improvement of subspace transport to eliminate the mishaps and make it safe for live freight.

(P.S. to Carla)

IT IS TWO weeks now since I went to the takeoff of the Nifleheim *Ark* and stood beside my daughter Lee, watching the whole show through her eyes, and gaining some of the understanding that made it possible for me to finish this story.

We were all together, Lee and Louis and the three youngsters. Carla, of course, was participating in the ceremonies.

Johnny, my youngest grandson, looked at the domed building in the center of the field and was disappointed.

"Just like any other building," he grumbled.

Lee nodded automatically. "Yes, dear, it is," she said, but something made her shiver as she said it. It was ordinary-looking, far more like a house than a spaceship. Nothing frightening at all . . . to look at. Yet it stood there, triumphant and menacing, the most impregnable enemy she had ever met. She hadn't even been able to stay away from the takeoff as she'd planned. She had to come: she was Louis Dooley's wife and Carla's mother, and Emma Tarbell's daughter, and they wouldn't let her stay home. She had to bring her other children, too, and any minute now, she'd have to watch the plain domed structure *disappear*.

"Centuries gone, man looked to the stars and prayed," the worn tape intoned. "He made them his gods, then his garden. . . ."

Leah shuddered and reached for her young son's hand, but he never felt her touch. The magic of the old, old words was wrapping itself around him.

". . . of thought, and at last his goal. We have not. . . ."

Inside the dome was all the equipment for separating and storing the uranium that could be had, for the simple extraction, from the atmosphere of Nifleheim. Inside, too, were quarters for humans and Ullerns to live side by side together. Inside was Carla's bridal home, and beyond the wall that held her bed was the dread machinery of subspace itself.

". . . reached that goal. This is not a beginning nor an end; neither the first step nor the last. . . ."

143

Lee looked around at all the others, the mothers who were supposed to be proud and pleased today, and saw the tense fists clenching, the tired eyes squinting, the hands reaching for a younger child's touch. She felt better then, knowing they shared the mockery of the moment.

She stood patiently, listening to Jo's speech, hearing him explain once more how Ullerns could venture forth on the surface of Nifleheim and actually benefit by the change . . . how changing shifts of Ullern workers could spend an adaptation period on the alien planet, expose themselves to the fluorine that would change their brittle skins to flexible teflon hides, while human hands inside worked the machinery that would process the desperately-needed uranium for transport back to Earth. Lee stood and listened to it all, but it meant no more than it had meant last year, or forty years before, when they started work on it.

Then at last, Carla was standing before her, with all the speeches and display finished, and nothing left to do but say goodbye. She reached out a hand, but Louis was there first, folding the slender girl in a wide embrace, laughing proudly into her eyes. . . .

Then Johnny, and Avis, and Tim, they all had to have their turns. And finally Carla turned to her.

Lee leaned forward, kissed the smooth young cheek, and said, before she knew herself what words were coming:

"Carla . . . Carlie, darling, aren't you *afraid?*"

Carla took both her mother's hands and held them tight.

"I'm terrified!" she said. And turned and left.

Thirty days on, thirty days off, and almost all the problems routine for the job—but the blues may be an occupational hazard for a woman in space. Startling Stories—*Summer, 1954.*

Stormy Weather

The time . . . For three days Cathy had watched and waited. Three days: measured in Earth-hours by creeping hands around the smug face of the chrono overhead; measured in mood and majesty by the slow progress of the dark ball of the Earth across the distant bright face of the sun.

Three days: twelve meals out of the chest freeze, duly warmed and eaten, but untasted; as many snatches at brief sleep that gave no rest; eighteen loggings of the instruments, checking new readings against prediction data from the analog. Three days: four thousand, three hundred and twenty minutes; how many seconds?

She could figure that out, but she couldn't, wouldn't, count the times she'd tried to call him. Or the endless stretches in between, waiting for him to call.

Where are you now? her need cried out within her. *Darling, I love you!*

How could he possibly not hear?

Mike! How could you go away?

She wouldn't call again. Not yet. Cathy moved restlessly

under the magneblanket in her bunk, and wide awake in her renewed determination, sat bolt upright and peeled herself out of its comfortless clutches. She pushed off from the metal frame, barefoot, and floated in aimless circuit of her small domain: one round room, three full lengths of her body in diameter; a tiptoe stretch, with arms upraised, from the light magnetism that held her metal-seeded sandals on the "floor" to the "ceiling" bulk-head that separated the living quarters here from the storage compartment "above."

She *wouldn't* call again. She couldn't afford to.

On the ceiling, near the chrono, a green bulb glowed, had glowed for three full periods now, twelve hours, to remind her that the tiny universe was rapidly becoming a closed system. The bulb went on when the u-v's did, as soon as solar radiation on the algae-air tank fell below full-activity point. It would keep burning, tingeing the round room faintly green, as long as the lamps kept working on the tanks outside. Beside the bulb, green numerals glared from a pale, violet-hued panel, offering the current index activity in the tank:

89.593.

She couldn't afford to use up oxygen now for anything but real necessities. And even if you stretched a psychological point to call this need essential, it was insane to draw on her reserves of air and heat both, trying to send a message he wouldn't even answer.

Wouldn't answer . . . All right, then keep the small reserves until *he* wants to call. That would be funny, wouldn't it? *Hilarious!* If he tried to call later, and she'd run her air too low by calling him to be able to answer.

Cathy tried to laugh at such absurdity, and found the humor of it was beyond her.

Serve him right!

The thought shocked her; she hadn't realized how angry she was beneath the doubt and worry. Just the same, she told herself, still trying to be funny, she didn't have to use all her oxygen and power now just to make sure she *didn't* answer when he—*if* he—called.

Besides, it might be useful to be able to answer a call from Control Central—or even *make* one if she had to. That's what they were paying her for, after all.

Eat; that's the thing to do. Time, and past time for a meal. *One message equals two meals,* she told herself primly in training-school sing-song.

Only she wasn't hungry.

"*Ping!*" The chrono chime startled her. She hadn't realized it was so late. "Instrument check," it reminded her softly. "1200 hours. Instrument check." Louder now: "Instrum—"

She switched it off in midword. They were paying her for this, too, she thought without interest, and reset the alarm for 1600 hours. She pushed off in the direction of the bunk, slid her feet into her sandals, began a slow, walking circuit of the room, logging the meter readings, resetting dials and controls.

Her mind was made up now. She would not—repeat, and underline, *would not*—make any effort to call Mike during the next period. After the 1600 check she could try again—once.

ALL quiet. All correct. Cathy fed her readings into the calcker, pulled a fresh tape out of the analog computer, and fed that data too into the softly whirring machine for swift comparison, knowing beforehand what the results would be. Everything checked well within the margin. She noted the minor variations meticulously on the analog corrector, reset the alarm systems, and checked her mental picture visually on the radar screen.

Everything in its place. A few tidy little asteroids, chasing their orbits around the vanishing sun, just as trim and true as the course of her own hollow cylinder of metal. Plenty of traffic to log, of course, but none to worry about. She was less than a million miles out from Earth now, and at that distance, Control Central still handled the live traffic.

All quiet . . . Bound to be quiet here, on the sunside swing of the Station's "rogue" orbit. A few more days, and she'd be inside Earth, slanting steadily "down" from the ecliptic, headed for perihelion just outside Venus. But by the time that happened, she wouldn't be aboard.

Just five more days to this tour. A week's time—one short week, if you looked at it that way—and she'd be back on Earth, while the station whirled on under the

147

care of a pleasant-looking blonde girl named Eileen whose height and weight and basal metabolism rate were just the same as Cathy's, and who, fortunately, liked the same music and films. More than that they were unlikely to know about each other ever—or at least not while they were both in Service.

Thirty days on, thirty off. A great life if you could take it. The pay was good. The food was better than you might think. If you didn't mind no gravity or solitude. The living conditions were pleasant enough, once you had your own permanent Station, especially if your alternate had somewhat the same tastes you did. Bring out a few replacements each new trip for reading and amusement, and find the changes made in your absence as well.

Five years of it, and you were set for life. Not that you could save much in Service—too much temptation to spend when you were Earthside. But besides the retirement pay, which was good, there were always jobs waiting for the glamorous heroes and heroines of the Space Service; and the best jobs of all were for the expert psychosomanticists who womanned—or manned—the Stations.

Cathy had almost four years of it behind her now. Seven more tours to retirement—and they'd both agreed it was foolish of her to quit. They could spend almost half the time together anyhow; and with both of them p-s-trained, no more was necessary. They could always keep in message-touch.

That's what they told each other, sanely, sensibly, after twenty days of wonder and enchantment back on Earth. No, not twenty, she reminded herself: nineteen. There was one day when they quarreled . . . .

That was even worse than now. That time she'd *known* his absence was angry and deliberate. Now she could find excuses, invent reasons . . . *Drunk? . . . doped? . . . dead?* . . . she asked herself brutally, marveling that she found these answers easier to contemplate than anger or indifference.

Because I don't believe them, she realized ruefully. But what other reasons could there be?

Pride. His foolish pride! Or just hard work? Something top secret so he couldn't even let *her* know? Or . . .

148

Sure, lots of reasons she could find, but none—the last included—that could make him just *walk out* without warning as he'd done. Unless the dream had been a warning after all: the scream in the dream that woke her from a period's sleep three long days back, just as the Station entered the penumbra of eclipse. He'd been gone when she came frightened-wide-awake that time; and she hadn't been able to reach him since.

THE coincidence was tempting, but she knew better. It *couldn't* be because of the eclipse. If it took radiating energy to message with, no one would ever be able to contact Earth from the outer Stations. . . .

Still, there might be something special about *this* eclipse. Some by-effect, some related phenomenon she didn't know about. It was also quite true that she hadn't heard from Control Central since she entered the shadow. Hadn't tried to call them, either. She could try now, of course, and then she'd *know*. But if she *didn't* try, she could keep the illusory comfort in her mind; a feeble sort of straw to cling to, but in the absence of anything more solid, she hesitated to let it go.

Besides, it was just as wasteful to make an unnecessary call to Control as to Mike. *One message equals two meals.*

Oxy at 88.974. *One meal equals two cigarettes.* And she still wasn't hungry.

Ought to sleep, then. She was afraid to sleep. . . .

Read a good film, then. She didn't feel like reading. She wanted a cigarette.

Four cigarettes is one message. *A message is only a message, but a good cigarette is a smoke.* Where did that come from?

And where are you now, my darling? Mike! Please, Mike. . . .

Sharply, she shut off the thought, and beneath it ran the thread of lonely melody again.

Gloom an' misery everywhere . . . Since my man an' I. . .

Cathy reached over to the calcker and fingered the roll of tape that wound out of its answend, as if she could find with her fingers some piece of information that her eyes missed when she read it through before. Something, maybe, to tell her why Mike and the sun had gone away together.

But the calcker didn't know about Mike. If she asked it, *Where is he now? Why won't he answer me?* it would buzz and click unevenly, and in the end tap out one terse rebuking symbol on the tape: Insufficient data.

Well, that was her problem, too. A scream in a dream, and the shadow of the sun; that was all she had to work with. Plenty of data about everything else, though: a wall full of it all around her, and a roll of it, neatly digested, right in her hand.

And the warning on the ceiling: *88.899.*

You don't take chances on a Station!

One cigarette, that's all, she promised herself. After all, she'd missed a meal. It was taking more of a chance, really, getting into this kind of state than using the extra little bit of air and heat.

Algae's not at top efficiency, but neither am I. Go ahead; pamper yourself a little. Better to have it now while the tank's still fairly high, still getting some solarays. If you're still wanting it tomorrow, you'll just be out of luck. . .

CATHY kicked off her sandals and floated over to her personal storage cabinet. She got out a cigarette, hesitated, and, holding it, made a quick automatic check of radar screen and indicator dials. No change; with everything quiet outside, she could watch for a while. She threw a switch to open the sunward port, retrieved her shoes, and walked back across the room to a padded piece of bulkhead from which she could keep both screen and viewport comfortably within her angle of vision.

Curled up against the foampad on the "floor," her metal soles and metal-seeded tunic were enough to keep her "sitting," even if she moved a bit from time to time. It took some conscious effort of the muscles to pull free from the light magnetism of floor, chair, and bunk. Settled into a reasonable facsimile of gravity-sitting, Cathy listened to the purring of the motor fade away as the heavy metal hatch slid off the port, filling the room with deep-empurpled light.

If things go on this way, ole rockin' chair will get

150

me. . . . With one long, angry inhalation, she lit her cigarette. Then she relaxed and watched the solar spectacle outside. Watched with an added guilty pleasure in her own delinquency through a thin veil of smoke that fanned out from the tip of fire in her fingers to the wide slits of air ducts round the room. . . .

She had watched at least a little while each day since it began. First a wedge of darkness, nothing more, nudging into the edge of the sun. Then a round black mallet squeezed at the giant ball of butter floating in fluid ice of space: shaped it into a fat crescent, then a thin and thinner one.

This time she found an almost total sphere of darkness cuddled inside the scant embrace of a lopsided new-moon sun: one arm, on top, much longer than the bottom one, because of the Station's relative position "under" the plane of the ecliptic.

But even as she watched, the long skinny arm on top grew visibly shorter; less than five hours from now the Station's orbit would intersect and enter the umbra of Earth's shadow. The "total" eclipse would last, then, for a full day and a little more. Twenty-six hours, seventeen minutes, thirty-nine seconds, the calcker said, and the figures stuck in her head like symbols of doom.

No sun up in the sky! Stormy weather!

There would be only a few more hours after that, two periods at most, before the Station raced inward under Earth's orbit, moving faster and faster into the full light of the sun again. Three days gone, and less than two to go—but all that time the green index figure on the ceiling would be falling.

At 50 percent, oxy production in the tank was just about equal to basic minimum requirements for one Cathy-sized individual doing a predetermined job in a known volume of space, with no waste motion, and no other unnecessary expenditure of air. According to the tape, the index wasn't likely to go below 57.000 this time —if she was careful. And that of course assumed continuous effective operation by the notoriously unreliable u-v's.

Cathy looked up at the green figure on the ceiling: 88.215.

It was falling faster now. Abruptly, she squashed out the not-quite-finished cigarette. The margin was just too narrow to fool around with. If the index did fall to fifty, it would mean accelerating the Station, using storage fuel from the great tank "overhead" to get back into the sunlight more quickly.

AT THE other end of the Station's long elliptical orbit, in the inner circle of the Asteroid Belt, such a maneuver was inevitably dangerous, and very possibly fatal. Getting even slightly off-course at any time made the analog predictions useless, and following an uncharted course out in the Belt, you were likely as not to find yourself disputing the right-of-way with a stubborn chunk of rock.

Cathy sat huddled against the cushioned bulkhead, alone and miserable, weary and wakeful, frustrated and fearful. The vast expanse outside the viewport seemed to have borrowed her mood for coloring.

When he went away, the blues came in and met me. . . .

Suddenly, she leaned over to the right, reached for a dial, and spun it fiercely, adjusting the polarization of the port plastic to compensate for the change in quality and intensity of the sunlight. Three days drifting into the shadow, and she hadn't thought to do that before! Now the crescent sun flared into sudden brilliance, and the small room acquired an almost cheerful glare.

She was surprised at the difference it made; the purplish light had seemed normal and inevitable. *Stormy weather . . .* three days of it. No Mike. No light.

"Three days, that's all," she said out loud, trying to make it sound like just a little while. She'd gone twenty-five years, after all, without even knowing him. Now it was just three days since they'd lost contact. At worst, it was only another week before she'd be back on Earth herself, and could *find out*. One week . . . seven days; just seven brief eternities, that's all!

Time is a subjective phenomenon, she told herself. Time is a trick of the mind. "A purely personal psychological defense against dimensions beyond understanding. . . ." *Who was it who said that?* It seemed very profound. An instructor somewhere, maybe. . .

Time is where you hang your hopes. At least nobody

had said *that*; that was Cathy, herself, original. Time-past is flat and gone, no more than a set of impressions in the cells of a brain. *My brain*. Time-future is tomorrow. But tomorrow never comes. It's always today, the time is *now*, a composite of memory and hope and longing focused on the pinpoint of perception that is *now*. . . .

Now is the time for all good Cathys to go to sleep. Got to sleep sometime. Close the hatch. Get in the bunk. Pull up the magneblanket . . . wonderful . . . good, good, *good* to be sleepy, relaxed . . .

"Alert for action. *Alert for action!* ALERT FOR ACTION."

The chrono speaker was louder and more incisive each time.

Cathy dived across the room to where two red bulbs glowed their warnings over agitated meter-needles. Quickly, reflectively, she fed new data into the calcker, ignoring the chrono speaker's increasingly urgent warnings till she could take time to switch it off. Then she hovered nervously over the whirring machine, waiting for the fresh tape to emerge, watching the radar screen beyond it for some sign of what the trouble might be.

Nothing there she didn't know about. Nothing but a little almost invisible interference fuzz in the far corner. Like windo tracks, or. . . .

She pulled at the tape as it began rolling out, and started it through the microfilm magnifier almost before there was enough length to let it ride the reel. Eagerly, she absorbed the steady stream of figures and symbols until, abruptly, everything fitted together, and the pattern was clear.

Just a little interference fuzz in one corner—a particicloud! A mass of fragmentary rocks and pebbles, the debris of some unidentified catastrophe in space: perhaps a minor everyday collision in the Belt; perhaps some greater mishap farther out in the System; possibly, though unlikely, a grand smashup between two extra-solar bodies light-years away.

IT DIDN'T matter now where the cloud of grit and gravel came from; it mattered very much where it was going. And it was headed straight *in*, irresistibly drawn by the

153

gravitational pull of the giant incinerator at the heart of the System. A tidy way to clean up solar trash—except that at its present velocity, the drift was due to cross the busiest space-lanes in the System, just outside Earth's orbit, and perhaps—if it diffused at all under the pull of planetary gravity—brush through the very edges of the atmosphere.

Once more, Cathy checked the coordinates and velocity of the cloud, and then the Stations Catalogue. No doubt about it: it was her baby. No other Station anywhere in range, and she was almost directly in line between the oncoming drift and Control Central's satellite around Earth.

There was nothing very complex about the operation. Standard procedure was to release a fizz-jet from the storage bay; position it inside the cloud and set it off; the whole job done at the remote control board, using coordinates and timing set forth with near-impossible precision on the calcker tape.

If it were done just so, the tiny particles of matter that composed the cloud would be reduced to powder fine enough to be *pushed* back, clear out of the System, by photon-power alone. And any specks or pieces that remained big enough to continue to respond to the sun's gravity would be impelled by the bomb burst to drift out sideways, perpendicularly away from the plane of the ecliptic; when they came floating back eventually, they'd be far out of the traveled space-lanes.

The operator's job was not so much difficult as delicate: a matter of steering the fizzer to its optimum placement, and then exploding it at the split second laid down by the calcker's figuring. It took practiced skill and close coordination—but Cathy had done it before, and as she got the data from the tape, found nothing out of the ordinary in this story beyond the edge of excitement provided by its imminent closeness to Earth.

She moved energetically now, logging data, setting up equations for the coordinates on the calcker, checking the analog, the screen, the dials and meters that belted her little world. When the call came through from Control Central twenty minutes after the first Alert, she registered it and replied without so much as a moment's delusion that it was Mike calling instead.

"Cath? Just checking. We got a particloud pattern on our screen in your sector."

"Yeah, I noticed."

"Everything under control?"

"I'm calcking the bomb-set now."

"How's it look from out there?"

What's the matter with them? Cathy wondered irritably, but kept her reactions out of her reply, or hoped she did. "S.O.P.," she answered tersely.

"Right. Check in when you get your set?"

"Better not. I'm eclipsed." She glanced at the ceiling. "Oxy's under 85 now, and a long way to go."

"Sorry."

Cathy recognized the personal pattern of the girl on the other end now: a kid named Luellen, just a few months out of school. No wonder she was nervous; this would seem like a Big Thing to her.

"Nobody told me," Luellen explained. "I guess I should have figured it out—"

"Forget it!" Cathy sent back briskly.

"Okay. We won't call again then unless it's urgent."

"Good. Anything goes wrong, I can still signal."

"Right. Signing out. . ." But before the contact was broken, another, more familiar, pattern cut in. ". . . Hey, Cath—you okay?" That was Bea Landau; she and Cathy had been in training together, and there was no excuse for anyone who'd spent four years behind a desk at Control Center kibitzing a message at a time like this.

"Sure I'm okay. Why?" This time Cathy didn't bother to conceal her annoyance.

"I dunno. Got some funny stuff around the edges there—I'm supervising the new girls today, and I was listening in on you—Listen, Cath, if anything's wrong, this is the time to—"

"*Nothing's* wrong. I just don't feel sociable. Get out, will you? I already said my oxy's low."

"Okay. But listen, Cath, if you want a hand, yell out."

"Sure. G'bye now."

DELIBERATELY, Cathy cut out of contact and went back

to work. But as the data piled up, she began to realize more fully that Control had some reason to be worried. This cloud wasn't just the usual nuisance that might clutter up the spaceways and perhaps make a mess of repair bills for somebody's Mars-ship. A whole lot of money, and probably plenty of Service brass would be sitting around holding its breath right now, she thought with a certain relish.

Not that the job was actually a tough one. The cloud was coming in from outside and on top. Made it a simple matter to hit—the bomb would set practically smack in front of the middle of it.

Not a tough job, but a crucial one. Just what the doctor ordered, she thought grimly, for a girl who wanted to forget her own troubles.

It was almost too simple, though. Fifteen minutes more or less had all the figuring finished, and everything checked and rechecked. Nothing else to do about it now till the cloud came into range, and by the tape it would be close to five hours yet before any action began.

Meanwhile, the space around her was clear and quiet. She opened the viewport again, and settled back into the foam-padded spot on the floor, consciously seeking a renewal of the pleasant apathy that had come last time, after she adjusted the plastic to let the sun come in.

But the mood was hard to find again. Part of her mind was busily retabulating the calcker's figures, and reevaluating the total problem, making certain of what needed to be done. For the rest, she was aware of an increasing sense of dullness and irritability as the good adrenal feeling of the first emergency wore off.

Well, dull is what I got to be right now, she told herself. Adrenalin equals oxygen, and don't forget it. She forced herself to relax, muscle by muscle, until she was little more than a collapsed heap on the floor: two great eyes drinking in the drama being staged outside her window; two ears alert for the first summons from the complex personality of the machine around her.

For more than an hour, she stayed that way; then the chime *pinged* again for the routine 1600-hour check. Cathy performed her chores mechanically, paying close attention only to what part of the data related to the cloud.

It was still holding shape and direction. Something better than three hours yet to wait before it was time for action.

She sat down again and remembered she had promised herself to call Mike again after this checkup.

But that was before the Alert. She couldn't do it now. Certainly not after snapping at Luellen just for keeping a contact open.

No, she wasn't even going to *think about* him any more; not till this business was done with, anyhow. Too easy to drift from memory and wistfulness into wanting to call; and such a swift slip from wanting to trying—

The bomb-set was absurdly simple. Usually, there was a certain amount of complicated geometry involved in the placement. But this one was straightforward. No tricky angle shots this time—

THE open viewport was a black-felt billiard table and the dark ball of Earth rested in the golden pocket of the sun. Off to one side, an unknown player held an invisible cue-stick; nothing of it showed but the blue-chalked tip, where Venus ought to be—

And me behind the eight ball. No, he is. One of us is.

Behind the eight ball. Maybe he wasn't on Earth at all. If he was on the other side of the sun for some reason—

She tried to remember whether she had ever messaged cross-sol, and couldn't recall. But if it made any difference, she'd have learned about it long before this. Sun . . . thermal energy . . . she wanted a cigarette.

83.323.

She was hungry now, she guessed. It was food she really wanted, not a smoke.

Messaging would make her hungry. It always did.

One message equals two meals. But that was only in terms of direct oxygen consumption. It didn't figure thermal energy used up at the time, or the air and heat both that went into extra eating afterwards. The heat didn't matter so much right now; the Station's thermal-erg reserve was a lot bigger than its oxy margin.

Sure, and it takes a lot more ergs to send than to receive a message, she reminded herself. Besides, she

157

didn't *want* to call him. He could reach her if he wanted to, pride said, and common sense approved.

Just can't pull my poor self together. Stormy weather. . . .

IT HAD been raining on Earth, the first time she heard the crazy old song, on a tinny-sounding tape made from an antique disk-record. That was the one time they'd been separated before. Two weeks after they first met, when they had their first, last, only, quarrel. For a whole day she couldn't reach him. She didn't have any pride that time—and she had lots of air.

On Earth the air is free.

She kept trying to find him all day, and couldn't. Then she heard the song.

It had all the tearing, tearful nostalgia so typical of the early twentieth-century folksongs. It sounded close and loud, for all the cracked acoustics of it, but she couldn't figure out where the sound was coming from till she realized she'd found him at last. He was listening to it, playing it for her, too, proud himself to say how he felt, but needing her back, and using this way to let her know, if she cared to hear.

A man can afford to be proud. Lucky for both of them that she knew *she* couldn't. He didn't try to find her at all; just sat listening to the tearful old tune, hoping she'd come and understand.

A woman couldn't afford to be proud. A Servicegirl couldn't take chances. Maybe that's why there were more women than men on the Stations, why women did better in psi-training than men. She'd heard something about new work with older people, where there was no sex differential in aptitude. A man, a young man, *had* to be proud. It made biologic sense. But it also meant somatic-semantic sets built-in . . . preconceptions that would naturally get in the way of free-associative interpretation of psi-somatic messages.

That meant it was up to her again, just like the last time. She was lucky to have found a guy who could psi at all. A guy worth having, that is.

But how could she do it? This time they hadn't quarrelled. She didn't know where or how to look for him.

No way of knowing even whether the scream in the dream had any meaning, or whether it was a product of her own subconscious fears.

Last month that wouldn't have occurred to her. But the psych tests didn't take into account the things that might happen when a girl met a guy.

Yes, they did, too. That's why you were supposed to report it when anything like this happened. She hadn't reported. She'd wanted to finish her term of Service. They never actually fired you, of course. But somehow the girls who fell in love always decided to quit—after a few visits with the psychers.

Maybe they were right, if she'd got to the point now where she couldn't tell the difference between a dream of her own and a message from Mike!

She ought to try just once more. . . .

81.506.

And outside, only the slimmest rim of light around the Earth.

You don't take chances on a Station!

It's not your own life you're playing with, Cathy. The Solar System has its eye on you.

No, it doesn't, either. Just a tiny corner of one eye, a veritable lewd wink of an eye. The sun can't see me now; it's got a cataract.

But the System depends on you, kid. How will all those lil chunks of rock know where to go if you don't show 'em the way?

"Traffic Control is the most vital agency in the Space Service. We are no stronger than the weakest link in. . . ."

Keep the vermin out of the skies. *Catherine Andauer, girl exterminator.* Somebody has to tell all the nasty little rogue rocks where to get off.

If things keep up this way, ole rockin' chair will get me. . .

If things kept up this way, she'd have to report in for psych leave, that's all.

If she could, that is . . . if she could still send a message at all. . . .

Meanwhile, there was a job to do, and no one to do it but her.

81.487, and the chrono said 1735 hours. Seventy minutes to go. Too late to sleep now.

Exercise.

That was the next best thing. Or maybe the best. Use up more oxygen, of course, but she could afford a *little* bit. And right now it was more important to stay alert. Stimulation could do more than relaxation sometimes.

She strapped herself into the massager and felt better almost immediately as rubber arms began to manipulate her stiff muscles and blood started pounding faster through her veins. She gave it ten minutes—less than she wanted, but a compromise with the green index figure. Then, in lieu of the meal she still didn't really want, she opened a bar of vi-choc concentrate and ate it slowly and determinedly, piece by piece, till it was all gone. Saved oxygen, too, she told herself, not heating a freeze-meal.

THE ceiling panel said 80.879 when the chrono read 1835, and the speaker said importantly:

"Final check before action. Commence last logging now. Initiate action in fifteen minutes. Last logging now. Final instrument check. Commence last. . . ."

She worked swiftly, surely, enjoying the feeling of urgency, as well as her own sense of competence. Meters and dials and familiar precision mechanisms—all things your eyes could perceive and your fingers could direct. Not like the strange uncharted stretches in the dark interior of self.

Check the logging against the analog. Run the last equations through the calcker one more time. Everything should check. Everything would be exactly. . . .

But it wasn't.

The cloud was not behaving in an orderly fashion. It was diffusing, as she'd known it might . . . toward Earth.

A three-body problem, in a sense: the third body composed of millions of specks and bits and pieces, and behaving in gravitational terms exactly as if it *were* a composite mass—of fluid!

She had set up general equations to meet the possibility beforehand, but now she had to work quickly, filling in new data and getting corrected results. She finished the

160

comping and was still rechecking when the chrono speaker pinged again to remind her:

"Space suit. Space suit. Prepare for open locks. Space suit. Space suit."

Cathy slid out of her sandals and kicked off to where the empty metal shell stood firm and tall inside its grapples against the wall. She floated into position "above" it, then pushed herself feet first "down" inside. When her toes slid into place into the fleece-lined shoe-pieces, the torso section encased her up to her shoulders. She wriggled her arms into the flexible sleeves and each finger carefully into place in the glove-ends. Then she pulled the headpiece out of its clamps overhead, settled it into place on the shoulders, and gave it a quarter-turn, pushing hard against the gasket pressure till she heard the closure latch into place.

She snapped on the headphone, tested the battery of switches and levers on the controls belt, turned off the magnetism of the shoe soles, and floated clumsily over to the compactly designed remote-control keyboard.

Six minutes to zero. Cathy threw the permissive switch that would allow the twin bays in the bomb-storage compartment at the other end of the Station to open, as soon as the timing mechanism went into action. Nothing left to do now but close the "gills" of the space suit, and open the valve on the built-in oxygen tank.

But it was too soon still for that. Two minutes ahead of time was S.O.P., just long enough to make sure the system was operating effectively. Actually, the whole space-suit procedure was an almost-unnecessary precaution. There were two solid bulkheads between Cathy and the bomb-stores, and between them twenty feet of liquid fuel. But Service practice on this point was firmly set: if any port in a space vessel is to be opened out of atmosphere, all personnel must first don space gear. Over-cautious, perhaps, but sensible in its way.

More important, actually, in this case was the always-present possibility that the Station attendant might actually have to leave the Station during the operation. It didn't happen often—but it could.

Five minutes to go, and time now for a final clearance check with Control Central if she were going to make one. Once the gills were closed, she had no further choice in the matter; *any* kind of long-distance messaging, even blank reception, would drain the suit's small oxy tank beyond the safety point.

Under normal circumstances, the final clearance was also S.O.P. But they wouldn't be expecting it now, with the complicating happenstance of the eclipse. And Cathy wasn't even thinking about Control Central at the moment.

Suppose he tried to call now?

Well, suppose he did! She'd been trying to get him for three solid days. If he tried once, and came up against a shut-out, he could damn well try again!

She *couldn't* call him now. If she *got* him, she wouldn't be able to stay in contact anyhow. There wasn't time.

It would be an hour, maybe more, after she closed the suit before she could open up again.

She stood there, struggling with the impossible, and suddenly his image was so sharply in her mind, his voice remembered in her ears, the imagined brush of his lips against her face so vividly real that, knowing the figure for the delusion it was, she was immersed in a salt wave of loneliness and misery beside which all that had gone before was insignificant.

FOR a moment she let herself be inundated by grief. But for a moment only. One sob escaped her; then her gloved fingers fumbled for the gill-valve switch.

Better be lonely than dead, she told herself, and wondered what the difference really was. But if he wouldn't answer anyhow, far better at least to be lonely alive than dead. Pride, this time, came to the aid of common sense; but with her finger on the switch, she still hesitated.

Three minutes still . . . In a swift compromise between desire and necessity, Cathy opened her mind to total blank reception; and even as she told herself once more on the thin top-conscious level that was still aware that she *couldn't* accept a call if it came—*she felt him,* and sent out a desperate searching hopeful answering cry:

Mike!

But there was nothing. Emptiness. Nobody there, until

she felt the forming of a pattern that wasn't his at all. Luellen's? She couldn't wait to find out. The ringing in her ears was *not* emotion; it was the warning chime still sounding to announce the start of action!

Her finger on the switch exerted the small necessary pressure, and the suit was closed at last. Through the clear plastic of the headpiece her eyes sought and found twin dials on the control board where slim red needles moved in unison from left to right . . . *one tenth around already!* The timing mechanism was already operating, swinging open the two hatches on opposite sides of the cylinder from which the bomb and its counterweight in mass would be released.

How long?

How long ago did it start?

A few seconds? Or a fraction of one? What should she be doing right now?

She could figure it out, of course, from the position of the moving needles, but there was no time for figuring now, and her mind, set for a routine pattern of familiar activity, refused to face the unexpected new demands.

She'd missed the opening note, and she couldn't pick up the beat. Like trying to remember the words to a song, starting in the middle of a line . . . *Jest can't pull my poor self together. . . .*

You damn well better, kid!

Then her mind focused on what her eyes were watching; the control comp tape glowing on the board in front of her acquired meaning as well as form and color. Still, for one further stretch of time, uncounted and unrecoverable, her fingers twitched and trembled uncontrollably inside the heavy gloves. One bead of sweat, tracking across her cheek, seemed irritant beyond endurance.

She cursed herself and Mike and the Traffic Control Service in general and its many officers, sections, and subsections in particular and in detail. Then she stopped cursing, or thinking about anything at all, and pressed down a button on the board, *knowing* it was right, without knowing which it was, or why.

The fingers of the gloves, activated by nerves and ganglia in the girl's hand, impressed her will effortlessly on keys and switches whose grooves and weights had been designed to suit their touch. Cathy herself, from that moment on, was a machine, a complex and delicate machine, within a jointed metal container. She was conscious of nothing, for the time, except the job at hand, and her capacity to perform it.

Girl, suit, and cylinder, bomb and dummy counterweight: they were one organism with one mind, one goal, one life in common; and between them they possessed every organ of perception or of motion that could conceivably be utilized to conquer the immediate objective.

THE bomb was underway now, curving through empty space outside, under the impetus of radio directives from the board. No way, no way at all for the girl at the board to know whether the time lost had upset her careful calculations. She followed the luminous pointer as it worked its way down the calcker tape; set her coordinates and velocities according to the predetermined course; but never for an instant was she unaware of the danger that the delay—how long, *how long?*—might have made the whole performance useless.

Useless or worse. When it was done, placement achieved as planned, and there remained just one more act to perform, Cathy depressed the button that would fire the bomb, not knowing as she did whether her act was one of dutiful efficiency, futile stupidity—or suicide.

Then the pinpoint of light on the screen that piped the bomb vanished from sight. And the irregular area of interference fuzz now centered on the screen began to spread out and retreat, dissolving as it went. Like that. Done. *Right!*

HE STROKED her head absently, the fear not quite gone from his eyes above his broad grin.

"You silly dame," he said tenderly. "Silly suspicious female. If you can't trust me when you can't see me, you better stick around after this."

Cathy smiled and stretched luxuriously, and woke from the wonderful dream to sweet reality.

"Hi, babe." *His* pattern this time. No mistake. "Awake now? Sure. Sure I'm here. I have been all along . . .

almost all along. Except four hours maybe, till they got my leg fixed up."

"Your leg? What . . . ?" But she didn't have to ask. She knew. He'd told her in the dream, while she was sleeping. The accident. The torn second's pain, and her own scream, feeling what he did as she slept, and then he was gone, and she was terrified.

He'd shut her out briefly, to keep the pain from her. And when he tried to call her back again, he couldn't find her.

His pride, she thought with a smile now. *It* was *his pride.*

He wouldn't share the pain. And she *couldn't* share her fear. From the first moment that she thought he'd left her, from the beginning of her harried searching for him, from when she'd let herself mix motives and meanings with the memory of her own scream—from that time on, it was increasingly impossible for him to make contact with her. From that time, till she fell asleep in the total-exhaustion aftermath of the day's work. "Okay, babe?" he asked. "You all right now?"

"I'm fine," she answered. "I'm just fine now. But Mike —don't go away again."

"Never," he promised, and she thought: *I can walk in the sun again.*

Reprinted the following year in the Martha Foley collection "Best American Short Stories, 1955," this story first appeared in The Magazine of Fantasy and Science Fiction—*November, 1954.*

Dead Center

They gave him sweet ices and kissed him all round, and the Important People who had come to dinner all smiled in a special way as his mother took him from the living room and led him down the hall to his own bedroom.

"Great kid you got there," they said to Jock, his father, and "Serious little bugger, isn't he?" Jock didn't say anything, but Toby knew he would be grinning, looking pleased and embarrassed. Then their voices changed, and that meant they had begun to talk about the important events for which the important people had come.

In his own room, Toby wriggled his toes between crisp sheets and breathed in the powder-and-perfume smell of his mother as she bent over him for a last hurried goodnight kiss. There was no use asking for a story tonight. Toby lay still and waited while she closed the door behind her and went off to the party, click-tap, tip-clack, hurrying on her high silver heels. She had heard the voices change back there, too, and she didn't want to miss anything. Toby got up and opened his door just a crack, and set himself down in back of it, and listened.

In the big square living room, against the abstract patterns of gray and vermilion and chartreuse, the men and women moved in easy patterns of familiar acts. Coffee, brandy, cigarette, cigar. Find your partner, choose your seat. Jock sprawled with perfect relaxed contentment on the low couch with the deep-red corduroy cover. Tim O'Heyer balanced nervously on the edge of the same couch, wreathed in cigar smoke, small and dark and alert. Gordon Kimberly dwarfed the big easy chair with the bulking importance of him. Ben Stein, shaggy and rumpled as ever, was running a hand through his hair till it, too, stood on end. He was leaning against a window frame, one hand on the back of the straight chair in which his wife Sue sat, erect and neat and proper and chic, dressed in smart black that set off perfectly her precise blonde beauty. Mrs. Kimberly, just enough overstuffed so that her pearls gave the appearance of *actually* choking her, was the only stranger to the house. She was standing near the doorway, politely admiring Toby's personal art gallery, as Allie Madero valiantly strove to explain each minor masterpiece.

Ruth Kruger stood still a moment, surveying her room and her guests. Eight of them, herself included, and all Very Important People. In the familiar comfort of her own living room, the idea made her giggle. Allie and Mrs. Kimberly both turned to her, questioning. She laughed and shrugged, helpless to explain, and they all went across the room to join the others.

"Guts," O'Heyer said through the cloud of smoke. "How do you do it, Jock? Walk out of a setup like this into . . . God knows what?"

"Luck," Jock corrected him. "A setup like this helps. I'm the world's pampered darling, and I know it."

"Faith is what he means," Ben put in. "He just gets by believing that last year's luck is going to hold up. So it does."

"Depends on what you mean by *luck*. If you think of it as a vector sum composed of predictive powers and personal ability and accurate information and—"

"Charm and nerve and——"

"Guts," Tim said again, interrupting the interrupter.

"All right, all of them," Ben agreed. "*Luck* is as good a word as any to cover the combination."

"We're all lucky people." That was Allie, drifting into range, with Ruth behind her. "We just happened to get born at the right time with the right dream. Any one of us, fifty years ago, would have been called a wild-eyed visiona——"

"Any one of us," Kimberly said heavily, "fifty years ago, would have had a different dream—in time with the times."

Jock smiled and let them talk, not joining in much. He listened to philosophy and compliments and speculations and comments, and lay sprawled across the comfortable couch in his own living room, with his wife's hand under his own, consciously letting his mind play back and forth between the two lives he lived: this, here . . . and the perfect mathematic bleakness of the metal beast that would be his home in three days' time.

He squeezed his wife's hand, and she turned and looked at him, and there was no doubt a man could have about what the world held in store.

When they had all gone, Jock walked down the hall and picked up the little boy asleep on the floor, and put him back into his bed. Toby woke up long enough to grab his father's hand and ask earnestly, out of the point in the conversation where sleep had overcome him:

"Daddy, if the universe hasn't got any ends to it, how can you tell where you are?"

"Me?" Jock asked. "I'm right next to the middle of it."

"How do you know?"

His father tapped him lightly on the chest.

"Because that's where the middle is." Jock smiled and stood up. "Go to sleep, champ. Good night."

And Toby slept, while the universe revolved in all its mystery about the small center Jock Kruger had assigned to it.

"Scared?" she asked, much later, in the spaceless silence of their bedroom.

He had to think about it before he could answer. "I guess not. I guess I think I ought to be, but I'm not. I don't think I'd do it at all if I wasn't *sure*." He was almost asleep when the thought hit him, and he jerked awake and saw she was sure enough lying wide-eyed and sleepless beside him. "*Baby!*" he said, and it was almost an accusation. "Baby, *you're* not scared, are you?"

"Not if you're not," she said. But they never could lie to each other.

II

Toby sat on the platform, next to his grandmother. They were in the second row, right in back of his mother and father, so it was all right for him to wriggle a little bit, or whisper. They couldn't hear much of the speeches back there, and what they did hear mostly didn't make sense to Toby. But every now and then Grandma would grab his hand tight all of a sudden, and he understood what the whole thing was about: it was because Daddy was going away again.

His grandma's hand was very white, with little red and tan dots in it, and big blue veins that stood out higher than the wrinkles in her skin, whenever she grabbed at his hand. Later, walking over to the towering skyscraping rocket, he held his mother's hand; it was smooth and cool and tan, all one color, and she didn't grasp at him the way Grandma did. Later still, his father's two hands, picking him up to kiss, were bigger and darker tan than his mother's, not so smooth, and the fingers were stronger, but so strong it hurt sometimes.

They took him up in an elevator, and showed him all around the inside of the rocket, where Daddy would sit, and where all the food was stored, for emergency, they said, and the radio and everything. Then it was time to say goodbye.

Daddy was laughing at first, and Toby tried to laugh, too, but he didn't really want Daddy to go away. Daddy kissed him, and he felt like crying because it was scratchy against Daddy's cheek, and the strong fingers were hurting him now. Then Daddy stopped laughing and looked

170

at him very seriously. "You take care of your mother, now," Daddy told him. "You're a big boy this time."

"Okay," Toby said. Last time Daddy went away in a rocket, he was not-quite-four, and they teased him with the poem in the book that said, *James James Morrison Morrison Weatherby George Dupree, Took great care of his mother, though he was only three. . .* So Toby didn't much like Daddy saying that now, because he knew they didn't really mean it.

"Okay," he said, and then because he was angry, he said, "Only she's supposed to take care of me, isn't she?"

Daddy and Mommy both laughed, and so did the two men who were standing there waiting for Daddy to get done saying goodbye to him. He wriggled, and Daddy put him down.

"I'll bring you a piece of the moon, son," Daddy said, and Toby said, "All right, fine." He reached for his mother's hand, but he found himself hanging onto Grandma instead, because Mommy and Daddy were kissing each other, and both of them had forgotten all about him.

He thought they were never going to get done kissing.

Ruth Kruger stood in the glass control booth with her son on one side of her and Gordon Kimberly breathing heavily on the other side. *Something's wrong,* she thought, *this time something's wrong.* And then, swiftly, *I mustn't think that way!*

Jealous? she taunted herself. Do you *want* something to be wrong, just because this one isn't all yours, because Argent did some of it?

But if anything is wrong, she prayed, let it be now, right away, so he can't go. If anything's wrong let it be in the firing gear or the . . . what? Even now, it was too late. The beast was too big and too delicate and too precise. If something went wrong, even now, it was too late. It was . . .

You didn't finish that thought. Not if you were Ruth Kruger, and your husband was Jock Kruger, and nobody knew but the two of you how much of the courage that had gone twice round the moon and was about to land on it was yours. When a man knows his wife's faith is

171

unshakable, he can't help coming back. (But: "Baby! *You're* not scared, are you?")

Twice around the moon, and they called him Jumping Jock. There was never a doubt in anyone's mind who'd pilot the bulky beautiful beast out there today. Kruger and Kimberly, O'Heyer and Stein. It was a combo. It won every time. *Every time.* Nothing to doubt. No room for doubt.

"Minus five . . ." someone said into a mike, and there was perfect quiet all around. "Four . . . three . . .

(But he held me too tight, and he laughed too loud. . . .)

(Only because he thought *I* was scared, she answered herself.)

". . . Mar—"

You didn't even hear the whole word, because the thunder-drumming roar of the beast itself split your ears.

Ringing quiet came down, and she caught up Toby, held him tight, tight. . .

"Perfect!" Gordon Kimberly sighed. "*Perfect!*"

So if anything was wrong, it hadn't showed up yet.

She put Toby down, then took his hand. "Come on," she said. "I'll buy you an ice-cream soda." He grinned at her. He'd been looking strange all day, but now he looked real again. His hair had got messed up when she grabbed him.

"We're having cocktails for the press in the conference room," Kimberly said. "I think we could find something Toby would like."

"Wel-l-l-l . . ." She didn't want a cocktail, and she didn't want to talk to the press. "I think maybe we'll beg off this time . . ."

"I think there might be some disappointment—" the man started; then Tim O'Heyer came dashing up.

"Come on, babe," he said. "Your old man told me to take personal charge while he was gone." He leered. On him it looked cute. She laughed. Then she looked down at Toby. "What would you rather, Tobe? Want to go out by ourselves, or go to the party?"

"I don't care," he said.

Tim took the boy's hand. "What we were thinking of was having a kind of party here, and then I think they're going to bring some dinner in, and anybody who wants to can stay up till your Daddy gets to the moon. That'll be pretty late. I guess you wouldn't want to stay up late like that, would you?"

Somebody else talking to Toby like that would be all wrong, but Tim was a friend, Toby's friend, too. Ruth still didn't want to go to the party, but she remembered now that there had been plans for something like that all along, and since Toby was beginning to look eager, and it *was* important to keep the press on their side . . .

"You win, O'Heyer," she said. "Will somebody please send out for an ice-cream soda? Cherry syrup, I think it is this week . . ." She looked inquiringly at her son. ". . . and . . . *strawberry* ice cream?"

Tim shuddered. Toby nodded. Ruth smiled, and they all went in to the party.

"Well, young man!" Toby thought the red-headed man in the brown suit was probably what they called a reporter, but he wasn't sure. "How about it? You going along next time?"

"I don't know," Toby said politely. "I guess not."

"Don't you want to be a famous flier like your daddy?" a strange woman in an evening gown asked him.

"I don't know," he muttered, and looked around for his mother, but he couldn't see her.

They kept asking him questions like that, about whether he wanted to go to the moon. Daddy said he was too little. You'd think all these people would know that much.

Jock Kruger came up swiftly out of dizzying darkness into isolation and clarity. As soon as he could move his head, before he fully remembered why, he began checking the dials and meters and flashing lights on the banked panel in front of him. He was fully aware of the ship, of its needs and strains and motion, before he came to complete consciousness of himself, his weightless body, his purpose, or his memories.

But he was aware of himself as a part of the ship before he remembered his name, so that by the time he knew he had a face and hands and innards, these parts were already occupied with feeding the beast's human

173

brain a carefully prepared stimulant out of a nippled flask fastened in front of his head.

He pressed a button under his index finger in the arm rest of the couch that held him strapped to safety.

"Hi," he said. "Is anybody up besides me?"

He pressed the button under his middle finger and waited.

Not for long.

"Thank God!" a voice crackled out of the loudspeaker. "You really conked out this time, Jock. Nothing wrong?"

"Not so I'd know it. You want . . . How long was I out?"

"Twenty-three minutes, eighteen seconds, takeoff to reception. Yeah. Give us a log reading."

Methodically, in order, he read off the pointers and numbers on the control panel, the colors and codes and swinging needles and quiet ones that told him how each muscle and nerve and vital organ of the great beast was taking the trip. He did it slowly and with total concentration. Then, when he was all done, there was nothing else to do except sit back and start wondering about that big blackout.

It shouldn't have happened. It had never happened before. There was nothing in the compendium of information he'd just sent back to Earth to account for it.

A different ship, different . . . different men. Two and a half years different. Years of easy living and . . . growing old? Too old for this game?

Twenty-three minutes!

Last time it was under ten. The first time maybe 90 seconds more. It didn't matter, of course, not at takeoff. There was nothing for him to do then. Nothing now. Nothing for four more hours. He was there to put the beast back down on . . .

He grinned, and felt like Jock Kruger again. Identity returned complete. *This* time he was there to put the beast down where no man or beast had ever been before. This time they were going to the moon.

III

Ruth Kruger sipped at a cocktail and murmured responses to the admiring, the curious, the envious, the hopeful, and the hate-full ones who spoke to her. She was waiting for something, and after an unmeasurable stretch of time Allie Madero brought it to her.

First a big smile seeking her out across the room, so she knew it had come. Then a low-voiced confirmation.

"Wasn't it . . . an awful long time?" she asked. She hadn't been watching the clock, on purpose, but she was sure it was longer than it should have been.

Allie stopped smiling. "Twenty-three," she said.

Ruth gasped. "What . . . ?"

"You figure it. I can't."

"There's nothing in the ship. I mean nothing was changed that would account for it." She shook her head slowly. This time she didn't know the ship well enough to talk like that. There *could* be something. Oh, *Jock!* "I don't know," she said. "Too many people worked on that thing. I . . ."

"Mrs. Kruger!" It was the red-headed reporter, the obnoxious one. "We just got the report on the blackout. I'd like a statement from you, if you don't mind, as designer of the ship—"

"I am not the designer of this ship," she said coldly.

"You worked on the design, didn't you?"

"Yes."

"Well, then, to the best of your knowledge . . . ?"

"To the best of my knowledge, there is no change in design to account for Mr. Kruger's prolonged unconsciousness. Had there been any such prognosis, the press would have been informed."

"Mrs. Kruger, I'd like to ask you whether you feel that the innovations made by Mr. Argent could—"

"Aw, lay off, will you?" Allie broke in, trying to be casual and kidding about it; but behind her own flaming cheeks, Ruth was aware of her friend's matching anger. "How much do you want to milk this for, anyhow? So the guy conked out an extra ten minutes. If you want somebody to crucify for it, why don't you pick on one

175

of us who doesn't happen to be married to him?" She turned to Ruth before the man could answer. "Where's Toby? He's probably about ready to bust from cookies and carbonation."

"He's in the lounge," the reporter put in. "Or he was a few minutes—"

Ruth and Allie started off without waiting for the rest. The redhead had been talking to the kid. No telling how many of them were on top of him now.

"I thought Tim was with him," Ruth said hastily, then she thought of something, and turned back long enough to say, "For the record, Mr. . . . uh . . . I know of no criticism that can be made of any of the work done by Mr. Argent." Then she went to find her son.

There was nothing to do and nothing to see except the instrument meters and dials to check and log and check and log again. Radio stations all around Earth were beamed on him. He could have kibitzed his way to the moon, but he didn't want to. He was thinking.

Thinking back, and forward, and right in this moment. Thinking of the instant's stiffness of Ruth's body when she said she wasn't scared, and the rambling big house on the hill, and Toby politely agreeing when he offered to bring him back a piece of the moon.

Thinking of Toby's growing up some day, and how little he really knew about his son, and what would they do, Toby and Ruth, if anything . . .

He'd never thought that way before. He'd never thought anything except to know he'd come back, because he couldn't stay away. It was always that simple. He couldn't stay away now, either. That hadn't changed. But as he sat there, silent and useless for the time, it occurred to him that he'd left something out of his calculations. *Luck,* they'd been talking about. Yes, he'd had luck. But —what was it Sue had said about a vector sum?—there was more to figure in than your own reflexes and the beast's strength. There was the *outside.* Space . . . environment . . . God . . . destiny. What difference does it make what name you give it?

He couldn't *stay* away . . . but maybe he could be *kept* away.

He'd never thought that way before.

"You tired, honey?"

"No," he said, "I'm just sick of this party. I want to go home."

"It'll be over pretty soon, Toby. I think as long as we stayed this long we better wait for . . . for the end of the party."

"It's a silly party. You said you'd buy me an ice-cream soda."

"I did, darling," she said patiently. "At least, if I didn't *buy* it, I got it for you. You had it, didn't you?"

"Yes, but you *said* we'd go *out* and have one."

"Look. Why don't you just put your head down on my lap and . . ."

"I'm no *baby*! Anyhow I'm not tired."

"All right. We'll go pretty soon. You just sit here on the couch, and you don't have to talk to anybody if you don't feel like it. I'll tell you what. I'll go find you a magazine or a book or something to look at, and—"

"I don't *want* a magazine. I want my own book with the pirates in it."

"You just stay put a minute, so I can find you. I'll bring you something."

She got up and went out to the other part of the building where the offices were, and collected an assortment of leaflets and folders with shiny bright pictures of mail rockets and freight transports and jets and visionary moon rocket designs, and took them back to the little lounge where she'd left him.

She looked at the clock on the way. Twenty-seven more minutes. There was *no* reason to believe that anything was wrong.

They were falling now. A man's body is not equipped to sense direction *toward* or *from, up* or *down,* without the help of landmarks or gravity. But the body of the beast was designed to know such things; and Kruger, at the nerve center, knew everything the beast knew.

Ship is extension of self, and self is—extension or limitation?—of ship. If Jock Kruger is the center of the universe—remember the late night after the party, and picking Toby off the floor?—then ship is extension of self, and the man *is* the brain of the beast. But if ship *is* universe—certainly continuum; that's universe, isn't it?—then the weakling man-thing in the couch is a limiting condition of the universe. A human brake. He was there to make it stop where it didn't "want" to.

Suppose it wouldn't stop? Suppose it had decided to be a self-determined, free-willed universe?

Jock grinned, and started setting controls. His time was coming. It was measurable in minutes, and then in seconds . . . *now!*

His hand reached for the firing lever (but *what* was she scared of?), groped, and touched, hesitated, clasped, and pulled.

Grownup parties at home were fun. But other places, like this one, they were silly. Toby half-woke-up on the way home, enough to realize his Uncle Tim was driving them, and they weren't in their own car. He was sitting on the front seat next to his mother, with his head against her side, and her arm around him. He tried to come all the way awake, to listen to what they were saying, but they weren't talking, so he started to go back to sleep.

Then Uncle Tim said, "For God's sake, Ruth, he's safe, and whatever happened certainly wasn't *your* fault. He's got enough supplies to hold out till . . ."

"Shh!" his mother said sharply, and then, whispering, "I know."

Now he remembered.

"Mommy . . ."

"Yes, hon?"

"Did Daddy go to the moon all right?"

"Y . . . yes, dear."

Her voice was funny.

"Where is it?"

"Where's what?"

"The moon."

"Oh. We can't see it now, darling. It's around the other side of the earth."

"Well, when is he going to come *back?*"

Silence.

"Mommy . . . when?"

178

"As soon as . . . just as soon as he can, darling. Now go to sleep."

And now the moon was up, high in the sky, a gilded football dangling from Somebody's black serge lapel. When she was a little girl, she used to say she loved the man in the moon, and now the man in the moon loved her, too, but if she was a little girl still, somebody would tuck her into bed, and pat her head and tell her to go to sleep, and she would sleep as easy, breathe as soft, as Toby did. . . .

But she wasn't a little girl, she was all grown up, and she married the man, the man in the moon, and sleep could come and sleep could go, but sleep could never stay with her while the moonwash swept the window panes.

She stood at the open window and wrote a letter in her mind and sent it up the path of light to the man in the moon. It said:

"Dear Jock: Tim says it wasn't my fault, and I can't explain it even to him. I'm sorry, darling. Please to stay alive till we can get to you. Faithfully yours, Cassandra."

IV

The glasses and ashes and litter and spilled drinks had all been cleared away. The table top gleamed in polished stripes of light and dark, where the light came through the louvered plastic of the wall. The big chairs were empty, waiting, and at each place, arranged with the precision of a formal dinner-setting, was the inevitable pad of yellow paper, two freshly sharpened pencils, a small neat pile of typed white sheets of paper, a small glass ashtray, and a shining empty water glass. Down the center of the table, spaced for comfort, three crystal pitchers of ice and water stood in perfect alignment.

Ruth was the first one there. She stood in front of a chair fingering the little stack of paper on which someone (Allie? She'd have had to be up early to get it done so quickly) had tabulated the details of yesterday's events. "To refresh your memory," was how they always put it.

179

She poured a glass of water, and guiltily replaced the pitcher on the exact spot where it had been; lit a cigarette, and stared with dismay at the burnt match marring the cleanliness of the little ashtray; pulled her chair in beneath her and winced at the screech of the wooden leg across the floor.

Get it over with! She picked up the typed pages and glanced at them. Two at the bottom were headed "Recommendations of U.S. Rocket Corps to Facilitate Construction of KIM-VIII." That could wait. The three top sheets she'd better get through while she was still alone.

She read slowly and carefully, trying to memorize each sentence, so that when the time came to talk, she could think of what happened this way, from outside, instead of remembering how it had been for *her.*

There was nothing in the report she didn't already know.

Jock Kruger had set out in the KIM-VII at 5:39 P.M., C.S.T., just at sunset. First report after recovery from blackout came at 6:02 plus. First log readings gave no reason to anticipate any difficulty. Subsequent reports and radioed log readings were, for Kruger, unusually terse and formal, and surprisingly infrequent; but earth-to-ship contact at twenty-minute intervals had been acknowledged. No reason to believe Kruger was having trouble at any time during the trip.

At 11:54, an attempt to call the ship went unanswered for 56 seconds. The radioman here described Kruger's voice as "irritable" when the reply finally came, but all he said was, "Sorry. I was firing the first brake." Then a string of figures, and a quick log reading—everything just what you'd expect.

Earth acknowledged, and waited.

Eighteen seconds later:

"Second brake." More figures. Again, everything as it should be. But twenty seconds after that call was completed:

"This is Kruger. Anything wrong with the dope I gave you?"

"Earth to Kruger. Everything okay in our book. Trouble?"

"Track me, boy. I'm off."

"You want a course correction?"

"I can figure it quicker here. I'll keep talking as I go. Stop me if I'm wrong by your book." More figures, and Kruger's calculations coincided perfectly with the swift work done at the base. Both sides came to the same conclusion, and both sides knew what it meant. The man in the beast fired once more, and once again, and made a landing.

There was no reason to believe that either ship or pilot had been hurt. There was no way of finding out. By the best calculations, they were five degrees of arc around on the dark side. And there was no possibility at all, after that second corrective firing, that Kruger had enough fuel left to take off again. The last thing Earth had heard, before the edge of the moon cut off Kruger's radio, was:

"Sorry, boys. I guess I fouled up this time. Looks like you'll have to come and . . ."

One by one, they filled the seats: Gordon Kimberly at one end, and the Colonel at the other; Tim O'Heyer to one side of Kimberly, and Ruth at the other; Allie, with her pad and pencil poised, alongside Tim; the Colonel's aide next down the line, with his little silent stenotype in front of him; the Steins across from him, next to Ruth. With a minimum of formality, Kimberly opened the meeting and introduced Col. Swenson.

The Colonel cleared his throat. "I'd like to make something clear," he said. "Right from the start, I want to make this clear. I'm here to help. Not to get in the way. My presence does not indicate any—*criticism* on the part of the Armed Services. We are entirely satisfied with the work you people have been doing." He cleared his throat again, and Kimberly put in:

"You saw our plans, I believe, Colonel. Everything was checked and approved by your outfit ahead of time."

"Exactly. We had no criticism then, and we have none now. The rocket program is what's important. Getting Kruger back is important, not just for ordinary humanitarian reasons—pardon me, Mrs. Kruger, if I'm too blunt —but for the sake of the whole program. Public opinion,

181

for one thing. That's your line, isn't it, Mr. O'Heyer? And then, *we have to find out what happened!*

"I came down here today to offer any help we can give you on the relief ship, and to make a suggestion to facilitate matters."

He paused deliberately this time.

"Go ahead, Colonel," Tim said. "We're listening."

"Briefly, the proposal is that you all accept temporary commissions while the project is going on. Part of that report in front of you embodies the details of the plan. I hope you'll find it acceptable. You all know there is a great deal of necessary, I'm afraid—*red tape,* you'd call it, and going through channels, and such in the Services. It makes cooperation between civilian and military groups difficult. If we can all get together as one outfit 'for the duration,' so to speak . . ."

This time nobody jumped into the silence. The Colonel cleared his throat once more.

"Perhaps you'd best read the full report before we discuss it any further. I brought the matter up now just to— to let you know the *attitude* with which we are submitting the proposal to you . . ."

"Thank you, Colonel." O'Heyer saved him. "I've already had a chance to look at the report. Don't know that anyone else has, except of course Miss Madero. But I personally, at least, appreciate your attitude. And I think I can speak for Mr. Kimberly, too. . . ."

He looked sideways at his boss; Gordon nodded.

"What I'd like to suggest now," O'Heyer went on, "since I've seen the report already, and I believe everyone else would like to have a chance to bone up some— perhaps you'd like to have a first-hand look at some of our plant, Colonel? I could take you around a bit . . . ?"

"Thank you. I would like to." The officer stood up, his gold Rocket Corps uniform blazing in the louvered light. "If I may say so, Mr. O'Heyer, you seem remarkably sensible, for a—well, a *publicity* man."

"That's all right, Colonel." Tim laughed easily. "I don't even think it's a dirty word. You seem like an all-right guy yourself—for an *officer,* that is."

They all laughed then, and Tim led the blaze of glory out of the room while the rest of them settled down to studying the R.C. proposals. When they had all finished, Kimberly spoke slowly, voicing the general reaction:

"I hate to admit it, but it makes sense."

"They're being pretty decent about it, aren't they?" Ben said. "Putting it to us as a proposal instead of pulling a lot of weight."

He nodded. "I've had a little contact with this man Swenson before. He's a good man to work with. It . . . makes sense, that's all."

"On paper, anyhow," Sue put in.

"Well, Ruth . . ." the big man turned to her, waiting. "You haven't said anything."

"I . . . it seems all right to me," she said, and added: "Frankly, Gordon, I don't know that I ought to speak at all. I'm not quite sure why I'm here."

Allie looked up sharply, questioning, from her notes; Sue pushed back her chair and half-stood. "My God, you're not going to back out on us now?"

"I . . . look, you all know I didn't do any of the real work on the last one. It was Andy Argent's job, and a good one. I've got Toby to think about, and—"

"Kid, we *need* you," Sue protested. "Argent can't do this one; this is going to be another Three, only more so. Unmanned, remote-control stuff, and no returning atmosphere-landing problems. This is up your alley. It's . . ." She sank back; there was nothing else to say.

"That's true, Ruth." Tim had come back in during the last outburst. Now he sat down. "Speed is what counts, gal. That's why we're letting the gold braid in on the job—we are, aren't we?" Kimberly nodded; Tim went on: "With you on the job, we've got a working team. With somebody new—well, you know what a ruckus we had until Sue got used to Argent's blueprints, and how Ben's pencil notes used to drive Andy wild. And we can't even use him this time. It's not his field. He did do a good job, but we'd have to start in with somebody new all over again . . ." He broke off, and looked at Kimberly.

"I hope you'll decide to work with us, Ruth," he said simply.

"If . . . obviously, if it's the best way to get it done

183

quick, I will," she said. "Twenty-eight hours a day if you like."

Tim grinned. "I guess we can let the braid back in now . . . ?" He got up and went to the door.

Another Three, only more so . . . Sue's words danced in her mind while the Colonel and the Colonel's aide marched in and took their places, while voices murmured politely, exchanging good will.

Another Three—the first ship she had designed for Kimberly. The ship that made her rich and famous, but that was nothing, because it was the ship that brought Jock to her, that made him write the letter, that made her meet him, that led to the Five and Six and now . . .

"I've got some ideas for a manned ship," he'd written. "If we could get together to discuss it some time . . ."

". . . pleasure to know you'll be working with us, Mrs. Kruger." She shook her head sharply, and located in time and place.

"Thank you, Colonel. I want to do what I can, of course . . ."

V

James James Morrison's mother put on a golden gown . . .

Toby knew the whole thing, almost, by heart. The little boy in the poem told his mother not to go *down* to the *end of town,* wherever that was, unless she took him along. And she said she wouldn't, but she put on that golden gown and went, and thought she'd be back in time for tea. Only she wasn't. She never came back at all. *Last seen wandering vaguely . . . King John said he was sorry . . .*

Who's King John? And what time is tea?

Toby sat quietly beside his mother on the front seat of the car, and looked obliquely at the golden uniform she wore, and could not find a way to ask the questions in his mind.

Where was James James's *father?* Why did James James have to be the one to keep his mother from going down to the end of the town?

184

"Are you in the Army now, Mommy?" he asked.

"Well . . . sort of. But not for long, darling. Just till Daddy comes home."

"When is Daddy coming home?"

"Soon. Soon, I hope. Not too long."

She didn't sound right. Her voice had a cracking sound like Grandma's, and other old ladies. She didn't look right, either, in that golden-gown uniform. When she kissed him goodbye in front of the school, she didn't *feel* right. She didn't even smell the same as she used to.

" 'Bye, boy. See you tonight," she said—the words she always said, but they sounded different.

" 'Bye." He walked up the driveway and up the front steps and down the corridor and into the pretty-painted room where his teacher was waiting. Miss Callahan was nice. Today she was *too* nice. The other kids teased him, and called him teacher's pet. At lunchtime he went back in the room before anybody else did, and made pictures all over the floor with the colored chalk. It was the worst thing he could think of to do. Miss Callahan made him wash it all up, and she wasn't nice any more for the rest of the afternoon.

When he went out front after school, he couldn't see the car anywhere. It was true, then. His mother had put on that golden gown, and now she was gone. Then he saw Grandma waving to him out of *her* car, and he remembered Mommy had said Grandma would come and get him. He got in the car, and she grabbed at him like she always did. He pulled away.

"Is Daddy home yet?" he asked.

Grandma started the car. "Not yet," she said, and she was crying. He didn't dare ask about Mommy after that, but she wasn't home when they got there. It was a long time after that till dinner was ready.

She came home for dinner, though.

"You have to allow for the human factor . . ."

Nobody had said it to her, of course. Nobody would. She wondered how much tougher it made the job for everybody, having her around. She wondered how she'd stay sane, if she didn't have the job to do.

Thank God Toby was in school now! She couldn't do

185

it, if it meant leaving him with someone else all day—even his grandmother. As it was, having the old lady in the house so much was nerve-racking.

I ought to ask her if she'd like to sleep here for a while, Ruth thought, and shivered. Dinnertime was enough.

Anyhow, Toby liked having her there, and that's what counted.

I'll have to go in and see his teacher. Tomorrow, she thought. I've got to make time for it tomorrow. Let her know . . . but of course she knew. Jock Kruger's family's affairs were hardly private. Just the same, I better talk to her.

Ruth got out of bed and stood at the window, waiting for the moon. Another ten minutes, fifteen, twenty maybe, and it would edge over the hills on the other side of town. The white hands on the clock said 2:40. She had to get some sleep. She couldn't stand here waiting for the moon. Get to sleep now, before it comes up. That's better. . . .

"Oh, *Jock!*

". . . the human factor . . ." They didn't know. She wanted to go tell them all, find somebody right away, and shout it. *It's not his fault. I did it!*

"You're *not scared, are you, baby?*"

Oh, no! No, no! Don't be silly. Who, me? Just stiff and trembling. The cold, you know . . . ?

Stop that!

She stood at the window, waiting for the moon, the man, the man in the moon.

Human factor . . . well, there wouldn't be a human factor in this one. If she went out to the field on take-off day and told KIM-VIII she was scared, it wouldn't matter at all.

Thank God I can do something, at least!

Abruptly, she closed the blind, so she wouldn't know when it came, and pulled out the envelope she'd brought home, switched on the bed light, and unfolded the first blueprints.

It was all familiar. Just small changes here and there. Otherwise, it was the Three all over again—the first un-manned ship to be landed successfully on the moon surface. The only important difference was that this one had to have some fancy gadgetry on the landing mech. Stein had given her the orbit calcs today. The rest of the job was hers and Sue's: design and production. Between them, they could do it. What they needed was a goldberg that would take the thing once around low enough to contact Jock, if . . . to contact him, that's all. Then back again, prepared for him to take over the landing by remote, according to instructions, if he wanted to. If he could. If his radio was working. If . . .

Twice around, and then down where they figured he was, if he hadn't tried to bring it down himself.

It was complicated, but only quantitatively. Nothing basically new, or untried. And no *human* factors to be allowed for, once it was off the ground.

She fell asleep, finally, with the light still on, and the blind drawn, and the blueprints spread out on the floor next to the bed.

Every day, she drove him to school, dressed in her golden gown. And every afternoon, he waited, telling himself she was sure to come home.

That was a very silly little poem, and he wasn't three, he was six now.

But it was a long time since Daddy went away.

"I'd rather not," she said stiffly.

"I'm sorry, Ruth. I know—well, I *don't* know, but I can imagine how you feel. I hate to ask it, but if you can do it at all . . . just be there and look confident, and . . . you know."

Look confident! I couldn't do it for Jock, she thought; why should I do it for *them?* But of course that was silly. They didn't know her the way Jock did. They couldn't read her smiles, or sense a barely present stiffness, or know anything except what she chose to show on the front of her face.

"Look confident? What difference does it make, Tim? If the thing works, they'll all know soon enough. If . . ."

She stopped.

"All right, I'll be blunt. If it *doesn't* work, it's going to make a hell of a difference what the public feeling was at the time it went off. If we have to try again. If—damn it, you want it straight, all right! If we can't save Jock, we're not going to give up the whole thing! We're not going to let space travel wait another half century while the psychological effects wear off. *And Jock wouldn't want us to!* Don't forget that. It was his dream, too. It was yours, once upon a time. If . . ."

"All *right!*" She was startled by her voice. She was screaming, or almost.

"All right," she said bitterly, more quietly. "If you think I'll be holding up progress for fifty years by not dragging Toby along to a launching, I'll come."

"Oh, Ruth, I'm sorry. No, it's not that important. And I had no business talking that way. But listen, babe, you used to understand this—the way I feel, the way Jock fel—feels. Even a guy like Kimberly. You used to feel it, too. Look: the single item of you showing your face at the takeoff doesn't amount to much. Neither does one ounce of fuel. But either one could be the little bit that makes the difference. Kid, we got to put *everything* we've got behind it this time."

"All right," she said again. "I told you I'd come."

"You do understand, don't you?" he pleaded.

"I don't know, Tim. I'm not sure I do. But you're right. I would have, once. Maybe—I don't know. It's different for a woman, I guess. But I'll come. Don't worry about it."

She turned and started out.

"Thanks, Ruth. And I am sorry. Uh—want me to come and pick you up?"

She nodded. "Thanks." She was glad she wouldn't have to drive.

VI

He kept waiting for a chance to ask her. He couldn't do it in the house before they left, because right after she told him where they were going, she went to get dressed in her golden uniform, and he had to stay with Grandma all the time.

Then Mr. O'Heyer came with the car, and he couldn't

188

ask because, even though he sat up front with Mommy, Mr. O'Heyer was there, too.

When they got to the launching field, there were people around all the time. Once he tried to get her off by himself, but all she did was think he had to go to the bathroom. Then, bit by bit, he didn't *have* to ask, because he could tell from the way they were all talking, and the way the cameras were all pointed at her all the time, like they had been at Daddy the other time.

Then there was the speeches part again, and this time *she* got up and talked, so that settled it.

He was glad he hadn't asked. They probably all thought he knew. Maybe they'd even told him, and he'd forgotten, like he sometimes did. "Mommy," he listened to himself in his mind, "Mommy, are you going to the moon, too?" Wouldn't that sound silly!

She'd come back for him, he told himself. The other times, when Daddy went some place—like when they first came here to live, and Daddy went first, then Mommy, and then they came back to get him, and some other time, he didn't remember just what—but when Daddy went away, Mommy always went to stay with him, and then they *always* came to get him, too.

It wasn't any different from Mommy going back to be with Daddy at a party or something, instead of staying in his room to talk to him when she put him to bed. It didn't feel any worse than that, he told himself.

Only he didn't believe himself.

She never did tell me! I wouldn't of forgotten that! She should *of told me!*

She did not want to make a speech. Nobody had warned her that she would be called upon to make a speech. It was bad enough trying to answer reporters coherently. She stood up and went forward to the microphone dutifully, and shook hands with the President of the United States, and tried to look confident. She opened her mouth and nothing came out.

"Thank you," she said finally, though she didn't know just what for. "You've all been very kind." She turned to the mike and spoke directly into it. "I feel that a good deal of honor is being accorded me today which is not

189

rightfully mine. We gave ourselves a two-month limit to complete a job, and the fact that it was finished inside of six weeks instead . . ."

She had to stop because everybody was cheering, and they wouldn't have heard her.

". . . that fact is not something for which the designer of a ship can be thanked. The credit is due to all the people at Kimberly who worked so hard, and to the Rocket Corps personnel who helped so much. I think . . ."

This time she paused to find the right words. It had suddenly became very important to level with the crowd, to tell them what she honestly felt.

"I think it is I who should be doing the thanking. I happen to be a designer of rockets, but much more importantly, to me, I am Jock Kruger's wife. So I want to thank everyone who helped . . ."

Grandma's hand tightened around his, and then pulled away to get a handkerchief, because she was crying. Right up here on the platform! Then he realized what Mommy had just said. She said that being Jock Kruger's wife was more important to her than anything else.

It was funny that Grandma should feel bad about that. Everybody else seemed to think it was a right thing to say, the way they were yelling and clapping and shouting. It occurred to Toby with a small shock of surprise that maybe Grandma sometimes felt bad about things the same way he did.

He was sort of sorry he wouldn't have much chance to find out more about that.

She broke away from the reporters and V.I.P.'s, and went and got Toby, and asked him did he want to look inside the rocket before it left.

He nodded. He was certainly being quiet today. Poor kid—he must be pretty mixed up about the whole thing by now.

She tried to figure out what was going on inside the small brown head, but all she could think of was how *much* like Jock he looked today.

She took him up the elevator inside the rocket. There wasn't much room to move around, of course, but they'd

190

rigged it so that all the big shots who were there could have a look. She was a little startled to see the President and her mother-in-law come up together in the next elevator, but between trying to answer Toby's questions, and trying to brush off reporters, she didn't have much time to be concerned about such oddities.

She had never seen Toby so intent on anything. He wanted to know *everything*. Where's this, and what's that for? And where are you going to sit, Mommy?

"I'm not, hon. You know that. There isn't room in this rocket for . . ."

"Mrs. Kruger, pardon me, but . . ."

"Just a minute, *please*."

"Oh, I'm sorry."

"What was it you wanted to know, now, Toby?" There were too many people; there was too much talk. She felt slightly dizzy. "Look, hon, I want to go down." It was hard to talk. She saw Mrs. Kruger on the ramp, and called her, and left Toby with her. Down at the bottom, she saw Sue Stein and asked her if she'd go take over with Toby and try to answer his questions.

"Sure. Feeling rocky, kid?"

"Kind of." She tried to smile.

"You better go lie down. Maybe Allie can get something for you. I saw her over there. . . ." She waved a vague hand. "You look like hell, kid. Better lie down." Then she rushed off.

He got away from Grandma when Sue Stein came and said Mother wanted her to show him everything. Then he said he was tired and got away from *her*. He could find his Grandma all right, he said.

He'd found the spot he wanted. He could just about wiggle into it, he thought.

The loudspeaker crackled over her head. Five minutes now.

The other women who'd been fixing their hair and brightening their lipstick snapped their bags shut and took a last look and ran out, to find places where they could see everything. Ruth stretched out on the couch and closed her eyes. Five minutes now, by herself, to get used to the idea that the job was done.

She had done everything she could do, including coming here today. There was nothing further she could do. From now on, or in five minutes' time, it was out of anyone's hands. but—Whose? And Jock's, of course. Once the relief rocket got there, it was up to him.

If it got there.

If he was there for it to get to.

The way they had worked it, there was a chance at least they'd know the answer in an hour's time. If the rocket made its orbit once, and only once, it would mean he was alive and well and in control of his own ship, with the radio working, and . . .

And if it made a second orbit, there was still hope. It *might* mean nothing worse than that his radio was out. But that way they would have to wait . . .

God! It could take months, if the calculations as to where he'd come down were not quite right. If . . . *if* a million little things that would make it harder to get the fuel from one rocket to the other.

But if they only saw one orbit . . .

For the first time, she let herself, forced herself to, consider the possibility that Jock was dead. That he would not come back.

He's not dead, she thought. I'd know it if he was. Like I knew something was wrong last time. Like I'd know it now if . . .

"Sixty seconds before zero," said the speaker.

But there is! She sat bolt upright, not tired or dizzy any more. Now she had faced it, she didn't feel confused. There was something . . . something dreadfully *wrong.* . . .

She ran out, and as she came on to the open field, the speaker was saying, "Fifty-one."

She ran to the edge of the crowd, and couldn't get through, and had to run, keep running, around the edges, to find the aisle between the cords.

Stop it! she screamed but not out loud, because she had to use all her breath for running.

And while she ran, she tried to think.

"Minus forty-seven."

She couldn't make them stop without a reason. They'd think she was hysterical . . .

". . . forty-five . . ."

Maybe she was, at that. Coolly, her mind considered the idea and rejected it. No; there was a problem that hadn't been solved, a question she hadn't answered.

But *what* problem? What . . .

"Minus forty."

She dashed down between the ropes, toward the control booth. The guard stepped forward, then recognized her, and stepped back. The corridor between the packed crowds went on forever.

"Minus thirty-nine . . . eight . . . thirty-seven."

She stopped outside the door of Control, and tried to think, think, *think* what *was* it? What could she tell them? How could she convince them? *She knew*, but they'd want to know what, why . . .

You just didn't change plans at a moment like this.

But if they fired the rocket before she figured it out, before she remembered the problem, and then found an answer, it was as good as murdering Jock. They could never get another one up quickly enough if anything went wrong this time.

She pushed open the door.

"Stop!" she said. "Listen, you've got to stop. Wait! There's something . . ."

Tim O'Heyer came and took her arm and smiled and said something. Something soothing.

"Minus nineteen," somebody said into a microphone, quietly.

She kept trying to explain, and Tim kept talking at her, and when she tried to pull away she realized the hand on her arm wasn't just there to comfort her. He was keeping her from making trouble. He . . .

Oh, God! If there was just some way to make them understand! If she could only remember *what* was wrong . . .

"Minus three . . . two . . ."

It was no use.

She stopped fighting, caught her breath, stood still, and saw Tim's approving smile, as the word and the flare went off together:

"Mark!"

Then, in a dead calm, she looked around and saw Sue. "Where's Toby?" she asked.

She was looking in the reserved grandstand seats for Mrs. Kruger, when she heard the crowd sigh, and looked up and saw it happening.

VII

The crash fire did not damage the inside of the rocket at all. The cause of the crash was self-evident, as soon as they found Toby Kruger's body wedged into the empty space between the outer hull of the third stage, and the inner hull of the second.

The headlines were not as bad as might have been expected. Whether it was the tired and unholy calm on Ruth Kruger's face that restrained them, or Tim O'Heyer's emergency-reserve supply of Irish whisky that convinced them, the newsmen took it easy on the story. All America couldn't attend the funeral, but a representative hundred thousand citizens mobbed the streets when the boy was buried; the other hundred and eighty million saw the ceremonies more intimately on their TV sets.

Nobody who heard the quiet words spoken over the fresh grave—a historic piece of poetry to which the author, O'Heyer, could never sign his name—nobody who heard that simple speech remained entirely unmoved. Just where or when or with whom the movement started is still not known; probably it began spontaneously in a thousand different homes during the brief ceremony; maybe O'Heyer had something to do with that part of it, too. Whichever way, the money started coming in, by wire, twenty minutes afterwards; and by the end of the week "Bring Jock Back" was denting more paychecks than the numbers racket and the nylon industry combined.

The KIM-IX was finished in a month. They didn't have Ruth Kruger to design this time, but they didn't need her: the KIM-VIII plans were still good. O'Heyer managed to keep the sleeping-pill story down to a tiny back-page notice in most of the papers, and the funeral was not televised.

Later, they brought back the perfectly preserved, emaciated body of Jock Kruger, and laid him to rest next to his wife and son. He had been a good pilot and an ingenious man. The moon couldn't kill him; it took starvation to do that.

They made an international shrine of the house, and the garden where the three graves lay.

Now they are talking of making an interplanetary shrine of the lonely rocket on the wrong side of the moon.

This story first appeared under a pseudonym, "Rose Sharon," in F&SF's short-lived sister magazine, Venture—*March, 1957.*

The Lady Was a Tramp

She had been lovely once, sleek-lined and proud, with shining flanks; and men had come to her with hungry hearts and star-filled eyes, and high pulse of adventure in their blood.

Now she was old. Her hide was scarred with use, her luster dulled; though there was beauty in her still, it was hidden deep. A man had to know where to look—and he had to care.

The young man left the conditioned coolness of the Administration Building and paused outside the door to orient. Then he strode briskly forward, ignoring the heat that wilted his uniform and collar and damply curled the edges of the freshly stamped papers in his breast pocket. He passed the inner tier of docks, refusing to look to left or right at the twin proud heights of gleaming Navy vessels.

Beyond them, alone in the outermost ring, the *Lady Jane* sat on her base in the concrete hole, waiting. In the white-light glare of the shadowless Dome, each smallest pit and pockmark of twenty years' usage stood out in cruel relief against the weathered darkness of her hull. Potbellied, dumpy, unbeautiful, she squatted without impatience inside the steel framework of supports, while her tanks were flushed and her tubes reamed clean. When the dock gang was done, and the ravages of the last voyage repaired insofar as could be, she would set forth once more on her rounds of the ports in space. Meanwhile, she rested.

The young man paused. It was his first good look at the *Lady Jane*. He half-turned back; but it was too late now. Fury, or training, or despair, or some of them, moved him on.

"That's him all right." Anita smiled, and turned a knob on the *Lady Jane*'s viewpoint screen; the figure leaped toward them with focused clarity, and the IBMan insignia showed up on the jacket sleeve.

"Mad dogs and eye-bee-men," Chan quoted softly, and leaned forward to study the young man with mock amazement. On the tenth "day" of lunar sunlight it was still possible to keep moderately cool inside an unsealed ship, and the central Administration Building was kept at a steady seventy, day or night. But out in the atmosphere dome, it was hot. Yet the young man walking briskly toward the ship wore formal greens, and his shirt was bound at his neck with a knotted tie. Chandra leaned back, picked up a tall cold glass, and shook his head.

"Look at him, Chan! He's a kid . . ."

Chan shrugged. "You knew that before. You got the papers . . ."

Impatiently, she shook her head. "I know. But look at him . . ."

"I wasn't any older—" Chandra began.

"Yes, you were! I don't know what your papers said, but—look at him. And you weren't an IBMan. And we were all younger then. And—darling, you were a man!"

He laughed and stood up, rumpling her hair as he passed. "Well, if that's all that's eating you, babe—hell, four of us kept you happy halfway home."

He ducked through the bunkroom door as she started to rise. "Don't shoot," he called back.

"It ain't so funny, honey." She stood watching the

screen. "What's bothering me is, who's going to keep *him* happy?"

Terence Hugh Carnahan, Lieutenant, U.N.N. Reserves, was twenty-four years old and newly commissioned. He was stuffed to the gills with eight full years of Academy training, precision, and knowledge. The shiny new stripes on his sleeve and the dampening papers inside his breast pocket were the prizes he'd worked for and dreamed of as long as it mattered. The fruits were sour now, and the dream was curdled. A man might approach the *Lady* incited by lust to a venture of greed, but the sight of her was enough to wipe out the last visions of glory.

The Lieutenant moved on, more slowly. He stopped as a three-wheeled red-and-white-striped baggage truck swung out in a wide crazy curve from behind the Navy ship to the left and careened to a stop at the *Lady*'s side.

A tall thin man in rumpled full-dress whites leaped out of the bucket, swinging a canvas suitcase in his hand. He climbed aboard the ship's waiting elevator and it started up.

Terry walked on and waited beside the truck for the cage to come down. When it did, he produced his ID card, got inside, and rode up in silence.

In the open lock, the man in the dirty whites was waiting for him. He held out his hand, and for the first time Terry saw the pilot's jets on his lapels; and the boards on his shoulders spelled Commander.

"You the new IBMan?" the pilot asked. "Where's your gear?"

"I sent it on this morning." They shook, and the pilot's slim fingers were unexpectedly cool and dry.

"Welcome to our happy home," he said. "Glad to have you aboard. And all that sort of thing. Manuel Ramon Decardez, at your service. They call me Deke."

"I'm Terry Carnahan."

"Come on in. I guess they're all waiting." Deke led the way through the open inner valve.

In the suit room, the pilot turned back. "Just take it easy, kid," he said. "It ain't like the Navy in here."

It wasn't.

The Lieutenant had been on merchant ships before. It

was part of his training to know the layout and standard equipment of every jump-ship ever made. He had been on inspection tours; and a *Lady* class ship was still in Academy use for cadet instruction trips. But that one was Navy-maintained and Navy-staffed.

This *Lady* had left the service thirteen years back. The crew quarters had been torn out to make an extra hold, and the rule book had gone by the wayside along with the hammocks.

"Up here," Deke said, and Terry followed him up the ladder to Officers' Country. Then he stood in the wardroom doorway and stared at the crazy carnival scene.

To start with, the overheads were off. The only light was diffused u-v out of the algae tanks that cut two-foot swaths along opposite bulkheads. In the yellow-green dimness, the scattered lounging chairs and coffee cups and a tray with a bottle and glasses on the table, gave a ridiculous cocktail-bar effect to the whole place. And the first thing he saw was a hippy blonde, in tight black slacks and a loosely tied white shirt, who detached herself from the arm of a chair—and from the encircling arm of what looked like a naked brown-skinned man inside the chair. She ran across the room to fling herself on Deke, who picked her up bodily, and kissed her with gusto.

"Where did you sneak in from?" she demanded. "We were waiting for——"

"Whoa, babe," Deke started. "If you mean——" He started to turn, began to move forward, to let Terry in, but from a shadowy corner a wiry little man in coveralls, with grease stains on his hands and his hair and his face, broke in.

"What the hell! These two give me a pile of pitch about haulin' myself up here to give the new kid a big hello, and all I find is that old s.o.b. instead!" These two appeared to be the blonde and the naked man. Deke was the s.o.b.

"You bitchin' again, Mike?" The voice was a bull-roar; it came from the only member of the *Lady*'s crew Terry had met before. The Captain came down the ladder from Control, sneakers and rolled-cuff workpants first, and then the tremendous bulk of chest and arms, bristled and wiry curling red-gold hair. The room had looked crowded before. With Karl Hillstrom's two-hundred-twenty pounds added, it was jammed. "Relax," he said. "Have a drink and relax. Nita said she saw the kid comin' . . ."

Deke had given up trying to interrupt. He turned back to Terry and shrugged. "I told you—" he started, and just then the blonde saw him.

"Oh, my God!" she said, and broke into helpless laughter; so did Deke. She took a step forward toward Terry, trying to talk. He ignored it.

"Captain Hillstrom?" he said formally, as loud as possible. He felt like a schoolkid in a lousy play, doing a bad job of acting the part of the butler at a masquerade.

The big man turned. "Oh, there you are!" He held out a burly hand. "You met Deke already? Anita, this is our new IBMan, Terry Carnahan. Anita Filmord, our Medic. And Mike Gorevitch, our chicf—" that was the grease-stained one—"and Chan—Chandra Lal, our Biotech."

Terry fished in his pocket for the orders the Captain had failed to request, and noted with relief meantime that the Biotech, Chan, now unfolding himself from his chair, wasn't entirely naked after all.

It wasn't till then that he fully realized the hippy blonde was nobody's visiting daughter or friend, but a member of the crew and an officer in the Naval Reserve.

The blonde officer put a drink in his hand, and his last clear thought that night was that Deke was quite right; it wasn't like the Navy. Not at all.

When they gave him his commission, at the Examiner's Board, they had also delivered elaborate and resounding exhortations about the Great Trust being placed this day in his hands: how the work of an IBMan on a merchant ship was both more difficult and more important by far than anything done by an officer of equivalent rank on a Navy ship.

He knew all that. The ranking IBMan officer, on any ship, was fully responsible for the operation and maintenance of all material connected in any way with either solar navigation or space-warp jumps. On a tramp, there was likely to be just one IBMan to do it all; Navy Transports carried a full complement of four officers and five enlisted men. Fresh Academy graduates came on board with j.g. status only, and worked in charge of an enlisted maintenance crew on the "jump-along"—that abstract mechanical brain whose function it was to set up the obscure mathematic-symbolic relationships which made it possible for matter to be transmitted through the "holes" in spacetime, enabling a ship to travel an infinite distance in an infinitesimal time.

On a Navy Transport, a full Lieutenant IBMan would be in charge of SolNav only, with two petty officers under him, both qualified to handle maintenance, and one at least with a Navy rating, capable of relieving him on duty at the control board during the five or twelve or twenty hours it might take to navigate a jump-ship in or out of the obstacle course of clutter and junk and planets and orbits of any given System.

Even the senior officer, on a Navy Transport, would never have to jump "blind," except in the rare and nearly unheard-of instance of an analog failure; only tramps and Navy Scouts ever jumped willingly on anything but a 'log-computed course The stellar analog computers were the Navy's Topmost Secret; when you used one, nothing was required except to make sure the jump-along itself was in perfect condition, and then to pull the switch. The 'log did the rest.

Merchant ships carried 'logs for their chartered ports of call—the *Lady* had two—but the charter ports were the smallest part of a merchant trip. The number of destinations for which Navy analogs were available was hardly a hatful out of the galaxies. Without a 'log to point the way for him, it was up to the IBMan to plot coordinates for where a hole ought to be. With luck and skill he could bring the ship out into normal space again somewhere within SolNav reach of the destination. With the tiniest error in computation, a ship might be lost forever in some distant universe with no stars to steer her home.

Terry Carnahan had been hoping desperately for a Navy Transport job—but only because it was the route to the Scouts: the Navy's glory-boys, the two-bunk blind-jump ships that went out alone to map the edges of man's universe. It was the Scout job he'd worked for those long eight years—and dreamed about five years before, while he sweated for credits to get into Academy.

He didn't argue with his tramp assignment; nobody argued with the Board. He knew that most of the men who drew Navy assignments would envy him; the money was in the Reserves. And most of the rest, the ones who drew Transport and liked it, were there because they couldn't jump blind, and they knew it.

He knew all that. But when his orders came, and they told him he drew a tramp because he was tenth in his class—that's what they said: tramp work was the toughest—he also knew how close he had come to the dream, because he also knew that the top five men had been sent to Scout training.

Eight years of the most he could give it just wasn't enough. The answer was *No!* For good.

But you didn't throw out eight years of training for a good job, either. Terry went for his psychs and medics, and met Captain (U.N.N. Reserve) Karl Hillstrom; he took his two weeks' leave and reported for duty.

That first night, he fell asleep with the bunkroom spinning around him, and an obvious simple solution to the whole mess spinning with it, just out of his reach, no matter how fast he turned. When he stopped whirling, the dreams began, the dreams about naked crewmen, one of whom might have been him, and a terrible wonderful blonde in a sea of stars, winkin' and blinkin' and nod in a herring tramp to the smiling moon-faced girl who asked him . . .

In the morning, Captain Karl Hillstrom showed him around Control. It was shipshape and shiny up here, and the IBMan plunged gratefully into routine, checking and testing his board and running off sample comps. He allowed himself only the briefest inspection of the jump-along and the keyboard and calckers attached. His first job would be solar navigation. Once they were clear of the System, there'd be three weeks on solar drive before they jumped—plenty of time to double-check the other equipment. Right now, the standard computers and solar 'log were what counted.

He worked steadily till he became aware of the Captain at his side.

"How does it look?"

"Fine so far, sir." Terry leaned back.

"Anything messed up there, you can blame it on me. I worked that board coming in."

Terry remembered now—they had lost their IBMan on Betelgeuse IV, last trip, and come back short-handed, and with half the trade load still in the holds. Since no one but an IBMan could jump blind, they'd had to come back to pick up a new man—Terry.

"I haven't found anything wrong, sir," Terry said.

"You can drop the 'sir.' We go mostly by first names here." There was an edge of irritation in the Captain's voice. "It's chow time now. You want to knock off?"

Terry hesitated. This wasn't the Navy; it was a lousy tramp. If the pilot was drunk half the time, and the Chief had a dirty neck, and the Captain looked like a pirate or stevedore (the first of which he was, and the second *had* been), the IBMan was certainly free to work or eat when he chose.

"I'd just as lief stick with it for a while," Terry said cautiously.

"Sure. Suit yourself. Galley's open. Take what you want when you want it . . ."

He disappeared. For a blessed two hours, alone with machines he knew and trusted, Terry ran off the standard tests and comps, noting with trained precision each tiniest deviation from perfect performance. The computer had never been built that could navigate without error. Maybe only in the tenth decimal, but that was enough for disaster. You had to know your 'log and your board and machines, and make your adjustments as automatically as a man makes allowance for the sights on a rifle he's known and shot for years.

It took Terry four hours to learn this board, and he had started his first dry run when the sandwich appeared on his armrest. A tall plastic glass with a straw in the top and a tempting froth came next.

"Well, thanks," he said, "but you didn't have to—"

"It's chocolate," she told him. "I ordered strawberry when your papers came in, but they haven't sent it yet."

"Chocolate is fine," he said weakly, and let himself look.

The loose-tied shirt and tight-fitting slacks of the evening had been replaced by standard-issue summer-weight fatigues. The blouse was zipped up, and she seemed to be wearing a bra underneath. Her shorts displayed no more than a reasonable length of shapely leg. She wore no makeup, and her face looked scrubbed and clean. You could hardly get mad at a woman for being good-looking. The sandwich looked toasted and crisp, and he found he was very hungry.

"Well, thanks," he said again, and took a bite, and picked up the pencil with his other hand.

"Karl had to go down to Ad," she said. He took his eyes off his paper, and figured that out. Administration office, she'd mean.

"They called him to bring down the Beetle 'log papers," she said. "He asked me to let you know—it'll be back in the morning."

He nodded, trying to match her casual air. The Betelgeuse analog was coming back from the shop tomorrow. And IBMan Carnahan would be due for his first installation—the first on his own command.

". . . we could finish your med-check in time for dinner," she was talking still. "You want to knock off up here pretty soon?"

He nodded again, and glanced over his board. The run he'd started would take most of an hour. Then some time for adjustments . . . "Sixteen hours all right?" he asked.

"Fine. Dinner's at nineteen."

He sat there and stared at his sandwich and thought it all over, including the staggering fact of the Commander's silver leaves on the woman's faded green shirt collar.

The milkshake turned out to be good, the sandwich delicious. The run on the board got fouled up, and after half an hour of grief, he had to admit his mind wasn't on it. There was a Manual on the wardroom shelf below that would tell him the things he wanted to know. He switched off the board and went down.

Page 532, Section Six, was explicit. The Medical Officer for a six-man crew had to have junior psych, as well as senior pharmacist's or nurse rating—besides being qualified sub for the Biotech. With Commander's rank, it meant she likely had more actual years of training than he did. And: "The Medical Officer shall be supplied with dossiers . . . psych ratings and personality profiles . . . responsible for well-being of personnel . . ."

It explained some things: the milk shake and strawberry order, for instance, and why she should bother with either one. It did nothing to change the first impression of last night; or to make him forget his dreams; or—certainly—to make him feel any more at ease with Commander Anita Filmord. There were some things a woman shouldn't know about a man . . . or at least some women . . .

There was very little Anita Filmord didn't know about Terry Carnahan three hours later. For the first half-hour she took smears and samples and scrapings with deft impersonal proficiency. Each labeled slide or tube went into its own slot or niche or clamp; then she threw a switch and sat down to confront him with a questionnaire. To the familiar humming background of the diagnostics, she asked him all the questions he had answered twice a year for the past eight years.

"They put me through all this when I got my orders," he said at the end. "How come . . ."

"We do it every time you come on board. I'll have to run samples on Karl this evening, too." The machine had run itself down. She pulled out the tape, tossed it onto her desk for reading later. "I don't know what you've been doing the past two weeks," she pointed out, and he felt himself flush at the certainty of what she meant. "And we've got a good long time to be shut up on this ship together." She stood there looking at him. Her smile faded. "The prospect isn't too appealing, is it?"

"You are!" he might have said. This wasn't the Navy. The way she was dressed last night, the way she acted . . .

Last night—was it one of those dreams? He couldn't be sure, but the memory came clearly . . . He had heard a door close, and the murmur of voices, one high and one low. Before he fell asleep again—or in his dream?—a tall figure had entered the bunkroom and flopped in the last empty sack.

Five men and one woman . . .

206

"You're goddamn right it's not!" he wanted to say, but he shifted his gaze four inches, and the leaves on the collar of her short-sleeved shirt were still a Commander's.

He threw out all putative answers and retreated to subordination.

"Yes, ma'am," he said blank-faced. "It surely is, ma'am." *Five men and one woman . . . and Deke had it all tied up!*

"I'm glad to hear you say so, Lieutenant," she answered deadpan. "But if anything should turn up—any problems or questions or troubles of any kind—remember, that's why I'm here." Her smile was just a bit mechanical this time. *Good!*

"Just come if you need me," she said. "Any time . . ."

Five men and one woman . . . and come, she said, *any time . . . maybe it wasn't just Deke. Maybe . . .*

He went to the spray room and stripped and turned on the shower full blast to shut out Chandra Lal's cheerful talk. When he was finished, Chan was still in a cloud of steam, the effects of a day cleaning algy tanks now removed. While Terry rubbed himself harshly dry, Chan resumed conversation.

"How do you like the old bitch?" he asked idly.

"I'm not an expert," Carnahan said, and rubbed faster.

"Who is? I've been here six years now, and I still get surprises. She may not look like much, but she's a hell of a mess of boat for five men to run . . ."

Five men and one woman . . . What the hell? Come off that track, boy. Chan was talking about the ship, not the Medic.

"You're right about that," Terry said, and escaped to his locker.

He wore his clean uniform like armor into the wardroom, accepted a cocktail, and sipped at it slowly. Deke, the pilot, and Captain Hillstrom were both drunk already, loudly replaying the ball game they'd just seen on the vid.

Hillstrom had shed his uniform as soon as he got back in the ship; he was bare-chested and rolled-cuffed again.

Deke at least dressed for dinner. So did Anita. Tonight,

the tight-ass slacks were red, and she did wear a bra—also bright red—under her clear plastic shirt.

Mike wasn't dressed and he wasn't drunk. He came up just in time to sit down and eat with the rest, his face and coveralls both, if possible, one layer greasier than the day before. Chandra did not dress, either: he emerged from the spray room, glowing, immaculate in the virtually nonexistent trunks he'd worn the night before. Anita poured him a drink.

Obviously, she wouldn't care how—or if—Chan was dressed.

And if she didn't, who should?

Not Karl Hillstrom, that was clear; or perhaps he was too drunk to notice.

Sleep didn't come easy that night. When all the crew's bunks but Deke's were filled, Terry gave up, and went out to the wardroom. He found Deke there, alone, watching a film. He tried to watch, too, but next to the screen, a red light on the Medic's door flashed, DON'T DISTURB! and his eyes kept seeing, instead of the picture, the curve of a thigh limned in the fiery red of her slacks, or perhaps of the bulb . . .

He got up and prowled the room.

DON'T DISTURB: ". . . *any time* . . ."

The door opened. Karl Hillstrom came out. It closed behind him, and the light flicked off. She was alone now. She could be disturbed.

"Hi . . . late-late show?" Karl poured himself a drink and held up the bottle. "How about you?"

"I had it," Deke said.

"Terry?"

"Thanks. I will . . . later." He poured his own, a big one, and took it back to his bunk.

. . . *any time* . . . Deke didn't have it tied up, not at all . . .

At two in the morning, he remembered vaguely some provision in the Manual for refusal to serve in ships with a crew of ten, on grounds of personality stress. That meant a psych Board of course—and it had to go through the Medic . . . well, she might have reasons to make it easy for him. This wasn't the Navy, but it was still under

Navy charter. *Lousy tramp!* He grinned, and promised himself to look it up, and went to sleep.

At three, he woke briefly, remembering she had said the Captain would have to have a new set of samples run that evening for his med records. Well, that could explain the DON'T DISTURB . . . At eight, they woke him to tell him the Beetle 'log was coming on board.

Mike Gorevitch drifted up from his engines to lend a hand, and the hand was a steady one, Terry found. By noon they were finished with a job that would have taken Terry more than a day by himself. His first installation was over. Over a shared plate of cold meat in the galley, the IBMan found himself inexplicably pleased at the Chief's terse invitation to have a look below.

"Nothin' you didn't see before better on a Navy boat," Mike said, "but some of the stuff is rigged up my own way. You ever get stuck with a duty shift down there, you'll want to know . . ."

Like every jump-ship, the *Lady* was Navy-built, -equipped, and -staffed. Even Hillstrom, who had made his stake in the Solar Fleet, had to get his Reserve Commission before they'd sell him his ship and lease him a stellar analog to hook onto the jump-along.

By now he had traded in that first cheap Sirius 'log for a prized Aldebaran, and had acquired a Betelgeuse besides. It was on Betelgeuse that Bailey, the IBMan who'd been with the *Lady* for nine of her thirteen years tramping, had lost his nerve. It was something that happened. The best jump-man reached the point where he'd figured he'd had it—the one more blind trip wouldn't work. Bailey quit cold, and declined even passage back.

This trip, the *Lady* carried a consignment of precision instruments for the new colony on Aldebaran III. But nobody ever got rich on consignment flight. It paid for the trip; that was all. The profit-shares came out of the other hold: the seeds and whisky and iron pigs and glassware and quick-freeze livestock embryos; the anything-and-whatsit barter goods that someone at some unchartered planet off the analog routes would pay for in some way. That was the lure that kept the crews on merchant ships: you never knew when you'd come back with the barter-hold full of uranium, or cast-gold native artifacts, or robin-egg diamonds.

And if you also never knew for sure *when* you'd come back, or *where from,* or *whether* . . . well, that was the reason why IBMen went upstairs fast. For a man who could handle the job, there was pay and promotion, and almost anything else he might want.

What Carnahan wanted, the *Lady* didn't have.

For Mike Gorevitch, that was not the case.

The *Lady* was a tramp. She was scratched and dented and tarnished with age. She'd lost her polish, and her shape was out of date. She'd been around, and it showed.

But she had beauty in her still, if you knew where to look, and you cared.

"There's a dance in the old girl yet," Mike said approvingly, when he saw the IBMan's hand linger with pleasure on the smooth, perfect surface of the shaft he'd ground the night before. "You read *Archy*?" he asked.

Terry shook his head. "What's that?"

"You might not like it," Mike said doubtfully. He opened a locker and pulled out a battered grease-stained book. "Here. You can take it up with you if you want."

That night, Terry slept. He took the Manual and Mike's book both to the bunk with him right after dinner, and found what he wanted in one, then returned to the other. Both of them helped, and so did exhaustion.

But somewhere in the night he woke long enough to note that it was Deke who came in last again, and to identify the pattern of repeated sounds from two nights back. It had not been a dream!

Five men and one woman . . . He wondered why Bailey had quit. Nine years, and then . . . If you took it that long . . . Well, he had the same way out if he wanted it . . . *any time* . . .

Next day, again, he worked at his board through the morning. This time it was Chandra who happened to be in the galley when Terry went down for his lunch. The pattern began to come clear: informal, haphazard, and unsystematic, but they were taking him over the ship, little by little.

The two of them sat on a white-painted bench in the Bio lab, and discoursed of algae and alien life-forms and also Anita. "Listen," Chan said abruptly, "has the blonde bombshell got you mixed up?"

"No," Terry said bitterly. "I wouldn't say that."

"It ain't like the Navy, is it, kid?" Chan smiled, and it didn't matter if you knew the man had been trained for years to create just this feeling of empathy and understanding; he created it all the same. If he couldn't, they'd be in a hell of a spot on an alien planet . . .

"Don't get me wrong," Terry said cautiously. "I like girls. If you think everyone sleeps in his own bed on a Navy ship . . ."

"I came out of Academy, too," Chan reminded him.

"All right, then, you know what I mean. But this kind of deal—one dame, and the five of us, and—I just can't see it. If I go to a whore, I don't want her around me all day. And if I have a girl, I damn sure don't want every guy she sees to get into . . . you know what I mean!"

"Yeah." He was silent a moment. "I know what you mean, but I don't know if I can explain . . . Look, it's a small ship and the payload counts. A girl friend for every guy would be nice, but . . . well, hell, kid, you'll see for yourself once we get going. All I wanted to say to begin with was if you got the idea it was all for one guy, you were wrong. Deke's always kind of hopped up before we go, and he's the guy we have to count on to get us out safe. She just naturally . . . anyhow, don't let him monopolize anything—not if you want it, that is."

"I don't," Terry said, and they went back to algae and aliens. And at least one thing emerged: Mike wasn't the only man on board who cared. Just what it was that mattered so much to him or to Chan, Terry wasn't quite sure: their work, or the *Lady* herself, or the dead dream she stood for. Whatever exactly it was, the feeling was something that Terry could understand—and that Deke and Hillstrom never could . . .

Hillstrom didn't have to. He owned the *Lady*. He wasn't obliged to understand her: only to pay the bills, and let the hired hands do their work for him. For *her* . . . ?

The hired help worked, all right. At least, Mike and Chan did, and Terry Carnahan. Even Deke put in a full morning up in Control, checking his board, and testing a dry run with Terry.

Even Deke? What the hell? Deke had been holding down the driver's seat on the *Lady* for four years now. He had to be good. And he was; the half-hour's test was enough to show his class.

In his bunk that night, Terry improved his acquaintance with Archy, the poet-cockroach, and Mehitabel the cat. Archy's opinions amused him; but in the determined dignity of the lady-cat's earthy enthusiasms, he found a philosophy sadly appropriate for the life of a *Lady* ship: and it was difficult to continue to feel entirely sad about the fit of the shoe while Mehitabel danced her wild free whirling dance, defiant and *toujours gai . . . wotthehell . . . wotthehell . . .*

Mehitabel, Mike, and Chandra all helped. But backing them all up was the Manual.

P. 549, at the bottom: "An IBMan specialist may exercise his privilege of declaring the psychological conditions on board a ship of the specified classes unfit for blind jump at any time before plotting navigation data to the jump-off point in question. In such cases, the ship will return by analog to Lunar Base; or if unequipped to do so, will remain in its current port, pending a hearing by the Commandant."

They wouldn't jump till after the Aldebaran hop. Six weeks out, two weeks in port: there was time to wait and find out whether one lousy tramp could ruin the work and the dreams of thirteen years.

As he fell asleep, the IBMan thought with surprise that grease and nudity were perhaps as fitting uniforms in their ways for engine maintenance and bio work as knife-edge trouser creases were for precision computing . . .

The thirty-foot-wide metal collar that encircled the lower third of the *Lady Jane* in drydock rose slowly out of the concrete pit. When the *Lady* had been lifted some twenty feet, the trucks moved in and extended supporting yard-wide jacks up into smaller collars, set in the underside of the wide, upper flange.

The outer lock, 'midships, swung open, and the elevator cage started down. Five figures in full-gear pressure suits emerged and took their places on the flange. They fastened the chains and winches securing the jacks in their sockets and belted themselves in position to keep a watch on the winches during the overland voyage.

One by one their voices cleared over the suit-to-suit. "All secure here . . . Okay . . . Check . . . Secure . . . That's it!" Hillstrom's was the last.

"All clear?" He waited five seconds, then waved the red flag at his side. The enormous pit jack sank downward, and the trucks started lifting alone. At fifty feet, the jet tubes were clear of the ramp. The trucks swiveled into alignment, and sixty-five earth-tons of wheelchair began to move the *Lady* away from drydock in lumbering state.

From his seat on the flange, Terence Hugh Carnahan surveyed man's moon, and found it good. Six hours away, the black knife-edge of lunar night sliced off the horizon. Ten minutes ahead, the mile-long launching tube yawned empty and waiting.

The suit-to-suit crackled with small talk and still smaller humor. Terry almost gave in to the urge to turn it off. He'd been through the launching routine a hundred times, in mockups and dry runs, but this was his first time to ride a live ship over the face of the moon from the dock to the tube. If the schoolboy dreams of glory were dead forever . . . if the battered old hulk of the *Lady* was all he could have . . . even she had her dubious virtues, and among them the brightest was this . . . this moment, now, the fulfillment of, not a child's dream, but the Big Dream of a man, of mankind, for the stars.

It was sacrilege, nothing less, to be approaching the launch site with a series of schoolboy *double entendres* supplying the background music.

He had actually reached for the switch, when a new voice floated in. "Still with us, Lieutenant?"

"Yes, ma'am!" He let his hand drop. The regulations made sense. Secured as they were in their seats, and spread round the bulge of the *Lady,* the audio was all the proof they had that each of them was still on post, alive and conscious. Even the Medic inside the sealed ship, watching the screens, couldn't be sure, from what she could actually see, whether a man immobile inside a suit was effectively operative.

They came up to the tube, and the great cranes reached out steel fingers, stripping and lifting the *Lady* out of her wheelchair wrappings, pushing and nudging and sliding her into place on the runway. Six moon-suited figures slid down the jacks into the trucks, and were toted back up to the airlock by the tube elevator.

There was no time for small talk now. Five hours to see for the last time that the ship was secure; once the word, *ready,* went down, it was too late to look any more.

Terry covered his section with swift, methodical care. Satisfied, he went to his chair, and strapped himself in; he did a last double check on his board; then he fastened his helmet back on and began the slow conscious relaxing of muscles and breathing that ended the ritual.

When the countdown began, he was off in a floating dream of sunshine and sparkling water. *Zero minus nine,* and he sat up erect. *Minus eight,* and he forced himself back into limpness before they hit *seven.* Breathe in . . . out . . . hold . . . *five* . . . out . . . *four* . . . in . . . *three* . . . out . . . *two* . . . innnn*none*-annnou-*out!*

Off and out . . . down and out . . . blackness and whirlpools and terror and kick back, up, out!

His finger punched the wake-up button before he was fully aware of consciousness again. The light ahead of him flashed green, and there was an instant's prideful notice that his was the second green on. Then he forgot to be proud, and forgot to be Terry Carnahan. Green lights flashed and steadied, then yellow and blue and red. The board was a Christmas-tree crossword constellation, each light a word or a number or place, their shifting patterns spelling out death and life.

Pressure eased, and the voices began—voices of engines and scanners and stresses and temps. Some he heard in the helmet, and some the board told him with signals and lights. A voice in the helmet allowed him to take it off: the voice of the Bio board. A key on the pilot's board, at the chair up ahead, was depressed by a finger; the think-board, in this chair, flashed questioning lights. The think-board replied, and new figures lit up ahead, for the hands to use—the hands and direction and eyes of the *Lady,* up there at the pilot's board, steering her free of the multitude of menacing mites and pieces and bits of matter and mass in the populous planet-plied system.

The dance of escape begat rhythm to suit itself, and the old girl whirled on her axis, and pushed her way out to the stars, with a dance in her yet, wotthehell and the think-board was metal-and-plastic but flesh-and-blood, too; part of her, of the streaming single mote which alone in this mote-filled single cell-of-Sol was bound to break out of bounds and escape to the endless entropic emptiness of Universe.

"Take a break, kid. We got a clear stretch here. Karl can take over."

He looked at the chrono, and didn't believe what he saw, and looked again. Five hours, and seventeen minutes past zero. Now aching muscles returned to sensation, and ego to Terry Carnahan.

Anita was standing beside him, one hand on a chair strap, the other held out to help.

"Whore!" he said. "Get away, bitch!"

She went away; Terry stayed where he was. What Deke could take, he could take, too.

He took it for six hours more, through the last of the dust and debris of the System. He drank from the flask when it nuzzled his lips, and swallowed the pills she put in his mouth, and gave back what she needed: the readings and scannings and comps and corrections that went to the driver's seat, to the pilot's board, to Deke with the strength of ten and a tramp in his heart.

He stayed there and took it until there was no more to do. Then he reached for the straps, and her hands were already there, unfastening him.

Bitch! he thought. *Tramp! You don't want me!*

He let her lead him out of the room, down the ladder, through yellow-green, to the door where the light would be flashing red outside.

And there he stopped. There was something important to ask her, when he found out what it was, he started to smile. *Which one do you want?*

Which one? How could she possibly tell?

As well ask, *Which one needs her?*

He laughed and stepped forward . . . and the tramp was his.

"Survival Ship," back in 1951, had led JM into some explorations of sex-role behavior toward a novel that never got written entire, but some stories out of her future history appeared; e.g., F&SF—December, 1958.

Wish Upon a Star

I WISH, I WISH, I WISH . . .

Sheik sat under the shadow of a broad-leaf shrub, his head back, eyes closed against the glare from overhead, mouth open for a shout of protest he could never voice.

He stifled the thought with the sound, pushed it out of his head as he pushed his body backward, throwing his weight straight-armed on the flat palms of his hands behind him. Flexing his calves below bent knees, he pulled against the long thigh sinews and tightened the slanting muscles of his back, driving all tension from his mind into his body as he raised his buttocks up off the ground and hung suspended, arching from knees to elbows, hands and feet rooted to the soil. Wholly intent on the immedate physical effort, he stayed so till the blood rushing to his head choked in his throat, and arms and legs were trembling beyond control. Then with a last summoning of purpose, he flipped over and sprawled contentedly collapsed on chest and stomach, head turned so one cheek also rested on the resilient softness of the granular stuff that made the plant beds. With each great breath of air

217

his nostrils sucked up the rich sweet damp aroma of the roots.

For a moment there was peace; and then, again, *I wish, I wish, I wish . . .*

Tears filled his eyes. He sat up and angrily and brushed them off. He was too old for crying. Crying wouldn't help. He was too old to be sitting idle here, wasting time, wasting wishes on absurdities. Old enough not to be bothered by anything Naomi said or did . . . but not yet old enough (smart enough?) to know better than to try to tell her anything.

She had listened so meekly, watched so quietly, while he repaired the rootpack she had broken, holding the torn parts—just *so*—together, tamping the soil down—just *so*—around the fiber, explaining as he worked why it was just *this* way. He let her silence fool him; well, it was no one's fault but his own. He should have known better by now.

When he was finished, she smiled, very sweetly. "It's so *comforting* to know you'll be here, Sheik," she said, "when *I'm* in charge. You're so *efficient*." Then a quick glance at the chrono, which she must have been watching all the time from the corner of her eye, or she couldn't have timed it all so perfectly. "Oh-oooh! I better run! I'm late for Sessions now . . ." And she was off, flashing a hand free of dirt or work, leaving him, trowel in hand, to realize he had just finished doing her job for her.

It wasn't fair. Naomi was twelve and a half, more than a year younger than he was. In Standard School she was behind him in almost everything; and never, never as long as she lived, would she be able to handle a plant, to feel it and *understand* it, as he did. But she was the one in Special Sessions classes now, learning the things he ought to know. They'd make her read all the books *he* wanted, whether she cared or not, and put her to learn in the lab, mastering all the mysteries and intricacies of advanced Bichem. While he, Yashikazu, would go on day after day, trowel in hand, taking her jibes now, and later—much later, when he replaced Abdur in charge of the plantroom—taking her orders as Ab took his orders from Lieutenant Johnson.

It just wasn't *fair!*

I wish, I wish I was . . .

He stopped it, cut it off sharply. He was not going to think that way any more. *I wish Sarah was here*, he finished the thought instead. Tonight, maybe, she would ask him again. He had nursery duty, but if he told Bob . . . *if* she asked him, that was . . . well, if she did, he'd get off duty somehow . . .

Without even closing his eyes, he could see her there now, as she had been the night before last, sprawled on the rootpacks beside him, her shining long legs golden under the ultras, her face in the shadow of the leafy shrub a deep dark brown, but somehow giving out the gold-glow, too. Her eyes were closed and her hand, smooth and cool, soft and small, lay inside his as he watched her in warm and perfect comradeship.

For most of an hour, they had barely moved or talked: they just lay there together in the private shadow, sharing what had been his alone, thinking and dreaming silently but not separately at all.

Nothing Naomi said or did ought to matter now, because things-as-they-were had given him this special thing, a place and a significance, to share with Sarah. Never before had he told anyone about the shadows—how he felt about them. (No one but Ab, of course, but that was different; Ab *knew*.) She had seen them, naturally, most every day of her life; everyone in the ship had. The nursery-age children spent at least an hour each day hullside, for ultra exposure and exercise as well as their basic Bichem. When they started with Standard School classwork, they were required to spend a half-hour of playtime every day under the lamps. But it was the light they came for; the shadows belonged to Sheik.

When he was just old enough to be allowed to go about alone, he started coming down hullside every chance he had; the shadows drew him. Later, the plants became important, too, and now he knew that they would be his work all his life. That was good in itself, but better because the shadows were part of the plants.

Nowhere else in the whole ship was there anything like it. Once in a while, the floorlight or one of the walls in the regular living and work rooms would go out of whack, and for a brief time the diffusion would be distorted and patches of dark-and-bright showed where people moved. But only here, where the thick rootpacks lined the whole inner shell of the ship's hull, where there were only struts instead of walls, and the great ultra lamps glared day and night overhead, only here were there real *shadows,* under the plants, stationary, permanent, and shaped.

The ultras were never dimmed. They shone, Sheik thought, with the same brilliant fixity of time and purpose as the pinpointed stars on the black satin of the lounge viewplate. And in the center of this same clump of shrubbery where he lay now there was a hollow spot where some of the oldest, tallest plants grew so thick no light could penetrate, where it was dark, *black,* almost as black as the space between the stars: the way, he thought, a planet's night must be.

And this spot, where he had taken Sarah, was—depending where you held your head—a moonlit planet night, a "twilight," "morning," or "afternoon" . . . all words in books, until they took on meaning here where the leaves and lights produced an infinitude of ever-changing shades and combinations of black, gray, green, brown, and gold.

He had never told anyone how he thought about that. Not Abdur; not even Sarah, yet. But if she asked him to take her here again, he thought, he could tell her; she would really understand.

He sat up sharply, the faint rustling sound like an answer to a prayer. *Sarah?*

Two plant stalks parted cautiously and a small, round, brown face stared into his own.

"What are *you* doing down here now?" Sheik demanded. How had the fool kid found him here?

"I *told* 'm I'd find you," Hari said triumphantly. "I *told* 'm I could. You better hurry. Ab's mad at you. He has to work onna mew-tay-shuns," the small boy said the new word carefully, "an' you're supposed to be our teacher this time."

Sheik scrambled to his feet. Nursery class here already? *That* late? He'd spent half the afternoon doing nothing, dreaming . . . Ab must be mad, all right!

"You forgot about us," Hari said.

220

He hadn't forgotten; he had just forgotten time. "Come on, shrimpy," he told Harendra gruffly. "Better hop on if you want to get back *quick*." He squatted and Hari climbed on his shoulders—a rare and special treat; it would make up for his seeming to forget. He started for Abdur's workroom at a trot.

Harendra was three years old now, almost four, but he was Yoshikazu's favorite in the nursery still. He had been Sheik's first full-charge baby; sometimes he didn't seem too sure himself which one was his father, Abdur or Sheik. Certainly he didn't care; he loved them both with the same fierce intensity. And it upset him if Ab was angry with the Sheik.

Abdur had been spending all his time the past few days struggling to save a planting of mutant seedlings newly developed in the Bichem lab. It was a high-protein lentil with a new flavor, but some mysterious lack in root-pack nourishment—the kind of thing that showed up only in actual growth conditions—made it essential to nurse each plant with extra care while the lab techs tried to find the cause of the trouble.

The intricate, patient skill with which Abdur tended the delicate young plants was fascinating to Sheik. And the young children, he thought, would be interested in the luminous unfamiliar yellow of the sickly leaves.

Abdur agreed with evident satisfaction to having the children visit the sick patch. He rebuked Sheik only briefly and without heat for his forgetfulness, and set out immediately for his plants, taking the way cross-ship, through the central living section, to reach the area on the other side of the hull without further delay. Yoshikazu took his troupe of six around by the hullside route, routinely replying to the inevitable routine questions at each step: why was this plant taller, the other stalk thicker, a leaf a darker green or different shape. To most of the grown people on board, the endless rows of plants covering the whole inner surface of the ship's hull were monotonous and near identical. Abdur knew better; so did Sheik; and the nursery kids noticed things sometimes that Yoshikazu hadn't seen himself.

But this time he didn't want to stop at every plant. It was a slow enough trip with their short legs, and he

221

hurried them past spots where he might otherwise have tried to show them something new or slightly changed. Then Dee, silly dimpled shrieking Dina, who, at barely two, should not (in Sheik's opinion) have come into the nursery class as yet, sat herself down on the rootpacks and refused to budge.

Yoshikazu bent to pick her up. He'd carry her, rather than waste time coaxing now. But she pointed to one root, growing wrong, malformed and upended, and stopped progress completely by spilling out a spurt of only half-coherent but entirely fascinated inquiry.

Well, he had been wrong; she *was* old enough. Sheik sat down beside her and got to work, framing his answers to her questions carefully, trying to give her a new mystery each time to provoke the next useful question. He pulled packing away from around the upended root, dug down, and placed the root where it belonged, giving all the children a chance to see how the other roots lay in the pack before he covered it. He explained how the roots drank nourishment from the soil, and floundered attempting to explain the action of the ultraviolet lamps.

All the while, Hari hung over his shoulder, watching; the boy had seen it all before, when Dina was too little to care, but he drank in every sight and every word as if it were the first time for him, too.

"It's like being tucked in," he broke in suddenly, offering his own level of lucidity in place of Sheik's complications. "Like when your daddy tucks you in at night and kisses you and you feel warm and good all over you and you grow in your sleep."

Dina's black eyes were shining with excitement. "I know," she said. "Every night when I sleep I grow." She lifted a hand to prove the point. "*Way* up!"

"Well, that's how it is," Hari nodded commendation to his pupil. "Only the lights don't have to go out for the plants to sleep, because they're asleep all the time. Underneath there. *That's* why they never go anyplace."

His voice lost some confidence at the end. He looked to Yoshikazu for approval, and Dina looked for confirmation.

Sheik hesitated, failed to find words for a more adequate explanation, and decided Hari had probably put across more than he could for right now. He nodded and smiled at them both. "Come on, now, or we won't have time to see the new plants." They all ran after him.

Lieutenant Johnson was on duty at the children's supper that evening. She strolled casually from one of the four tables to another, listening to a scrap of conversation here, answering a question there, correcting a younger child somewhere else, reminding Fritzi—who at eleven had just become a table leader—to keep her group quieter.

At Sarah's table she paused only briefly; the officer on duty never had to stop there except for a greeting. Sarah and Sheik had seven in their group, more than anyone else, but they never had trouble. They were a good combination; Sheik glowed inwardly with his awareness of this, and with the feeling that the same thought was passing through Johnson's mind as she looked from one end of the table to the other. He didn't need any smiles from Johnson to keep him happy tonight, though. In the lounge, just before, Sarah *had* asked him. As soon as he could swap his evening duty, he was to meet her and take her down hullside again.

He caught her glance across the table as the Lieutenant walked away and saw her wink at him. With astonishment he thought, *She's as happy as I am! She wants to go, too!*

He knew, though he could not see as she bent over the carving, how her breasts had begun to swell under her shirt, and he knew by heart, though they were hidden behind the table, the long clean curves of those golden legs. Mechanically he added lentils to carrobeet top and passed a plate down, reminding Adolph Liebnitz that there was a fork at his place, and he should use it. He answered a question of Irma's without ever knowing what she asked, filled another plate, kept his eyes off Sarah thinking, *This time . . . this time I'll . . .* Added a little extra greens to Justin's plate, skimping on the carrobeets the kid hated . . . *This time I'll . . .* Looked up, caught Sarah's eye again, felt himself going hot and red, and dropped the thought.

He was in a warm daze still when Lieutenant Johnson mounted the rostrum to conclude the meal with the evening prayer. Sheik chanted the familiar words of

223

thanksgiving, suddenly meaningful, and looked directly at Sarah as they finished, saying to her and her alone, "Survive in Peace!"

The Lieutenant read off the cleanup assignments, and then, just as casually as if she were making a routine announcement instead of delivering a stomach punch, added, "There will be gameroom play for Classes Three and Four till bedtime. Special Sessions girls are invited to attend a staff meeting in the wardroom immediately after senior supper."

Sarah threw him a look of mild disappointment. "Tomorrow?" she mouthed. He didn't answer, pretended not to see. Tomorrow? Sure. What difference did it make to *her*?

And then he was angry at himself. It wasn't Sarah's fault. And you couldn't blame her for being excited about a wardroom meeting. It had to be something *big* for the Sessions to get asked in to wardroom. He tried to meet her eye again, but everyone was getting up; people were moving; he caught a glimpse of her back, and then couldn't see her at all. Desultorily, he drifted with the other older children to the lounge and stood staring at the big screen.

The sun was big now, filling one whole sixteenth sector. Maybe the meeting . . . ? He couldn't get excited. There'd been too many false alarms when they began decelerating almost a year ago, rumors and counter rumors and waves of excitement about how the tapes were coming out of the calckers, how it was *the* planet . . . No, it was poisonous, ammonia atmosphere . . . No, it was just a barren sun . . . It was the right one after all; it had a perfect earth-type atmosphere, one-third the mass . . .

Meaningless words, after all, to those who had been born on board *Survival;* words out of books. The older people had been more excited than the kids. "Earth-type" *meant* something to them.

But that was a year ago, and every day since, the sun had grown bigger on the plate, and no day had brought any real news, except somewhere along the way it had been confirmed officially that there *were* planets —type as yet unknown. Bob said he thought it would be four or five more months before they came in close enough to give the calckers anything to work on.

Last year, when they first began decelerating, Bob had talked a lot to Sheik, times when they were by themselves in quarters, the little ones napping or asleep for the night. It was the first time, really, since Sheik's nursery years that he and his father had been close. From the time he was six, when he was assigned for training in the plant rooms, Abdur had grown to fill the role of father-advisor more and more. But when the bright sun started to grow faintly brighter on the viewscreen, Bob's excitement was uncontainable; he poured it out on his son, a boy incredibly grown to where, by the time a landing was likely to take place, he would be in effect one of the men.

And the men, Bob told him, would have to work together when that happened. Things on a planet would not be quite the same as on board ship. For weeks, Bob reminisced and daydreamed, talking about Earth and its homes and families and governments, about the launching of the ship, *Survival,* and how and why things were set up on board ship as they were.

Some of it Sheik had heard in class; other parts he was cautioned to forget except in private. Everyone knew that the *Survival* was Earth's first starship, a colonizing expedition sent to find a planet—*if* there was one—suitable for the spillover of the world's crowded billions. Everyone knew the voyage might take years or decades; the ship was completely self-contained; the ion drive made it possible to carry fuel enough for a hundred years. There were living quarters on either side of those now in use that had never been unlocked; if a third or fourth generation grew up on board ship, they'd be needed.

But if it took that long, it would do Earth no good. If the ship could not return with news of an established colony within fifty years, then it was under orders not to return at all, but to remain and start over altogether in the new place.

This much was common knowledge, and one further fact: that the original crew of twenty-four had included twenty women and four men for obvious biological race-survival reasons.

What they didn't tell in classes was why all of the men were subordinates, none of them trained for astrogation, electronics, communications, or any of the skilled jobs of ship control; why all the officers were women. The children took it for granted as they grew; the ship was the way things were and always had been; the readers that spoke of families and pets and churches, towns and villages and lakes and oceans, aircraft and weather, were fascinating, and in a quaint way, true, no doubt; but reality was the ship with its four family units, domestic fathers, energetic women, school dorms, communal meals.

Bob's talk of men who "ran their own families" and ruled their homes, of male supremacy in the environment of a hostile world, of wives and husbands cleaving one to one faithfully, first intrigued Sheik, then excited him, while he regarded it as fairy-tale stuff. But when his father pointed out one day that there were just as many boys as girls among the children—a fact Yoshikazu somehow had not thought about before—everything the old man said struck home in a new way.

"Then *why* did they put the women in charge of everything?" he demanded for the first time.

Bob's answer was incoherent, angry and fantasizing. Later Sheik took his puzzlement to Ab, who explained, tight-lipped, that women were considered better suited to manage the psychological problems of an ingrown group, and to maintain with patience over many, many years, if needed, the functioning and purpose of the trip.

"Then when we land . . . ?"

"*When* we land, there will be time enough to think about it! Who's been talking to you about all this?"

"Well, I was asking Bob," Sheik said cautiously. "But . . ."

"But nothing," Abdur said sharply. "If you're smart, Sheik, you'll forget it now. If anyone else hears this kind of talk from you, your father will be in trouble. Or I will. Forget it."

And for the most part, he did. Bob never spoke of it again. And Ab spoke only as he always had, of sun and rain, forests and gardens, sunsets and hillsides and farmlands *outdoors* on a planet.

Sheik stared at the giant sun on the viewscreen; if they had found their planet, if they landed here, he was almost a man . . .

No. He *was* a man. He could do everything a man could do, and he was very strong, stronger than any of the girls. And Sarah, he thought, was very close to womanhood. She was the oldest of the girls; it would be natural. One man and one woman, Bob had said . . . the thought was exciting. There was no other woman he would want to have. Naomi or Fritzi or Beatrice, the other older girls, were *nasty*. As for the crew—Lieutenant Johnson, maybe, but—but when he thought of Sarah the idea of being at the call of four others besides was obscene somehow.

Sheik laughed abruptly and turned and left the lounge. He had spent enough time today dreaming fantasies. There was work to do.

Still, when the last of the little ones was tucked in bed, and the quarters were quiet, Sheik found himself pacing restlessly in the tiny pantry-service room. He had his schoolbooks with him, and had meant to study for the morning's class. But when he tried to read, plant shadows and Sarah's legs and all the things Bob had said raced through his mind, blurring the print. He wished Bob would come back from wherever he was. The kids were asleep; there was only one hour till he himself had to be in dorm, and he was obsessed with the need to go hullside, to find his cool shadow-corner and lie there where peace was always to be found.

And obsessed, foolishly, with the idea that after the meeting Sarah might, just *might,* go down to look and see if he was there . . .

Bob didn't come. After a while Yoshikazu closed his book, wrote a quick note, "Hullside. Back in a minute," and went out.

He had never done such a thing before. He had broken rules, yes, but not when the children were in his care. But, really, what could happen? If one of them woke up, if anything went wrong, half an hour could not mean life or death. And . . .

And he didn't care. He *had* to go.

Quickly and quietly, exhilarated beyond previous experience by the sense of his guilt, he went down companionways towards the hull. He closed the last hatch behind him and stood on the top step looking down into the shadowed vastness of hullside. He was above the lamps. Beneath them was bright yellow light; then pale green, new leaves at the top of the plant stalks. Darker green below. Brownish-green stalks, some slender swaying things, some thick as his own arm. And underneath, the shadows. He started down, quietly still, but beginning already to feel more at ease.

Then he heard the voice. Bob's voice. Urgent, persuasive.

"I tell you it's *true*. This time it's true. I got it straight."

"Hell, Bob, every time they send in a tech to film something secret, you think that's *it*. You said the same thing six months ago, and how many times before that?" That was Sean, Sarah's father, who ran the livestock rooms.

"This time I know I'm right," Bob said quietly. His voice was convincing, even to Sheik.

"Well, if it is, what do you want us to do, Bob?" Abdur, this time, also quiet. The voices were coming, Sheik realized, from Abby's little private room near the seedbeds.

"Just that I think it should have been announced. I want to know what they're up to, with that meeting. Ab, have you ever stopped to think that maybe when the time came, *the women wouldn't want to land?*"

Silence, shocked silence; Sheik stood like a statue on his step.

"Come off it, man." Sean. "They're not *that* crazy."

"It's not so crazy, Sean," Abdur said thoughtfully, and then: "But I don't see what we could do about it if they didn't. *And* I don't think they'd hold back, even if they wanted to."

"You got a lot of trust in human nature, Ab."

"No-o-o-o. Well, yes. I guess I do. But that's not why. Listen, Robert, what do you think kept you from going off your nut those first five years?"

"What do you want me to say?" Bob asked bitterly. "God?"

"Well, He may have helped. But that wasn't what I meant. You were in bad shape for a while. After Alice . . ."

"Watch yourself, Ab." Bob growled.

"Take it easy and listen a minute. After what happened—how come you didn't do the same thing?"

Sheik eased himself down to a sitting position on the top step and listened.

A lot of it made no sense. Alice had been one of the women, of course; there were nineteen now. Funny he'd never thought of *that* before! She must have died when he was still a baby. Most of the kids wouldn't even know the name.

And Bob, Bob had had something to do with Alice. The conversational scraps and fragmentary references were incomplete, but Sheik had a picture, suddenly, of something that had happened to his father, of something like what was, maybe, happening with him and Sarah, and wasn't *supposed* to happen.

He tried to think how he would feel, what he would do, if Sarah suddenly—were no more. He could not imagine it. Nobody ever died. Nobody on the ship was more than forty-five. If Bob had felt that way, and then Alice died, he could see why his father was— *funny,* sometimes. Why he imagined things and made up stories about the time on Earth.

The twin revelation—the knowledge that what he thought and felt for Sarah had happened to *other* people, often, and the shocked glimpse of grief inside his father —almost obscured the more immediate importance of what the men said down there.

"Indoctrination," Ab was saying.

Alice was the only one who hadn't had it. She had been the ship's doctor; "they," the planners, had thought someone on board, the "stablest" one, should be free of "post-hypno." Words, some new, some old but out of context here. *Indoctrinated* . . . the women were indoctrinated, too; they *couldn't* refuse to land the ship. Ab said so.

The others agreed with him. Bob didn't, at first, but after a while, though he kept arguing, Sheik knew even Bob was convinced.

Gradually, the voices turned more casual; the conversation slowed. Sheik thought it must be getting close to dorm curfew. He raised the hatch above him cautiously, hoisted himself up through it and let it down with silent care. He reached his own family quarters again without meeting anyone.

Inside, he put his note down the disposall, checked on the sleeping children, and arranged himself in the galley with a book on his lap, his feet on the counter, and a yawn of boredom on his face. When Bob returned, he hung around hopefully a little while, but Bob was not feeling talkative.

Sheik had a few minutes till curfew still; without planning it, he found himself in the nightlit empty lounge, at the big screen, watching the giant sun, almost imagining he could see it grow bigger and closer against the dead black of space, straining his eyes absurdly for the planet . . .

Planet!

The pieces began to come together.

Voices came down the corridor, and a far part of his mind remembered the wardroom meeting, Sarah, the evening's plans. Just coming out now? Maybe he could see her still. That was silly—curfew soon. Well, tomorrow . . . Just coming out *now*? That was some meeting . . .

Meeting! And Bob said he knew *for sure* this time the tapes on the planet were through: It was a good one. They could land on it, and live.

Live on a planet.

His stomach felt funny for a minute, and he thought that was foolish, what was there to be *afraid* of?

Live on a planet. He thought the words slowly and purposefully. Planet. Plants. Plants on a planet. On a planet, plants grew everywhere, by themselves, *naturally*. That's what Ab said. He said they grew all over, so you'd have to *tear them out* to make a place to build your house.

House. Family. Inside-outside. They were all words in the books. Hills, sunsets, animals. *Wild* animals. Danger. But now he wasn't afraid; he *liked* the thought. Wild animals, he thought again, savoring it. Houses, inside and outside; inside, the family; outside, the animals. And plants. The *sun*shine . . . daytime . . . and night . . .

Shadows!

The light brightened around him. On a planet, there would be shadows all the time everywhere.

"Sheik . . ."

"Yes, ma'am." He turned. The response was automatic . . . "indoctrinated"; . . . even before his mind reoriented.

The room was daylit again. Five of the women were standing just inside the door. Lieutenant Johnson was smiling, watching him.

"Better hop, boy. Curfew."

"Yes, ma'am." He moved past the others. Johnson, closest to the doorway, reached out a hand and rumpled up his hair.

"Do your dreaming in bed, Sheik," she said tenderly, as if he were in the nursery still. But something was in her eyes that made him know she did not think he was a little boy. He felt better when he got outside.

The girls' dorm was to the right; he could see the last of the senior class girls disappearing through the door. If he moved faster . . .

He turned to the left, walked up to the boys' dorm, and almost missed hearing the sharp whispered noise from the cross-corridor beyond.

He looked back. No one in sight. Raced up the corridor, and she was *there,* waiting. Waiting for *him.*

"Sheik! Shhh . . . I just wanted to make sure . . . Tomorrow night?"

"Sure," he said.

Her eyes were shining. Like the Lieutenant, she was looking at him *differently.* But it was a different kind of difference, and he liked it. Very much.

"Sure," he said again. "Tomorrow night for sure."

But neither one moved. A gong sounded softly. Curfew time.

"You better get back," she said. "I have a pass."

Even her whispering voice was different. She was vibrating with excitement. It was *true!*

"Okay," he said. "Listen, Sarah. Let's not wait. What about tonight?"

"Tonight?"

"After inspection."

"You mean . . . ?"

"Sneak down. It's easy," he promised out of the practice of an hour ago, and lied. "I've done it lots of times."

"Who with?"

He smiled. From inside the lounge they heard voices. "Listen, I got to get back. Right now. I'll meet you in Cargo G in half an hour. Then I'll show you how."

"But, Sheik . . ."

He didn't wait for her answer. He didn't dare. Johnson or one of the others would be out for inspection any minute now. He ran on his toes, silently, back down the corridor, tore off his clothes, jumped into bed, pulled covers up, and did not open his eyes even to peek and see what officer it was when she came in to inspect the row of beds. He just lay there, astonished at what he had said and what he was—beyond hesitation—going to do.

He thought of the times he had waited and wanted and hoped for Sarah to ask him, to notice him, to pick him to dance with or play with or for a work partner. Now, all of a sudden, he had thrown himself at her head, suggested . . .

He began to be horrified. It wasn't the idea of breaking curfew rules. Yesterday, even this afternoon, that would have shocked him, but now—knowing about the planet changed all *that*. What bothered him now was the brazenness of it, the way he had practically begged her to come, and hadn't even waited to find out . . .

He wouldn't go. She'd never go. He was crazy to think . . .

She was laughing at him now.

I wish, he thought miserably, *I wish I was . . .*

Only he didn't. He didn't envy girls any more.

He lay very quietly in bed for fifteen minutes. Then he got up and pulled on his shorts. He looked at the six other beds in the schoolboys' dorm. Joel, the youngest, was nine, still a kid. The others were twelve, thirteen, eleven, eleven, twelve. Five of them who would soon be men. Like Bob and Ab, Bomba and Sean, and Sheik himself. He left the dorm, slipped down the corridor, thinking as he went of the words he had read somewhere, that he "moved like a shadow."

I wish, he thought, and turned round a corner to safety, *I wish that she comes.* And then: *I wish that we land on a planet very soon.*

232

The basic subject of this story is binary sex; there are points of view from which two-sex creatures may seem pretty incomprehensible; this one appeared in Worlds of Tomorrow, —October, 1963.

The Lonely

TO: The Hon. Natarajan Roi Hennessy, Chairman, Committee on Intercultural Relations. Solar Council, Eros.
FROM: Dr. Shlomo Mouna, Sr. Anthropologist, Project Ozma XII, Pluto Station.
DATE: 10/9/92, TC.
TRANSMISSION: VIA: Tight bcam, scrambled. SENT: 1306 hrs, TST. RCDV: 1947 hrs, TST.

Dear Nat:

Herewith, a much condensed, heavily annotated, and top secret coded transcript of a program we just picked up. The official title is GU #79, and the content pretty well confirms some of our earlier assumptions about the whole series, as this one concerns us directly, and we have enough background information, including specific dates, to get a much more complete and stylistic translation than before.

I'd say the hypotheses that these messages represent a "Galactic University" lecture series broadcast from somewhere near Galactic Center, through some medium a damn sight faster than light, now seems very reasonable.

This one seemed to come from Altair, which would date transmission from there only a few years after some incidents described in script. Some of the material also indicates probable nature of original format, and I find it uncomfortable. Also reraises question of whether Altair, Arcturus, Castor, etc., relay stations are aimed at us? Although the content makes that doubtful.

Full transcript, film, etc., will go out through channels, as soon as you let me know which channels. This time I am not pleading for declassification. I think of some Spaserve reactions and—frankly I wonder if it shouldn't be limited to SC Intercult Chairmen and Ozma Sr. Anthropoids—and sometimes I wonder about thee.

Cheery reading.
Shlomo

TRANSCRIPT, GU #79, Condensed Version, edited by SM, 10/9/92, TC. (NRH: All material in parens is in my words—summarizing, commenting, and/or describing visual material where indicated. Straight text is verbatim, though cut as indicated. Times, measurements, etc., have been translated from Standard Galactic or Aldebaran local to Terran Standard; and bear in mind that words like "perceive" are often very rough translations for SG concepts more inclusive than our language provided for. —SM)

(Open with distance shot of Spaserve crew visiting Woman of Earth statue on Aldebaran VI. Closeup of reverent faces. Shots of old L-1, still in orbit, and jump-ship trailing it. Repeat first shot, then to Lecturer. You may have seen this one before. Sort of electric eel type. Actually makes sparks when he's being funny.)

The image you have just perceived is symbolic, in several senses. First, the statue was created by the Arlemites, the native race of Aldebaran VI (!! Yes, Virginia, there *are* aborigines!!) in an effort to use emotional symbols to bridge the gap in communications between two highly dissimilar species. Second: due to the farcical failure of this original intent, the structure has now become a vitally significant symbol—you perceived the impact—to the other species involved, the Terrans, a newly emerged race from Sol III. (Note that "you perceived." We must accept the implication that the original broadcasting format provides means of projecting emotional content.) Finally, this twofold symbol relates in one sense (Shooting sparks like mad here. Professional humor prctty much the same all over, hey?) to the phenomenon of the paradox of absolute universality and infinite variety inherent in the symbolism.

(Next section is a sort of refresher-review of earlier lectures. Subject of the whole course appears to be, roughly, "Problems of disparate symbolism in interspecies communications." This lecture—don't laugh—is "Symbols of Sexuality." Excerpts from review:—)

The phenomenon of symbolism is an integral part of the development of communicating intelligence. Distinctions of biological construction, ecological situation, atmospheric and other geophysical conditions, do of course profoundly influence the radically infantile phases of intellectual-emotional-social development in all cultures . . . (but) . . . from approximately that point in the linear development of a civilization at which it is likely to make contact with other cultures—that is, from the commencement of cultural maturity, following the typically adolescent outburst of energy in which first contact is generally accomplished . . . (He describes this level at some length in terms of a complex of: 1, astrophysical knowledge; 2, control of basic matter-energy conversions, "mechanical or psial;" 3, self-awareness of whole culture and of individuals in it; and 4, some sociological phenomena for which I have no referents.) . . . all cultures appear to progress through a known sequence of i-e-s patterns . . . (and) . . . despite differences in the *rate* of development, the composite i-e-s curve for mature cultural development of all known species is familiar enough to permit reliable predictions for any civilization, once located on the curve.

(Then progresses to symbolism. Specific symbols, he says, vary even more, between cultures, than language or other means of conscious communication, as to wit—)

It is self-evident that the specific symbols utilized by, for instance, a septasexual, mechanophilic, auriphased species of freely locomotive discrete individuals, will vary greatly from those of, let us say, a mitotic, unicellular, intensely psioid, communal culture. (Which makes it all the more striking, that) it is specifically in the *use of symbols,* the general consciousness of their significance, the degree of sophistication of the popularly recognized symbols, and the uses to which they are put by the society as a whole, that we have found our most useful constant, so far, for purposes of locating a given culture on the curve.

(Much more here about other aspects of cultural development, some of which are cyclical, some linear—all fascinating but not essential to understanding of what follows.)

Sexuality has until recently been such a rare phenomenon among civilized species that we had casually assumed it to be something of a drawback to the development of intelligence. Such sexual races as we did know seemed to have developed in spite of their biological peculiarity, but usually not until after the mechanical flair that often seemed to accompany the phenomenon had enabled them to escape their planet of origin for a more favorable environment.

I say more favorable because sexuality does seem to develop as an evolutionary compensation where (some terms untranslatable, some very broad, but generally describing circumstances, like extra-dense atmosphere, in which the normal rate of cosmic radiation was reduced to a degree that inhibited mutation and thus, evolution) . . .

As I said, this seemed almost a freak occurrence, and so it was, and is, here in the heart of the Galaxy. But in the more thinly populated spiral arms, the normal rate of radiation is considerably lower. It is only in the last centuries that we have begun to make contact with any considerable numbers of species from these sectors—and the incidence of sexuality among these peoples is markedly higher than before.

Recently, then, there has been fresh cause to investigate the causes and effects of sexuality; and there has been a comparative wealth of new material to work with.

(Here he goes into a rexiew of the variety of sexual modes, ranging from two to seventeen sexes within a species, and more exotica-erotica of means, manners, and mores than a mere two-sexed biped can readily imagine. Restrain yourself. It's all in the full transcript.)

But let me for the moment confine myself to the simplest and most common situation, involving only two sexes. Recent investigations indicate that there is an apparently inevitable psychological effect of combining two essentially distinct subspecies in one genetic unit. (Sparks like mad.) I perceive that many of you have just experienced the same delight-dismay the first researchers felt at recognizing this so-obvious and so-overlooked parallel with the familiar cases of symbiosis.

The Terrans, mentioned earlier, are in many ways prototypical of sexuality in an intelligent species, and the unusual and rather dramatic events on Aldebaran VI have added greatly to our insights into the psychology of sexuality in general.

In this culture, dualism is very deep-rooted, affecting every aspect of the i-e-s complex: not just philosophy and engineering, but mathematics, for instance, and mystique.

This cultural attitude starts with a duality, or two-sided symmetry, of body-structure. (Throughout this discussion he uses visual material—photos, diagrams, etc., of human bodies, anatomy, physiology, habitat, eating and mating habits, etc. Also goes off into some intriguing speculation of the chicken-or-egg type: is physical structure influenced by mental attitudes, or is it some inherent tendency of a chromosome pattern with *pairs* of genes from *pairs* of parents?)

In this respect, the Terrans are almost perfect prototypes, with two pairs of limbs, for locomotion and manipulation, extending from a central—single—abdominal cavity, which, although containing some single organs as well as some in pairs, is so symmetrically proportioned that the first assumption from an exterior view would be that everything inside was equally mirror-imaged. Actually, the main breathing apparatus is paired; the digestive system is single—although food intake is through an orifice with paired lips and two rows of teeth. In both "male" and "female" types, the organ of sexual contact is single, whereas the gamete-producers are pairs. There is a single, roundish head set on top of the abdomen, containing the primary sensory organs, all of which occur in pairs. Even the brain is paired!

I mentioned earlier that it is typical of the sexual races that the flair for physical engineering is rather stronger than the instinct for communication. This was an observed but little-understood fact for many centuries; it was not till this phenomenon of dualism (and triadism for the three-sexed, etc.) was studied that the earlier observation was clarified. If you will consider briefly the various sources of power and transport, you will realize that—outside of the psi-based techniques—most of these are involved with principles of symmetry and/or equivalence; these concepts are obvious to the two-sexed. On the other hand, the principle of unity, underlying all successful communication—physical, verbal, psial, or other—and which is also the basis for the application of psi to engineering problems—is for these species, in early stages, an almost mystical quality.

As with most life-forms, the reproductive act is, among sexual beings, both physically pleasurable and biologically compulsive, so that it is early equated with religio-mystic sensations. Among sexual species, these attitudes are intensified by the communicative aspects of the act. (Cartoon-type diagrams here which frankly gave me to think a bit!) We have much to learn yet about the psychology of this phenomenon, but enough has been established to make clear that the concept of unity for these races is initially almost entirely related to the use of their sexuality, and is later extended to other areas—religion and the arts of communication at first—with a mystical—indeed often reverent attitude!

I hardly need to remind you that the tendencies I have been discussing are the primitive and underlying ones. Obviously, at the point of contact, any species must have acquired at least enough sophistication in the field of physics—quanta, unified field theory, and atomic transmutation for a start—to have begun to look away from the essentially blind alley of dualistic thinking. But the extent to which these Terrans were still limited by their early developmental pattern is indicated by the almost unbelievable fact that they developed ultra-dimensional transport *before* discovering any more effective channels of communication than the electromagnetic!

Thus their first contacts with older civilizations were physical; and, limited as they still are almost entirely to aural and visual communication, they were actually unable to perceive their very first contact on Aldebaran VI.

(Shot of Prof. Eel in absolute sparkling convulsions goes to distance shots of planet and antiquated Earth spaceship in orbit: L-1 again. Then suborb launch drops, spirals to surface. Twenty bulky spacesuited figures emerge —not the same as in opening shots. This looks like actual photographic record of landing, which seems unlikely. Beautiful damn reconstruction, if so. Narration commences with Aldebaran date. I substitute Terran Calendar date we know for same, and accept gift of one more Rosetta Stone.)

The time is the year 2053. For more than six decades, this primitive giant of space has ployed its way through the restrictive medium of slow space. Twice before in its travels, the great ship has paused.

First at Procyon, where they found the system both uninhabited and uninviting; and at the time they did not yet know what urgent cause they had to make a landing. (Our date for Procyon exploration, from L-1 log, is 2016, which fits.)

Then at Saiph, two decades later, where they hoped for just a bare minimum of hospitality—no more than safe footing for their launches, in which they could live while they tried to ensure their future survival. But this system's planets offered little hope. One Earth-size enveloped in horror-film type gases and nasty moistures. (One more with dense atmosphere of high acid content: probe from ship corroded in minutes.)

They limped on. A half decade later they came to a time of decision, and determined not to try for the next nearest star system, but for the closest one from which their radio had received signs of intelligent life: Aldebaran.

What they had learned between Procyon and Saiph was that those of their crew who were born in space were not viable. The ship had been planned to continue, if necessary, long beyond the lifespan of its first crew. The Terran planners had ingeniously bypassed their most acute psychosocial problem, and staffed the ship with a starting crew of just one sex. Forty females started the journey, with a supply of sperm from one hundred genetically selected males carefully preserved on board.

Sex determination in this species is in the male chromosome, and most of the supply had been selected for production of females. The plan was to maintain the ship in transit with single-sexed population and restore the normal balance only at the end of the journey.

The Terrans have apparently reached a level of self-awareness that enables them to avoid the worst dangers of their own divisive quality, while utilizing the advantages of this special (pun intended—Prof. Eel was sparking again) ambivalence. Their biological peculiarities have, among other things, developed a far greater tolerance in the females for the type of physical constraints and social pressures that were to accompany the long, slow voyage. Males, on the other hand, being more aggressive, and more responsive to hostile challenges, would be needed for colonizing a strange planet. (Dissertation on mammals here which says nothing new, but restates from an outsider's—rather admiring—viewpoint with some distinction. Should be a textbook classic—if we can ever release this thing.)

That was the plan. But when the first females born on the trip came to maturity, and could not conceive, the plan was changed. Three male infants were born to females of the original complement—less than half of whom, even then, were still alive and of child-bearing age.

(Well, he tells it effectively, but adds nothing to what we know from the log. Conflicts among the women led to death of one boy, eventual suicide of another at adolescence. Remaining mature male fails to impregnate known fertile women. Hope of landing while enough fertiles remained to start again pretty well frustrated at Saiph. De-

cision to try for nearest system eight light years off—
with Aldebaran still farther. Faint fantastic hope still at
landing, with just one child-bearer left—the Matriarch,
if you recall?)

Remembering the reasons for their choice of Aldebaran,
you can imagine the reaction when that landing party,
first, lost all radio signals as they descended; then, could
find no trace whatsoever—to their senses—of habitation.
The other planets were scouted, to no avail. The signals
on the Mother Ship's more powerful radio continued to
come from VI. One wild hypothesis was followed up by
a thorough and fruitless search of the upper atmosphere.
The atmosphere was barely adequate to sustain life at
the surface. Beam tracing repeatedly located the signal
beacon in a moutain of VI, which showed—to the Terrans
—no other sign of intelligent life.

The only logical conclusion was that they had followed
a "lighthouse beacon" to an empty world. The actual explanation, of course, was in the nature of the Arlemites,
the natives of Aldebaran VI.

Originating as a social-colonizing lichen, on a heavy
planet, with—even at its prime—a barely adequate atmosphere, the Arlemites combined smallness of individual
size with limited locomotive powers and superior air and
water retentive ability. They developed, inevitably, as a
highly psioid culture—as far to one end of the psichophys-
ical as the Terrans are to the other. (My spelling up
there. I think it represents true meaning better than
"psycho.") The constantly thinning choice was between
physical relocation and a conscious evolutionary measure
which this mature psioid race was far better equipped to
undertake: the Arlemites now exist as a planet-wide diffusion of single-celled entities, comprising just one individual, and a whole species.

(Visual stuff here helps establish concept—as if you or
I just extended the space between cells.)

It seems especially ironic that the Arlemites were not
only one of the oldest and most psioid of peoples—so
that they had virtually all the accumulated knowledge of
the Galaxy at their disposal—but were also symbiote

products. This background might have enabled them to comprehend the Terran mind and the problems confronting the visitors—except for the accidental combination of almost total psi-blindness in the Terrans, and the single-sexed complement of the ship.

The visitors could not perceive their hosts. The hosts could find no way to communicate with the visitors. The full complement of the ship, eventually, came down in launches, and lived in them, hopelessly, while they learned that their viability had indeed been completely lost in space. There was no real effort to return to the ship and continue the voyage. The ranks thinned, discipline was lost, deaths proliferated. Finally, it was only a child's last act of rebelliousness that mitigated the futility of the tragedy.

The last child saw the last adult die, and saw this immobility as an opportunity to break the most inviolable of rules. She went out of the launch—into near-airlessness that killed her within minutes.

But minutes were more than enough, with the much longer time afterwards for examination of the dead brain. It was through the mind of this one child, young enough to be still partially free of the rigid mental framework that made adult Terrans so inaccessible to Arlemites, that the basis was gained for most of the knowledge we now have.

Sorrowingly, the Arlemites generated an organism to decompose the Terrans and their artifacts, removing all traces of tragedy from the planet's surface. Meanwhile, they studied what they had learned, against future needs.

The technological ingenuity of these young sexuals will be apparent when I tell you that only four decades after the departure of that ill-fated ship, they were experimenting with ultra-dimensional travel. Even at the time of the landing at Aldebaran, ultra-di scouts were already exploring the systems closest to Sol. Eventually—within a decade after the child's death—one of these came to Aldebaran, and sighted the still-orbiting Mother Ship.

A second landing was clearly imminent. The Arlemites had still devised no way to aid this species to live in safety on their planet, nor did they have any means to communicate adequately with psi-negatives whose primary

242

perceptions were aural and visual. But they did have, from the child's mind, a working knowledge of the strongest emotional symbols the culture knew, and they had long since devised a warning sign they could erect for visual perception. The statue of the Woman of Earth was constructed in an incredibly brief time through the combined efforts of the whole Arlemite consciousness.

They had no way to know that the new ship, designed for exploration, not colonizing, and equipped with ultra-di drive, which obviated the long slow traveling, was crewed entirely by males. Even had they known, they did not yet comprehend the extreme duality of the two-sexed double-culture. So they built their warning to the shape of the strongest fear-and-hate symbols of—a female.

(Shot of statue, held for some time, angle moving slowly. No narration. Assuming that emotional-projection notion—and I think we must—the timing here is such that I believe they first project what they seem to think a human female would feel, looking at it. I tried women on staff here. They focused more on phallic than female component, but were just as positive in reactions as males.???? Anyhow, like I said, no narration. What follows, though out of parens, is my own reaction.)

It seems more a return than a venture.

The Woman waits, as she has waited . . . always? . . . to greet her sons, welcomes us . . . home? . . . She sits in beauty, in peacefulness, perfect, complete, clean and fresh-colored . . . new? . . . no, *forever* . . . open, welcoming, yet so impervious . . . warm and . . . untouchable? . . . rather, *untouched* . . . almost, but never, forgotten Goddess . . . Allmother, Woman of Earth . . . enveloped, enveloping, in warmth and peace . . .

One stands back a bit: this is the peace of loving insight, of unquesting womanhood, of great age and undying youth . . . the peace of the past, of life that is passed, of that immortality that nothing mortal can ever achieve except through the frozen impression of living consciousness that we call *art*.

The young men are deeply moved and they make

243

jokes. "Allmother," one hears them say, sarcastically, "Old White Goddess, whaddya know?"

Then they look up and are quiet under the smiling stone eyes. Even the ancient obscenely placed spaceship in her lap is not quite absurd, as it will seem in museum models—or tragic, as is the original overhead.

(Prof. Eel goes on to summarize the conclusions that seem obvious to him. Something is awfully wrong; that's obvious to me. How did they manage to build something so powerful out of total miscomprehension? What are we up against, anyhow? And, to get back to the matter of channels, what do you think this little story would do to Spaserve brass egos? Do you want to hold it top secret a while?)

End of Transcript

TO: Dr. Shlomo Mouna, Sr. Anthropologist, Ozma XII, Pluto
FROM: N. R. Hennessy, Solar Council Dome. Eros
DATE: 10/10/92
TRANSMISSION: VIA tight beam, scrambled. SENT: 0312 hrs. RCVD: 1027 hrs.

Dear Shlomo:

Absolutely, let me see the full package before we release it elsewhere. I've got a few more questions, like: Do they know we're receiving it? How do we straighten them out? Or should we? Instinct says yes. Tactics says it is advantageous to be underestimated. Think best you come with package, and we'll braintrust it. Meantime, in reply to your bafflement—

"L" class ships, you should have known, are for "Lysistrata." Five of them launched during brief Matriarchy at beginning of World Government on Terra, following Final War. So sort out your symbols *now*.

And good grief, where did the *other* four land?

NRH

Oklall. Written mostly in 1946-47, when the Feminine Mystique was at its most pervasive, this poem's central image (in 1976) seems trendy. It first saw print in the Canadian collection, 1973.

Auction Pit

Prologue

Striped shirt or morning pants, white tie or none,
Smooth-shaven some, others strong of shoulder,
Men jostle lightly, push up to the platform,
With intricate courtesy, Queensbury rites, in the pit
Where the women are auctioned.

In the old days,
Till they stripped off the superstructure,
Hoopskirted ladies were trained to a gentler strain, spirit
Unlikely as limb was to show through the swaddling.
Then there were auctioneers, mothers and maiden aunts,
And elder sisters.

Streamlining, sequin sheath, and strictly divided
Breast-moulding bathing suit, have done for the body
What the unparallelled
High-educational fine opportunities
Offered by charm mags,

Moom-pitcher palaces, as well as success schools,
Business schools, sororities, and secretaryships
Have done for the mind and soul.

The girls cry their own wares now,
With style and strident art, full worthy
The masters of the antique trade.

Procession

This first in line today, she knows her points:
Displays the supple limbs and arching back.
This girl can be had for money, advertise
The swing of hips and sway of short fur
Chubby on her shoulders.
Here is no art nor artifice. She sells
Nothing but flesh for the bare bottom price of cash.

That slender piece back there, the one
With the whispering talk and the willowy walk: who has
The price for this must offer more than money.
Bid your attention, Gentlemen,
The soft voice sibilates:
                                    I am not strong,
But I am sweet; I shall need all your care;
I'm woman-weak, and chill seeps from me
Through the flesh and spirit;
But for the warmth you give, I'll flower-worship
You as my sun, and thank you prettily
For all you pay.

This other is rounder and firm of step:
She would scorn money, needs no lingering care.
Her face is pretty, and sweet with love.
She sells simplicity; her body
Is built to a biologic frame; she'll take
Her pay in kind, from the strong-shouldered man:
The seed to form large noisy children;
The arm to build a wall against the world.
She wants no more.
For a man of simple and sturdy ways

She is cheap at the price, and the salt of
The earth; many will want her, but bidding
Is little likely to go high. She understands
No art of contract, and her needs are
Elementary, and the truth is
There are quite enough of her to go around.

They pass; they come and go.
The girl-child, dimpling, asks indulgence; and the
Spinster, cased in starch, shaped in her dress by an
Imperious iron, flat as a board, disdains affection,
Asks security.
And many more: this one in tweeds wants family; and that
In chiffon asks a lover's eyes to follow her eternally without
Results. Each one goes by. From time to time
A single bid, offered in ignorance, or out of passion,
Is seized upon, and then the crowd cries:
"Love—A marriage made in heaven,"
And the two depart, leaving the rest with sadness
In their hearts. But for the most,
The price runs high and low through the fleshy procession.
From one shape to the next across the boards, small choice
Except as fancy stretches with the purse.

Distinction

White Tie, eyeing the trading from an advanced
Position of disinterest to one side, straightens
His stance at the sound of a crisper cry
Than has been heard yet from the crowded stalls.
This straight proud woman mounts the steps
To sale, and displays
Indifference quite elaborate as his own. She cries no price,
But stipulates just that the bidding be precise.
This is not mother, daughter, whore, nor wife,
But courtesan; she has no choice, most feminine of women,
But to mould her rich
Endowment of nuance to what price buys her.

She sells suggestion:
                    of cleverness to carry off

The chic complexity of social stipend.
                    intelligence to build a sounding
Board, if she accept the bid of brain-prestige.
                    self-centered grace to shower on black
And silver service in a rich man's home.
                    of sensual calculation to fulfill
Desire, if admiration is her wage.

Love, money, home, adventure, intellect,
Society, fine clothes, fine words, or eminence . . .
Some few or all of these White Tie must bid . . .
And heavily, for now the price runs high.
All things to all these men, she waits to learn
What butcher, bravo, prince, or puritan
Will top the offers and command
Her being. A chimera, she changes shape to suit
Each bid, and as the price soars so her charms increase.

White Tie, impatient at the boorish crowd,
Spurning the men unworthy of this creature,
Always a spender and a self-willed man,
Must have the woman, and he crowns
Each bid with casual grace and smiling scorn.
She will be his; she was ordained for him.

Epilogue:

Off in a corner of the market place
a curious creature stands
in some confusion at the furious trading:
nor buyer, nor seller,
not engaged in commerce:
clearly untrained to perform although
just as clearly in the shape of woman.

Men brushing by, stop,
finding it beautiful
and pleasing among them.

From time to time the curious creature
falls into conversation with such men

—timid or haughty, too poor or too rich
to buy hastily—as bid infrequently
and can enjoy such strangely-neutral
entertainment while they wait
for an appropriate enticing cry
to prick them back to business from the auction block.

Some kindly souls,
instinctively protective-masculine,
stop to direct—or help—
it to the crowded stalls:
a woman lost should be
returned to cover:
this one, in proper form,
might be a piece worth bidding
high and paying pretty for.

A few rude fellows rub against it now and then,
thinking, a woman-body for the asking:
but these are frightened easily by conversation
and stumble off pulling their pockets for the price
of something satisfying to a man's desires.

A curious creature:
not for sale;
yet not free.
Nor can it understand why,
being already among the men,
it must depart and make
a journey back on some one
single arm: selected,
signed and sealed—and delivered?

The men are wiser:
they are familiar
with profit as a function
of possession: happiness
surely lies in what they call
their own.

The curious creature mingling

in their midst will not
be owned.

They fondle it in passing,
smile and speak perhaps, pass by:
press forward to complete their bids
for proper women on the auction block.

Hallall. *An intensely personal exploration from a "curious creature"; first published in F&SF—October, 1974.*

In the Land of Unblind

You know how it is

indown you close your eye(s) and let take
your self between a stumblecrawl and lazyfloat

I mean when

you get past the rubbage really *indown* there's
no seefeeltouch not
the skinside *upout* way
blindbalance cannot tell if a touching is over
or under or on the feeling is inside your skin

I mean

indown you know in the land of unblind the one
eyed woman is terribilified
no light
but the infires' flickerdimglow and
they all keep their eyes closed so
scrabbleswoop and stumblesoar fly
creep in fearableautiful nolightno
dark of eacheveryother's infires

(No need to cover or to show
they   canwillnot   looksee
except   the   one-eyed   me
I wonder what would happen if
a person took a light *indown*)

                                    Before

I opened up one apple-eye I too
flewstumbled graspgropegleaned
in   holystonemaskhunger   then

                              one time
indown in that hell-eden innocence I touched
a man and he touched me   you know the way
it happens some times later or before or inbe
tween we touched *upout*

                                I mean

where skins can touch and some
place or other we remembered as
in the other we felt fate upon us
blindunblind future past which

                              one is when
upout his openwide eyes full of hunger and
some kind of hate   I tasting somehow hate
fulhunger over all the skins inside my mouth

            I love you!   he said
            Witchcraft! I had to come!
            You must come! Magic!
            I love you!

                                          so
I came we loved our skins touched inside some
times almost remembering *indown*

                              not quite then
oneanother soundless *indown* timestill blindun
blind I touched a man and touching me he spoke
words I c/wouldnot hear just scramblescared
                              a way you know
                              it happens some
time in betweenafterbefore when meeting *upout*
all our eyes and ears and mouths were open

            I love you!   he said
                    252

We had to come together!
Remember!   he said   *beforewords—*

                 I c/wouldnot
                 I love you
        I said   *Witchcraft!*
all the skins inside my mouth tasting sweet
sour terror as I ran he spoke

                (again?)

        Open your eyes!   he said

                  One time (soon?)
indown still fearful
           (fearful still for still I do
           not open more than one)
I opened up my first *indown*eye seeing stir a
livesome ghost of memory pastfutureinbetween
that time I touched no man but
           (then?)
                one time
upout you know before or after
my first man was there (again?)
skinsight airvoice was all we
unshared how it waswouldbe to touch *indown* I
did not know he did not know there was *indown*
not to remember full of fear he went away but
           (then?)
           one time
indown one eye just-slit open in dimglowing
flickerdrift infires a man touched me and I
could see *indown* the face I touchedspoketo of
course he c/wouldnot hear
         so
          but
           when
             you know
we met *upout*eyes open all the hungerskinside
my mouth turned sweet remembering beforewords

I love you!   he said
Witchcraft! I had to come!
You made me come! Magic!
I love you!   he said with words
                                    but
he did not know echopremonitions stirring
from under *upout*skintouch he couldwouldnot
premember how *indown* we touched his hunger
fear soured all the skins inside my mouth
I had to go
                    away
                          (again?)
                                    one time
indown I met a man with one eye
open like my own in flickerdim
infireglow seeing each how horribleautiful
eachotherself fruit flower and fester touching
so we spoke beforewords so
                                    you know
the waysometime(s) you meet *upout* all eyes and
ears and mouths wide open great new hungers
pungentsweet
on all the skins inside remembering *indown*
bebackwords neverquite to know which place
time was wherewhen or waswouldbe we first
felt fate upon us so
                    We love   (we do not say)
                    We had to come
                    Witchcraft!   (we laugh)
we love skins touch *upout*side premembering
sometimesalmost like *indown*touchtalk still
                                    and yet
                                    I wonder
                              what it's like
                    indown for the two-eyed?

254